CODE OF HONOR

Knights Of Honor
Book Three

Alexa Aston

Copyright © 2017 by Alexa Aston
Print Edition

Published by Dragonblade Publishing, an imprint of Kathryn Le Veque Novels, Inc

All rights reserved. No part of this book may be used or reproduced in any manner whatsoever without written permission, except in the case of brief quotations embodied in critical articles or reviews.

Table of Contents

Prologue 1
Chapter One 14
Chapter Two 21
Chapter Three 27
Chapter Four 38
Chapter Five 48
Chapter Six 54
Chapter Seven 62
Chapter Eight 73
Chapter Nine 84
Chapter Ten 91
Chapter Eleven 99
Chapter Twelve 106
Chapter Thirteen 114
Chapter Fourteen 123
Chapter Fifteen 130
Chapter Sixteen 139
Chapter Seventeen 147
Chapter Eighteen 154
Chapter Nineteen 162
Chapter Twenty 173
Chapter Twenty-One 181
Chapter Twenty-Two 190

Chapter Twenty-Three	199
Chapter Twenty-Four	206
Chapter Twenty-Five	215
Epilogue	223
About the Author	226

PROLOGUE

Sandbourne Castle—1350

AS THEY CRESTED the hill, Michael Devereux gazed with pride as he caught sight of his home. Sandbourne Castle stood in the distance, surrounded by rolling green hills. Cottages dotted the landscape. Animals grazed in the pastureland. A lump formed in his throat. He'd been away from home over a year and had missed his mother more than anyone. He couldn't wait to entertain her with stories of his first year as a page fostering in Sir Lovel's household.

He spurred on his borrowed horse, wanting to reach the keep as soon as possible after three long days on the road in blistering heat, accompanied by a knight Sir Lovel provided to see him safely to his parents' doorstep. Michael differed from the other boys in this. They all had fathers or other close family members who escorted them home for their summer visit.

Not Michael.

The Earl of Sandbourne wrote that he was too busy to dance attendance upon his only son, much less send one of his soldiers to see that the boy reached Sandbourne without any problems. Sir Lovel graciously provided Michael with an escort, much to his embarrassment. It only gave the other pages and squires something new to tease him about. They already taunted him unmercifully because he was so plump. His mother assured him as he grew older and taller, the extra weight would come off. For now, Michael tried to ignore the wicked names the other boys called him to his face and pretend he didn't know how they talked about him behind his back.

Thank the Christ Geoffrey and Raynor had put an end to the harshest cruelty. The two squires, both seven years older than he was, had been gone when Michael first arrived at Sir Lovel's to foster. When they returned, they put a stop to the worst of it, boxing a few ears and bloodying a few more noses to get their point across. Now the other boys simply called him Tol—which stood for Tub of Lard. Michael found it a tolerable nickname and so he endured it. He couldn't let Geoffrey and Raynor fight all of his battles. He was eight, after all, and needed to learn how to stand up for himself.

But it still angered him that his father hadn't spared the days it would have taken to come and bring him home for summer. Michael envied the joyous reunions he'd witnessed between family members as he lurked in the shadows of the great hall. Already, he'd been the only child fostering who hadn't returned home the previous Christmas. His father told Sir Lovel that his boy needed to toughen up, so Michael had spent the holy holidays keeping mostly to himself. Sir Lovel had graciously included Michael in his family's festivities, but he'd slipped away at the earliest chance during the many celebrations held between Christmas and Epiphany.

Why did his father hate him so much?

From Michael's earliest memories, the earl never showed him any sort of affection. He never once referred to Michael by name. The nobleman was brusque with his only child, paying him little attention. Only his saintly mother spent time with him. Nurtured him. Taught him to read. Rode around Sandbourne with him and introduced him to its tenants. It was his strong desire for his mother's company that had him eager to return home now. Without her, life seemed drab. She always invented creative stories to tell him and showered him with attention and love.

Michael gave a shout to the familiar gatekeeper, who opened the gates at his command. Michael assumed he was expected since Sir Lovel had sent news of his return to Sandbourne, but no one stood to greet them as they made their way toward the inner bailey.

Turning to Sir Oderic, his escort, he said, "We should ride to the stables. We can have someone care for the horses before we go into the great hall. I know you need to quench your thirst and Cook can provide you with a small meal."

He did not miss the look of pity in the soldier's eyes as the man spoke up after hours of silence on the road. "I'll see to our horses, young master. I can also find myself food and drink without your help. Why don't you go and find your mother? I'm sure she'll be happy to lay eyes upon you after you've been away for so long."

Michael threw a leg over the saddle and jumped down from the horse Sir Lovel had allowed him to ride on this journey home. He owned no horse of his own, which suited him since he had no fondness for the huge, intimidating animals. That would have to change because part of his training would include caring for horses once he became a squire.

Gratitude toward Oderic flooded him. The knight had always treated him with a good bit of kindness. "Thank you, good sir. I'm anxious to find Mother and speak to her." He reached up and took his small bag of clothing attached to the pommel. "Will I see you before you leave Sandbourne? We could sup together tonight in the great hall."

Oderic shook his head. "Nay, young man. I'll wet my whistle and have a bit of bread, but I'll return immediately to my liege lord's estate."

Michael heard in Oderic's voice what the knight did not bother to express aloud. That he believed he would not be welcomed by the Earl of Sandbourne. That the nobleman would probably pound away, pumping the soldier for information about how his son's training progressed.

And as an honorable knight who upheld the code of chivalry, Sir Oderic couldn't lie. The answers he would give would not be ones the earl wished to hear. For Michael was the slowest of all Sir Lovel's pages and lagged behind in every activity assigned to him. His chubby fingers made him clumsy. His thick legs saw that he finished last in every physical task, especially in delivering messages around the castle and its grounds. He was, for all intents and purposes, a miserable failure.

Yet Michael believed he would overcome these obstacles. He didn't know how or when, but Geoffrey had told him that he, too, had been slow to grasp things at first. Geoffrey shared with Michael that he'd made a terrible page. And look at him now. Geoffrey de Montfort was the finest of all Sir Lovel's squires. Even the nobleman himself said that Geoffrey was the bravest of them all and would be the first to be knighted amongst their group.

Michael gave Sir Oderic a curt nod. "Thank you for the safe conduct back to Sandbourne. I'll see you when I return at summer's end."

The knight gave him a rare smile. "I'll return for you in six weeks' time. We'll have much to discuss on our journey."

He watched Oderic head toward the stables. So it had already been decided that his father would not accompany him back to Sir Lovel's. The knowledge cut Michael to the quick, but he resolved to push it aside. He would find his mother and enjoy spending the afternoon with her.

And push the dread of speaking with his father into a dark corner of his mind. For now.

Michael entered the keep. He stopped a servant girl unfamiliar to him and inquired where his mother might be.

"So you're the young master?" she asked pertly.

"Aye."

"I heard you were coming home." She studied him a moment. "You're not at all what I expected."

He shrugged. What could he say? He was short. Pudgy. His stained clothes reflected three days of travel without being changed. He knew he looked less an earl's son than most.

"You can try—"

"Michael?"

He turned and saw his father's long-time steward coming his way. Alarm filled Michael at having to see his father so soon.

"The earl is waiting for you. Follow me."

Michael reluctantly fell into step behind the man as he mounted the staircase. So much for spending an enjoyable afternoon in the company of his beloved mother. Instead, he prepared himself for the tongue-lashing he would receive. Reaching into his pocket, he stroked his good luck charm, a pink rock he and his mother had found as they walked around the estate one afternoon. He always kept it within reach. His fingertips brushed against it now, as he willed the small stone to bring him courage for the encounter ahead.

They reached the door to the solar.

The steward paused. "Go on in. The earl is expecting you. He saw you ride through the gates." He nudged Michael.

So his father had seen his arrival. Michael wondered why he hadn't taken the time to come greet his son in person as he would any guest that graced Sandbourne. It made him question whether his mother even knew her boy was expected for a visit. It wouldn't surprise him if the knowledge had been kept from her.

He pushed the door open, throwing his shoulders back and holding his head high. Preparing for the worst. Hoping for the best—though knowing that was unlikely.

His father sat in his favorite chair, holding a pewter cup, as he nibbled from fruit and cheese which sat on a platter on the table next to him. He glanced up. Already the earl wore a frown on his face, as if merely the sight of his son caused him great disappointment.

"Close the door," he barked.

Michael did so and approached timidly.

"Don't be such a mouse. You're a man. Act like one," his father commanded, as if simply uttering the words would make it so. In the earl's world, it did. No one dared cross the nobleman. His orders had to be followed swiftly, without hesitation. And if the Earl of Sandbourne became displeased in any way?

Pity the soul who drew his wrath.

"You're filthy, boy," his father admonished. "Don't even think of sitting down and spreading the dust that clings to you."

Michael wished he'd had time to wash the stains of travel from his hands and face and change his gypon and *cotehardie* before this meeting occurred.

His father's nose crinkled in disgust. "You haven't lost any of that fat on you. I'd hoped Lovel would have worked it off you by now."

What was he supposed to reply?

"I do work very hard in service to Sir Lovel, Father."

The earl snorted. He stared at Michael without speaking, his eyes roaming up and down in judgment. "God's teeth, but I believe you've actually *gained* weight!"

Michael shuffled uneasily. "I can promise you that I put my heart and soul into every task which I am assigned. And I eat no more than the other pages do."

"Hmph."

Michael hesitated, wondering if he should speak. He decided he would try to be the man his father expected. That would mean taking the initiative in their conversation.

"Would you like to hear about what I've learned so far, Father?"

"I know what you should've learned, boy," the earl snapped. "How to curb your appetite, for one. How to polish armor till it gleams. How to sharpen a sword. How to deliver a message, quickly and quietly. How to sit a horse. Are you still afraid of horses? Or has Lovel stamped that fear out of you?" The earl's eyes flashed in interest for the first time.

The mention of it caused the pit of Michael's stomach to shrivel as memories flooded him. He'd been put on a horse at a very young age—and promptly fell off. Over and over. One aggravated horse stomped on his foot so hard that the animal broke it. Michael spent weeks off his feet as the bones healed. He'd finally learned to tolerate being around horses during his year away from Sandbourne, but they'd never be his friend. Once again, he had Raynor Le Roux to thank. The squire had spent numerous hours with Michael once he'd discovered Michael's fear of the large beasts. Raynor's teaching skills and patience paid off. Michael no longer was ridiculed by the others regarding his lack of finesse upon a horse.

"I ride as well as any boy that fosters with Sir Lovel," he said, which was the truth. But he didn't reveal how he still panicked each time he first sat in the saddle. How his heart raced. How it pounded so violently that he thought it might tear away and jump from his chest.

Then as he became used to the horse under him, the panic would slowly subside. He'd learned to control the animal with the reins and his thighs. Raynor had taught him that mastering being in the saddle was as much a mental game as a physical effort. Michael was proud of how far he'd come along in the past year. He would show his father how different he'd become. How much he'd grown up in such a short amount of time.

Summoning every bit of bravery he possessed, he said, "Mayhap tomorrow we can ride out together, Father. I'd love to see the land around Sandbourne and hear about what you've done this past year while I've been gone."

There, he'd spoken up. Ventured to address his father in conversation instead of only waiting to reply to a question. Showed his interest in their property. After all, one day he would hold the title of earl. Geoffrey had told him 'twas never too early to learn about the estate you would inherit.

His father eyed him with more interest now. "Mayhap Lovel *is* making something of you. I don't remember you being so bold in the past." The stern look the earl wore had Michael wishing the ground would open up and swallow him whole. "However, I am curious as to how you behave around a horse nowadays."

The earl stood. "Let's go to the stables. I want to see you saddle a horse. You do know how to saddle a horse?"

"Aye, Father."

Without further conversation, his father strode from the room. Michael raced to keep up with him, sweat breaking out along his hairline. He knew the basics. What each piece did and where it should be placed.

But pages didn't saddle horses—only squires did so. He'd watched Geoffrey and Raynor do it many times. Raynor was kind enough each time he took Michael out to ride to explain over and over what he did as he drew each piece mounted on the wall and affixed it to the horse. Raynor claimed the repetition would do Michael good and that he'd be able to saddle a horse in his sleep when the time came.

But that time would be sometime in the future. His father wanted to see his progress. Now.

Michael tamped down the reluctance flooding him and told himself to get control of the emotions rushing through him. He did so when the other boys teased him. His greatest skill had been learning to take their cutting words in stride and let them wash off him as water spilling from a bucket might. As they left the keep, he slowed his breathing so that it became deep and even—another thing Geoffrey had taught him to help calm himself when his nerves threatened to spin out of control.

I can do this.

Repeating those words over and over, he hurried after his father. The older man's long strides kept Michael running as he tried to keep up.

They crossed the bailey, passing many people hard at work. No one spoke a word to them. 'Twas so unlike Sir Lovel's, where every person shouted a greeting and rewarded one another with a smile. Sandbourne ran efficiently, but Michael understood now that it wasn't a happy place to live and work. He'd been out in the world a bit now and could see how his father's oppression blanketed those who lived on the estate.

Michael swore in that moment that when he finally gained the title, everything would change.

Everything.

They approached the stables and entered. He was glad to be out of the strong sunlight. By hurrying across the bailey, he could already sense the sweat gathering in his hair and drizzling down his back. His palms, too, had broken out as if he'd dipped his hands in the horse's trough. Michael wiped them against his thighs. He wondered how he'd be able to lift a heavy saddle and hoist it on whichever horse his father selected, much less if he could hold on to it without it slipping from his grasp.

If only Geoffrey and Raynor were here to cheer him on. Their constant support had changed how Michael viewed himself. Others might see him as slow and fat, but Michael had learned he possessed a keen mind and a clever wit. Even Geoffrey told him that he spoke as well as one thrice his age. One day, the fat would melt away as his mother promised and his body would catch up. He would become one of the finest knights in all the land. Why, he might even serve in the king's guard someday.

Michael heard voices and pulled himself from his reverie. Laughter came from one of the far stalls. His father stopped a moment and listened, then charged ahead like a foot soldier rushing into battle.

Alarm exploded inside Michael as the tinkling laughter sounded again. 'Twas his mother's gentle laugh, which always sounded to him like bells merrily pealing. He ran to catch up to where his father now stood, feet apart, glaring into a stall.

Michael stopped next to his father and looked inside. The stall held an ebony horse Michael had never seen before. Next to it stood his mother and Sir Thirkell, one of his favorite knights in his father's employ. Thirkell and his friend, Sir Charles, had told Michael stories about King Arthur and the Knights of the Round Table from the time he was a babe. Michael had thought back on those stories during the nights he had trouble falling asleep. He used his fascination with the tales to push aside the taunts from that day.

"Michael!" his mother cried in joy as she caught sight of her son. "Do you like him? It's your new horse, Tempest. Sir Thirkell just brought him home. We were feeding Tempest bits of carrot. He's a greedy little thing."

"My lord," Thirkell said, acknowledging the earl's presence before he looked to Michael. "Young Master Michael. 'Tis good to have you home for your summer visit."

His mother stepped behind the knight and stumbled as she squeezed by him in the narrow stall. Thirkell caught her by the waist as she toppled forth. She gave him a tentative smile as he righted her.

With that, his father exploded. "Get your hands off my wife!"

His mother took a step forward. "I only—"

The earl struck his wife hard. She spun in a full circle and fell to her knees, blood dripping from her mouth, her eyes haunted with fear. Michael knew it wasn't the first time his father had injured her. He'd seen the bruises she tried to hide. He remembered the times she'd been bedridden for a week at a time, unable to walk after one of her husband's beatings for the slightest infraction.

Thirkell gave his the nobleman a look that chilled Michael's heart. The knight bent and lifted the countess to her feet and steadied her. He turned and faced his liege lord.

"I have sworn an oath to protect your family, my lord. That includes your lady and your son. I simply brought the countess to the stables to see the horse she wished purchased for Master Michael's homecoming." Thirkell paused. "I am sorry if I offended you by preventing her from falling."

The earl's eyes narrowed in a way that brought terror to Michael. "I've seen the looks you give one another when you think no one sees," he said, his tone more menacing than Michael ever remembered. "I know the slut sneaks off to your bed."

Thirkell's brows shot up. "I sleep in the barracks with a hundred other of your men, my lord. No woman—much less the lady of Sandbourne—ever graces my bed. You dishonor your wife by claiming so."

Michael saw his mother shrink against the stall's wall as the knight spoke. Blood stained the front of her light blue *cotehardie*. He turned back to view his father. Michael knew his father would never back down from the accusation, no matter how outlandish it was.

"You dare to call me a liar?" the earl demanded.

Thirkell shook his head. "Nay, my lord. You are simply mistaken. Nothing untoward has gone on this day, or any other day. I am in your service and loyal to you and the Devereux name."

Michael saw the blur as his father moved toward Thirkell. His brain refused to comprehend what happened so quickly.

Yet seconds later, he watched the knight's eyes go wide. Thirkell's hands flew to his throat, where a red gash angrily crossed his flesh. Michael glanced and saw the dagger his father always carried dangling from his hand. Blood dripped from the blade. Michael looked on as the knight crumpled to his knees. Thirkell tried to speak and then fell forward with a dull thud. Michael's jaw dropped open. No words came out. He watched the blood begin to pool under the knight's head, saturating the hay.

His father approached his mother, a gleam of madness in his eyes. Michael remained frozen in fear, unable to move.

"You have tested me, woman. Beyond what any man should endure. You've played me for a fool many times while you've dallied with other men. 'Tis time I rid myself of you, a woman who pawned off a child on me."

His mother took a step forward. Michael wanted to cry out for her to run away, but he couldn't speak.

"I have never been unfaithful for a single moment, Husband," she declared. "Michael is your son. No one else's."

His father moved with lightning speed and slapped his mother, knocking her against the wall. His fists pounded her face. Pummeled the soft flesh of her body.

Michael had to act. He must save her. Even if his father did the same to him as he did to Sir Thirkell. He had to be a man—for his mother's sake.

The earl's blows had forced his wife to the ground. He savagely kicked her now. Michael heard a rib crack and her gasp of pain. He slammed into his father, knocking him aside. Michael rode his father's back and began to choke him as the earl tried to regain his feet. Distantly, he heard his mother wheezing, a pitiful sound that broke his heart.

Suddenly, his father pried away the fingers from his throat and tossed his son off. Michael hit the ground so hard it knocked the breath from him, as if he'd fallen from a horse. He tried to suck in air, but his lungs seemed to freeze up. Before he could breathe, his father grabbed him, fists bunching into Michael's clothes as the earl lifted his son to his feet. Then an explosion of stars danced before Michael's eyes because his father brutally backhanded him.

Pain rippled along his cheek. He brought a hand to his face and touched the blood. His father's signet ring had sliced open his cheek.

Michael staggered to his feet and yelled, "Stop!"

The earl did so. It shocked Michael that his words had finally gotten through the fog of madness surrounding the man.

"No more, Father," he ordered, his voice quivering.

The earl gave him a grim smile. "You're right. I won't put up with this any longer." He glanced at his wife, now curled in a fetal position, her face already swelling. "Behold your mother for the last time, boy."

Michael sucked in a quick breath. *Would his father kill his mother right now?*

"You and I will never see this slut again. She's betrayed me for the last time. I'll find witnesses to her adultery. Pay them if I have to. She can spend the rest of her days on her knees in a convent, thinking on her multitude of sins and hoping God will forgive her many betrayals. As of this day, she is dead to me—and to you." His eyes shifted to the trembling, bloodied woman lying in the hay. "I won't be humiliated by a whore anymore. I'll see that you are locked away. That no one will ever know where you've gone. May God have mercy on you, for I have none left in my heart for you or your wanton ways."

Michael gazed at the broken woman on the ground. Her lips moved, but no words came out. Their eyes met. In them, he saw relief. Michael realized she would be glad to escape her marriage to this monster and the frequent punishments he doled out for imagined offenses.

As their eyes remained locked, Michael hoped his mother understood what was in his heart. That he loved her. That no matter what his father said, her son would someday find her.

And when he became the Earl of Sandbourne, Michael would bring her home and reinstate her to the position of honor she so richly deserved after all of her suffering.

Michael ran and kissed her swelling cheek before the earl could stop him. He then drew himself up and latched on to Tempest's mane. He willed himself to leap upon the horse bareback and surprised himself when he realized he sat atop the beast.

Looking down at his father, he declared, "You are a stranger to me and no longer my father. You've never called me by name. I have no love for you. I will never forgive you for what you've done this day. I'll never set foot on Sandbourne land again until your body lies cold and rotting in the ground."

Before the earl could stop him, Michael spurred Tempest on with a swift kick. The Earl of Sandbourne jumped aside. Michael hung on for dear life as he steered the horse out of the stables and galloped away from his home.

To a new future.

CHAPTER ONE

Kinwick Castle—1365

MERRYN DE MONTFORT took her fifteen-month-old son from Tilda and smiled as he babbled some nonsense. Knowing he had her attention, Hal then blew a bubble and laughed heartily. He was a sunny child and reminded her of how Geoffrey had been as a young boy, full of good cheer and light.

"He looks more like your brother, Hugh, every day, my lady," the servant said. "I should know. I cared for Hugh from the day he arrived." She paused and grinned at the babe. "I do see a bit of you in Hal, as well. You and Master Hugh looked fairly alike till you turned two. Then you went your own separate ways in your looks."

Merryn laughed. "That's nonsense, Tilda. Hal resembles his father. Look around his eyes. And his mouth. He is Geoffrey made over, from his coloring to his dark hair."

The woman shook her head sagely in disagreement. "The little lord has the Mantel family mouth, my lady. Of that, I'm certain."

Merryn bounced Hal slightly, causing his eyes to go wide before he giggled. No matter what her longtime servant said, she believed her boy would grow up to look like his father. Already, Hal reminded her of Ancel at that age. At almost eight years of age now, Ancel strongly favored Geoffrey.

She was happy Ancel would soon come home for his summer visit. Even though he fostered at Winterbourne, the adjoining estate to Kinwick, Merryn missed seeing her eldest son on a daily basis. She was grateful she and Geoffrey often received invitations from Hardie and

Johamma to visit Winterbourne and catch a glimpse of Ancel performing his duties as a page to the earl. Even so, it surprised Merryn how much her sweet boy had grown in the past year.

"My lady! They've been sighted. They're coming through the gate," a servant informed her.

Joy filled Merryn's heart as she hurried from the solar and down the staircase. She took care not to jostle Hal too much. While she missed Ancel, as any mother would, she ached every day from the pain brought by the separation from her daughter, Alys, who fostered with the queen at the royal court. For the first seven years of life, her oldest child had been her mother's shadow. Alys aided Merryn in growing and picking herbs and had all the makings of a future healer. In fact, the girl proved more knowledgeable than Merryn at the same age. Since Alys lived in London, Merryn hadn't seen her only daughter since the Christmas season. The bond between them was strong and she missed Alys more than words could explain.

Now, her daughter would remain at Kinwick for a longer period since she was not expected at her young age to go with the royal court on its entire summer progress. Merryn couldn't wait for Alys to see how much Hal had changed in the last few months.

Catching sight of Geoffrey astride Mystery, peace washed over Merryn. Her husband was the best part of her world. She was happy to have Geoffrey home after he'd been on the road this past week. He'd been back at Kinwick two years now after their long separation and she loved him more with each passing day. He galloped across the inner bailey, a broad smile on his face as he spotted her. She blew him a kiss—and couldn't wait for his lips to be against hers in a real one.

Other knights in the escort party followed closely behind him. Merryn spied Alys, sitting in front of Sir Michael Devereux. The knight had only been at Kinwick a year now, but he proved to be one of her favorites. His loyalty was beyond question and he had a way with all of the children on the estate. Hal seemed drawn to Michael like a moth to a flame and she had watched the two playing in front of the fire in the great hall many nights. Merryn wished that Michael would find a wife, for he would make a perfect father. Mayhap, she should begin to think of a woman to place in his path that would suit him.

She raised a hand in greeting, catching her daughter's eye.

"Mother!" Alys cried, waving her dainty hand back and forth.

She smiled as Michael lowered her daughter to the ground. Alys took off running up the stone stairs leading up to the keep. Merryn watched her approach and returned the girl's smile. Merryn could already see the budding beauty within Alys. One day she would steal men's hearts.

Alys reached the top of the stairs and clung to her mother for a moment. They both shed tears of happiness at being together again. Hal began squirming in her arms, trying to get a glimpse of his sister.

"Oh, Mother." Alys stroked the babe's cheek. "He has grown into a little man."

Merryn laughed. "He was barely toddling about when you were here at Christmas time. And now we have to watch him every minute of the day. He is faster than a comet streaking across the night sky."

Alys held out her arms. "Hello, little brother." She took the child and ruffled his dark hair. "Do you remember me? I'm your sister. The eldest child. Never forget that."

Merryn laughed. "'Tis a good thing Ancel is not here. He hates it when you mention that. He should return from Winterbourne in time for the noon meal tomorrow."

The girl sniffed. "Well, I am the firstborn. I arrived a good minute before Ancel did. I'll always be the oldest de Montfort child." Her eyes twinkled. "And I shall never let either brother forget it."

Merryn found herself spun around and in Geoffrey's arms. He pressed his mouth to hers in a lingering kiss. As always, just a simple touch from her husband melted her bones to liquid. Breaking the kiss, he gazed at her with love before brushing his lips tenderly against her forehead. Her husband always made her feel treasured.

Then he reached and snatched Hal from Alys' arms. "How's my boy?" He tossed the babe into the air and caught him. Hal squealed in delight. Geoffrey repeated the gesture several times before setting Hal on his feet. Hal bolted toward the doors where Tilda stood with a slice of cheese, his current favorite food.

Geoffrey put an arm about Merryn and Alys and drew them close. "I'm glad to be at Kinwick, once again, with my two girls."

"I'm a young lady, Father," Alys sternly reminded him. "The queen says so."

He laughed. "Far be it from me to disregard what Queen Philippa has said." Geoffrey squeezed both of them again. "Come, let's go inside. I know your mother wants to hear all about your time at court."

They bypassed the great hall and headed upstairs. Alys stopped at her bedchamber to wash and change her clothes, promising she would hurry. Merryn and Geoffrey continued on to the solar, where he did the same. Though she couldn't wait to hear what news Alys brought, Merryn felt a pang of regret as her husband doffed his clothes and changed into new ones. She wished they had some time to themselves.

"I see how you're looking at me, Wife," Geoffrey teased. He pulled his gypon over his head and laced it before drawing the rust *cotehardie* over it. "You wish to worship my body."

Merryn placed her palm on his chest and felt his heart jump. "Mayhap you can worship mine later this evening, my lord," she said saucily.

He yanked her close for a searing, possessive kiss. Much too short but ever so sweet. Then released her.

"Alys already chides us for all the kissing we do. I suppose we'll need to behave ourselves." He winked. "At least for now."

The door flew open at that moment. Alys entered with a parchment in her hand.

"A missive has come. Tilda said the messenger was given something to eat. He told Tilda that he's to wait for a reply." Alys handed it to her father, curiosity written across her face.

"Hmm. 'Tis addressed to Lord and Lady de Montfort in a hand I don't recognize." Geoffrey seated himself at the table and broke the seal.

Merryn came and placed her hands on his shoulders and peeked at the writing. She read:

To my dearest brother Geoffrey and his wife, Merryn –

It's been far too long since we have seen one another, Brother. I know being a dozen years older than you meant that we never spent much time together, yet I still remember your sweet, mischievous face to this day. Having lived far in the north till a year ago has made us strangers in this life, but I wish to remedy that.

I have remarried at the king's command and now reside at Hopeston Castle, only two days' ride from Kinwick. My fondest desire is for you to come and meet your nieces, Elysande and Avelyn. Elysande, my older girl, is to be married in a week's time. I hope you'll choose to attend so she can meet her uncle and aunt and her cousins—if you've been blessed with children.

Please come as soon as you can, Geoffrey. I'm sorry we lost touch for so many years. I would have us spend some time together as a family before the wedding. Elysande, as I was, will become a bride to a man from the north. This might be the only chance for you to meet her.

I pray I'll see you soon, Geoffrey. My best to you and yours.

Love,
Your sister, Mary

"This is a surprise," Geoffrey said, looking over his shoulder at Merryn. "I haven't seen Mary since she married many years ago. When I left to foster with Sir Lovel, she also left home to marry. My other sister, Eloisa, married and went to live in Wales the following year." He paused, a thoughtful look on his face. "And to think Mary is now close to us." He rested a hand atop Merryn's. "What do you say, my love? Shall we attend my niece's wedding and bring all our children with us so they may discover their cousins?"

"I am anxious to visit Mary." Merryn grinned. "Who knows? She might have some wonderful stories to share about her baby brother."

Her husband stroked her hand with his thumb for a moment before he rose. He brought her hand to his lips and kissed it tenderly. "You and Alys should pack, my love. I'm off to let Gilbert know what we're up to and choose a group of soldiers to accompany us to Hopeston."

Geoffrey left the solar and hurried down to the training yard, a spring in his step. The thought of reuniting with his older sister after so long a time and introducing Mary to his family brought him a great deal of happiness. His family meant everything to him.

Especially after the long years apart from them.

He reached the yard where soldiers dueled in pairs, his captain of the guard watching them compete with a careful eye. Geoffrey joined Gilbert and stood observing silently for a few minutes. It didn't surprise him to see that Michael Devereux had already joined in the exercises, despite their long trip from London. Michael proved to be one of the most eager knights that had sworn fealty to the de Montforts, and Geoffrey was happy to have the knight's service for as long as possible.

Michael fought against Hammond, another loyal knight who had been Kinwick's most talented swordsmen—until a year ago.

Michael Devereux's arrival had changed that.

Geoffrey watched the men battle one another. Stripped to the waist, the soldiers' muscles flexed as they waged war. Though both proved swift on their feet, Michael's movements were a shy more fluid. That gave him the advantage, which he now used to best Hammond. Applause broke out among the soldiers. Many of the pairs had stopped to watch the duel between Kinwick's best.

"I wish I had a score of men with half their talent," muttered Gilbert.

Geoffrey smiled at his captain. "You are a master swordsman yourself, Gilbert. You know how I value you and your way of teaching the men."

Gilbert nodded at the compliment. "Thank you, my lord," he said gruffly.

"I'll need ten of the men to accompany me tomorrow for a visit to my sister's. My niece is to wed in a week's time, and we've been invited to the wedding."

"Shall I choose which soldiers will make up the escort party?"

"Nay. I will do so myself. Carry on."

Geoffrey walked toward Michael. Hammond had already gone to the trough and dunked his head in, shaking his hair out.

"Michael? A word?"

The young knight's laughter stopped as he turned away from his companion's antics. Seeing his liege lord addressed him, he stood tall. "Aye, my lord?"

"I know we only just arrived from London, but I would like you to lead an escort party to my sister's home."

Michael didn't hide his delight in being asked to be in charge of the guard. He flashed a broad smile. "Of course, Lord Geoffrey. When would you like us to leave? And which knights will go?"

Geoffrey thought a moment. "I have great trust in you, Michael. I will allow you to select the men. Including yourself, I would like a guard of ten to bring myself and my family to Hopeston Castle, which we can reach in two days."

"When do we leave, my lord?"

"After we break our fast tomorrow."

Michael grew serious. "Then I will speak to the men at once and make the preparations for our journey." He paused. "Thank you, my lord, for having faith in my abilities."

Geoffrey gave the younger knight a fond smile. "You have come a long way since yours days as a page, Michael."

Michael broke out in a grin. "I have, indeed, my lord. If you'll excuse me?"

"Of course."

Geoffrey watched the soldier make his way toward Hammond. After a moment's conversation, Hammond eagerly nodded in agreement. The two men slapped each other on the back, and Michael went to speak to another knight. Satisfied, Geoffrey turned back toward the keep, ready to spend time in private with his wife.

CHAPTER TWO

Hopeston Castle

"The only explanation I can think of is that you've gone mad." Avelyn fell back onto the bed dramatically, her arms spread wide.

Elysande shook her head at her younger sister's behavior and sat in a chair next to the bed. She took Avelyn's hand in hers, knowing their time together drew to a close. She couldn't imagine a life without her sister in it. They had been as thick as thieves growing up and loved each other as sisters—but more importantly—as friends. Elysande's head ached thinking she would no longer be able to share everything with Avelyn on a daily basis.

Avelyn sat up. "This is your chance to escape living with the tyrant," she said, her eyes large. "You cannot stand Lord Holger. You wished Mother had never married him."

"But she had to," Elysande pointed out. "King Edward requested the match. No matter how you feel, you don't say no to the king. Mother had no choice but to marry Lord Holger and bring us south with her."

"Well, I think you're lucky. You'll get away from this dreary place and all of Lord Holger's bluster. He's nothing but a fool." Avelyn sighed. "I wish Papa would have betrothed me to someone as he did you."

Elysande stroked her sister's cheek. "He planned to do so. He told me as much. Father worked to have my betrothal contract signed first since I am two years older, and then he wanted to concentrate on finding a husband for you." She paused. "He didn't know how sick he would become or how fast death would occur."

Avelyn sat up and gave her a hug. "I know. I miss him so very much. He was a good father, but he was also a good man."

Elysande brushed aside a tear before it fell. "He was, indeed." She stood and restlessly began to pace their bedchamber. "But as much as I wish to escape from Hopeston, I don't want to leave you behind."

"Or the horses."

Elysande nodded. "Or the horses. Morningstar is due to foal soon. How can I miss that? And yet, in her condition, I can't take her with me." She continued roaming aimlessly about the room. "Do you think my new husband will even care? Will he allow me to send for Morningstar and her foal? Or will he allow me to dress like this?"

She glanced down at her man's clothing, which she wore far more than her smock and kirtle. Then she collapsed upon the bed. "I don't like to do anything that's ladylike in nature. I'm going to make a terrible wife."

Avelyn flopped beside Elysande, her hand resting under her head as she lay on her side. "Maybe Hendry will fall so in love with you that he'll allow you to dress as a boy. Or should I say a man? You are twenty now."

Elysande rolled over to her side and faced Avelyn. "I wish I could be feminine like you are. You love pretty clothes. You look good in anything you wear. You enjoy sewing tapestries and mending tunics. I've never been good at the womanly arts."

Avelyn sighed. "I'm still jealous of you. Except for the part where you'll have to move north to live. I much prefer the milder weather in the south. 'Tis the only good thing that has come from Mother's new marriage. I wonder when Lord Holger will get around to finding me a husband. Not that he even knows my name. He never calls either of us by name, Elysande. That's wrong. It's as if he doesn't acknowledge that we even exist."

"Lord Holger is an idiot. He probably can't remember our names. But Mother will see that he does his duty. She will insist that he find a husband for you."

"Do you suppose Hendry has any brothers?" her sister mused. "If I could marry one of his brothers, we wouldn't have to be separated."

Elysande shrugged. "I know so little about him. We only saw each other for a few moments when the betrothal contracts were signed four years ago. He barely said a word and looked so skinny and pale. Hendry mispronounced my name, and I had to tell him twice it was *EL-a-sund*. Twice!" As she tried to remain calm, she revealed something that had cut her to the quick. "What I remember most was that when he left, he told me that he didn't enjoy riding!"

Avelyn gave her a sorrowful look. "You never told me that."

"How could I? Horses are my life. I like them better than I do most people. How can I marry a man who refuses to like riding? What kind of man *is* that?"

"Elysande! Calm yourself," her mother ordered as she entered the chamber and closed the door. "You met the boy a long time ago. Surely, he has matured during these past few years. And so what if he doesn't care for riding? Not everyone is as horse mad as you are."

Elysande bit back the sharp retort that threatened to escape. No sense in alienating her mother in the short time they had left together. Yet, even that thought brought misery to her. She had put off thinking about her upcoming marriage for years. It seemed to be in the distant future. And now, it was right around the corner. Soon, she would return to the north, the place of her birth, far from her sweet mother and beloved sister. She looked at the pair and shuddered.

"I have some wonderful news to share with you," her mother said. "I just received word that my brother, Geoffrey, and his wife, Merryn, will attend your wedding. They are bringing their three children with them—your cousins. I haven't seen Geoffrey since he was a boy of seven. 'Tis more than twenty years that have passed. I can't wait to see how he turned out and meet his family."

Elysande rarely saw this kind of glow on her mother's face. She wondered if her mother would be alive a score from now. Glancing at Avelyn, Elysande tried to picture her sister twenty years in the future.

Slightly heavier after birthing babies. Faint lines about her eyes and mouth. Elysande could not imagine going that long without seeing her only sibling. It made her want to burst into tears.

Her mother chattered on about her former life at Kinwick Castle and the trouble she and her sister Eloisa used to get in to. She told a few stories about their baby brother and how good-natured Geoffrey had been. How she loved playing games and telling stories to him.

The more animated she became, the more she seemed like the mother Elysande had grown up with. A nurturing woman who loved her husband and children and would do anything for them.

"Do you miss Father?" she asked.

Her mother startled at the question and then frowned. She looked to Avelyn. "Leave us, child. I wish to speak to your sister alone."

Elysande saw the protest forming on Avelyn's lips and shook her head. Avelyn picked up on the cue and left the room without a backward glance.

Once the door closed, her mother warned, "I've asked you never to speak of your father, Elysande."

"Are you afraid of Lord Holger, Mother? Does he beat you? Is he unkind? I can't leave you in his care if something is wrong between you." She went and put an arm about her mother, wanting to comfort her.

Mary shrugged. "'Tis the way of the world. Holger leaves me alone for the most part. I run his household in the manner I see fit. Is he a fool? Of course. But for the most part, I have a free hand and don't have to spend much time in his company."

"I have no intention of running a household," Elysande proclaimed. "And I fear Hendry won't have changed much. He was weak and sick then. He will be the same now." She began pacing again, the words spilling from her. "I plan to twist this new husband of mine round my little finger. I won't dance to his tune. *He* will dance to mine."

Her mother gave her a stern look. "You would be wise to have a change of heart, my sweet girl. Hendry's father is a hard man. Lord

Ingram's reputation is chilling. Since he has no wife, you will be mistress of the castle even before Hendry claims his father's title." She came and put both hands firmly on Elysande's shoulders.

"You must do our family name justice. You are a Le Cler. You must behave appropriately. It's important that you give Hendry many sons to make him—and Lord Ingram—happy. You know the way of things. Our family lost your father's title to a cousin because I only gave birth to females." Her mother's fingers dug into her shoulders to emphasize her point. "Why do you think we wound up here? I don't want the same to happen to you. I want you settled and secure."

Mary's grip loosened. She cupped Elysande's cheek. "I have so much to get ready for. Your uncle and his family will arrive ahead of the wedding party so that we may visit before the celebration begins. I want everything to be perfect for him." She kissed her daughter's cheek and left.

Sobering thoughts flooded Elysande. She hadn't given much thought to her mother's remarriage. She didn't like Lord Holger, so she ignored him for the most part. That wasn't hard to do since she spent most of her time in the stables or in the pasture with the horses. But what was her mother's life really like? Elysande could see that her mother wasn't happy with this new husband. Not as she had been with her first.

And it hadn't been her decision. With no male children to inherit, they'd been turned from their home and sent south. Her mother had never laid eyes upon Lord Holger, but the king had ordered they marry at once, her father barely in his grave. Elysande couldn't believe she'd never thought these matters through. She'd ignored everything about marriage, including burying in the back of her mind her own upcoming marriage like some silly fool.

With her wedding merely days away, she would soon leave her loved ones behind. With such a great distance between them, she might never see Avelyn or her mother again. That paralyzed Elysande with fear.

It worried her that her mother had shared that Lord Ingram was a harsh man. Elysande remembered the nobleman from the signing of the contracts. How tall he'd stood. How he dominated a room with his loud voice and harsh laugh. Lord Ingram was the exact opposite of his son in every way. Elysande had been scared of the man. She'd avoided him until he and Hendry had left.

Elysande became anxious thinking about the marriage act. What if Hendry was still sickly and couldn't perform his husbandly duties? What if no babes came? Would Lord Ingram use her ample dowry to put her away in a nunnery and find his son a new, more fertile wife? Was that how things worked? She had no idea and realized how little she really knew about how the world worked.

And a darker thought flittered in the back of her mind. What if the father stepped in for the son? If he were that controlling a man, would he try to control her? Elysande realized, in that moment, how noblewomen were truly nothing but pawns.

With no say, she had no choice but to go through with her wedding.

CHAPTER THREE

"W E'RE ALMOST THERE!" Geoffrey de Montfort called out, his words carrying on the slight summer breeze.

Michael Devereux heard the excitement in his liege lord's voice and looked ahead to the castle that loomed large before them in the distance. He'd been lost in conversation with Ancel, Geoffrey's son who fostered with the Earl of Winterbourne, and hadn't realized how close they'd come to Hopeston Castle.

He looked back at Ancel, the very image of Lord Geoffrey. The boy already stood taller than most his age. His eyes took in everything about him. Michael had put Ancel through his paces in the dueling yard when he arrived home and was impressed with how quickly Ancel moved with a weapon in hand.

So unlike Michael at that same age. He'd been pudgy and short, slow in swinging a sword or running an errand. Laughed at unmercifully by the other boys who fostered with Sir Lovel. Yet his mother had been proven right. As Michael matured, the rolls of baby fat fell away. He shot up in height till he towered well over six feet. It took time to become accustomed to his new body as he grew into it, but once he had?

Everything changed.

He'd spent hours observing soldiers training in the yard and remembered everything he saw. Michael put those lessons to good use. Suddenly, the sword or mace that had seemed so foreign and unfriendly in his boyish hands now became a natural extension of his body. He became the one feared by all in the training yard, known for his fluid moves and quick thinking.

Though Michael could have remained in service to Sir Lovel, he changed his mind when he heard that Geoffrey de Montfort had returned to Kinwick Castle. Rumors abounded for years as to where the dashing knight had gone since he'd disappeared the day after his wedding. Finally, the king decided the nobleman must be dead and had arranged for Geoffrey's widow to remarry. Yet news traveled faster than lightning when Lord Geoffrey reappeared before the marriage could take place. No one learned where the Earl of Kinwick had been during those missing years, but Michael knew he must hurry south to serve the man he'd idolized as a child.

With reluctance, Sir Lovel had dismissed him from his service, telling Michael if he ever had a change of heart that he could return.

Michael made his way to the de Montfort estate and had spent the last year in happiness. Lord Geoffrey had matured since they'd last seen one another. He was a bit quieter than the gregarious youth Michael remembered, but Geoffrey still proved himself a leader amongst men. Michael knew he could learn much from the earl in the coming years.

Before he assumed his own title of nobility. Once his father lay dead.

Michael enjoyed the people of Kinwick. The estate was a happy place, full of kindness and love. Lord Geoffrey was responsible for some of those high spirits, but Michael placed most of the reason that Kinwick thrived at Lady Merryn's doorstep. The countess was a famous beauty, but that only told a small part of the story. She was wise beyond her years and had run the entire estate in her husband's absence. It flourished under her hand. She had a quick wit and a kind heart. Michael believed he and every knight in the de Montfort service were a little bit in love with her.

Surprisingly, the three de Montfort children brought him immense pleasure. Michael had never been around young children, but he found them to be delightful company. He'd only begun to know Lady Alys since her return from the royal court in London but, already, he could see Lady Merryn's hand in the child. Alys was thoughtful and interesting and full of good cheer. She'd entertained Michael on the entire journey back from London when they went to retrieve her for her summer visit to her home. He looked forward to seeing Alys mature as the years progressed.

Michael saw Ancel on a more regular basis since he fostered with Lord Geoffrey's neighbor and was a more frequent visitor to Kinwick. He could tell that the little boy would grow to be a skilled knight and an intelligent liege lord to all his people. Michael hoped that someday he could have a son much like Ancel.

Most of all, he adored the babe. Hal now toddled about and got into more mischief than seven children combined, yet the boy's sunny nature had stolen the hearts of everyone in the keep and beyond. His capacity for language grew by leaps and bounds every day. Michael enjoyed whittling toy soldiers for the boy. They would play with them in the great hall, spreading them out before the fire. Hal moved the soldiers around as Michael told him of battles that Knights of the Round Table had fought. Then Hal would direct Michael on how he wanted the toys placed. The two had spent many enjoyable hours in one another's company.

Michael wondered if he would ever have children. He supposed he must, in order to pass down the Devereux family's title and estates.

The thought soured his cheerful mood. He rarely thought about his boyhood home, which he hadn't seen in ten and five years. Keeping the promise he'd shouted out to the miserable man who had sired him, Michael had never returned. Only when the earl rotted in his grave would Michael come back to Sandbourne, laying claim to his title and tracking down which convent his mother had been banished to. If she still lived, he planned to restore her to the place of honor she richly deserved.

Until he came in to his title and the fortune that accompanied it, it was foolish to waste time thinking about it.

They approached the gates of Hopeston, and Michael captured the excitement spreading throughout the traveling party. He knew Lord

Geoffrey, now a score and ten, had not seen his sister since the year he left to foster at Sir Lovel's as a boy of seven. Between their reunion and the joyous occasion of the upcoming wedding of Geoffrey's niece, 'twas a happy time for all. Michael appreciated being part of the guard that accompanied the de Montforts to their destination.

The gatekeeper called out a friendly greeting and swung open the gates. They rode into the outer bailey and continued on through the inner one. Arriving at the keep, Michael watched a dignified woman make her way down the stone stairs, her skirts held aloft from her ankles. A younger girl followed closely on her heels. Michael assumed she was the bride-to-be.

"Mary!" Lord Geoffrey called, leaping off his horse and running to her. He captured his sister in his arms and twirled her about, their laughter warming Michael's heart. As an only child, he'd had no sibling to share anything with. If he ever did marry, he would fill Sandbourne with a dozen babes who would not only be blood kin but close friends who could depend upon one another through thick and thin.

He dismounted and aided Lady Merryn by taking Hal from her arms and setting him on the ground. The child quickly took off, but Ancel pounced on his brother and scooped Hal up in his arms despite his howling protests. Michael then lifted Lady Merryn from the saddle. She thanked him before she rushed to meet her sister-in-law and niece. Michael helped Alys from the horse she had insisted on riding by herself today on the last leg of their journey.

"You did a fine job, my lady. I think you were born to the saddle."

The corners of her mouth turned up in a pleased smile. "I've always loved to ride. Queen Philippa likes that about me." Alys joined Ancel, who now had Hal by the hand. Alys grabbed the child's free hand and the twins made their way to their parents with their baby brother in tow.

Michael, as head of the small guard that had accompanied the de Montforts to Hopeston, awaited his orders. After much hugging and cheek kissing, Lord Geoffrey broke away and came to him.

"See to all the horses, Michael, and then you and the men are to join the family in the great hall after you're settled in the Hopeston barracks. The noon meal will be served in two hours' time, but my sister, Mary, has thoughtfully provided ale and some bread and cheese to tide us over till then."

"At once, my lord," Michael promised.

Geoffrey strode away as Michael motioned for the knights to take the family's horses by their reins so they could take the animals to the stable. As they gathered the riderless horses and began to head in the direction Lord Geoffrey had indicated, Michael heard Lady Mary apologizing for her daughter's absence. Michael knew of two nieces at Hopeston, and he hoped the missing one wasn't ill. 'Twould be a shame if she missed her sister's wedding and the opportunity to know her extended family.

Remounting Tempest, he followed the nine knights ahead of him to the stables. A groom met them and showed where to house each animal in the vast structure. Michael saw that the men thoroughly rubbed down all the horses and fed them a good measure of oats before instructing the soldiers to drop their gear in the barracks and return to the keep.

As was his custom, he walked the stable area again, making sure everything was up to his own personal standards. Sir Lovel—and even Geoffrey and Raynor—had impressed upon Michael never to walk away from a task and assume that it had been accomplished as ordered. He must check each individual's work and be satisfied before moving on.

Michael counted the horses in his head, looking in on each. Everything appeared to be in order. Every animal had been cared for properly. He could leave and join the other men.

As he started to make his way back to the front of the stables, a voice startled him. He looked around but saw no one. Curious, he retraced his steps and went beyond where the de Montfort horses had been located. Rounding a corner, he heard the voice again. This time he distinguished it as female.

What would a woman be doing in the stables?

Michael continued till he found the source. He looked into the stall and saw a young man winding cloth around a horse's tail.

"Now Morningstar, you must be patient, my love. 'Tis best if you let me wrap this around your tail. It will keep from having all the hairs in your tail swish and get in the way when your sweet babe comes."

The clothing might be a man's, but the voice was that of a woman. He saw her profile now. The delicate, upturned nose. The flawless, milky skin. She was tall for a female, her breasts small, her willowy figure like a young sapling. A long, dark blond braid spilled down her back to her waist.

She must have sensed his presence because she turned toward him. Large, amethyst eyes dominated her face.

The most beautiful face he'd ever seen.

He sucked in a quick breath. His stomach lurched oddly as their eyes met.

"I am Michael. Do you need help?"

She pursed full, pink lips in thought. "I suppose you can stay in case I need an extra pair of hands. Have you ever helped foal a horse?"

"No." He grinned. "But I'm a fast learner."

"Good. I need a little more fresh straw. I swept out her stall this morning and placed a new bed of straw within, but my girl has been restless. Bring about three pitchforks full. I'll show you where to place it."

He did as told, retrieving the clean hay and spreading it where she requested.

"Are you serious about learning?" she asked.

"Of course. I may need to know about this someday." He thought of the day when he would own a stable full of prime horseflesh as the Earl of Sandbourne. Understanding the birthing process would be good knowledge for him.

She stroked the horse. "Do you see these wax-like beads at the end of her teats?"

Michael squatted. "I do. They're easily visible. What do they mean?"

"Morningstar began dripping this late last night. Some droplets of milk also have appeared. That tells me she will deliver soon." She patted the horse fondly. "And look here. A day ago her vulva began to swell and relax. It stretches in preparation for her to allow the foal to pass through the birth canal."

He looked carefully where she indicated. "I see." He stood again.

The mare snorted and began pacing around the stall. He noticed the space was actually two stalls that had been joined together. The wall between them had been knocked down. He decided to ask about it.

"Aye, it was an idea I tried. Many dams like to move about during the process. I suggested we give them more room to do so." She crossed her arms and leaned against the stall's wall as she watched the horse move restlessly about.

"She's a bit cranky now. It's all a part of it. She also drinks and expels her waste more frequently, but that tells me that everything is going as planned. She may want to be left alone now at this stage." The woman indicated for him to exit the stall. She followed and came to stand next to him, just outside. "We can give her a bit of privacy but still be on hand in case she needs us."

Michael supposed this woman must be a groom's daughter, if not the head groom, due to her knowledge.

"Have you been around horses all your life?"

A brilliant smile, bright as the noon sun, danced across her face. It drew him in like a siren's call to a sailor. "I live for horses."

He heard the love and devotion in her words and admired her for becoming informed in an area most women knew nothing about.

Of course, most women did not dress as she did. She wore all brown, her gypon and *cotehardie* barely covering her hips. Tight pants reached down to hug her long legs.

He wondered idly what she looked like under her man's clothing.

They watched the horse pace nervously for some minutes. The mare walked and then lay down. Moments later, she came to stand again. She repeated that process several times. The horse also kicked at her abdomen more than a few times and pawed the ground. Michael was fascinated by what he observed.

"Look. There. See how she breaks into a sweat along her neck and flanks?" the woman pointed out. "That's another sign that tells us the chain of events is progressing as it should."

Michael watched her studying the mare. A tightness banded his chest. His pulse beat rapidly. He'd never experienced such feelings when viewing any woman, much less one dressed as a man.

"I think we can go in again," she whispered. "Keep your voice low and nonthreatening. Morningstar will go through three stages now. She may be fine on her own or we might have to help her along."

"And you'll know what to do?"

"Of course," she said, looking at him as if he were an idiot.

"So what will be this first part?"

"Positioning her foal. She's been nervously pacing. The standing and lying down are her way of helping to place the foal in a proper position so it will easily come through the birth canal."

Without warning, the woman gripped his forearm. "Look!" she said, her soft voice growing more animated.

He watched as the mare expelled a rush of fluid from her body.

"That helps lubricate the birth canal. Now the strong contractions will begin."

She continued gripping his arm without realizing it, standing close to him. Michael inhaled a faint scent of violets surrounding her. Her fingers almost seared through his armor as if scorching stronger than a burning fire. Though she only stood next to him, he began to feel aroused. He bit his tongue, trying to tamp down the arousal.

The woman released her grasp and fell to her knees as the mare positioned herself on her side. The animal got up and down several times as before, extending her long legs as she strained with each contraction.

He knelt, watching the labored breathing of the horse.

"There! The foal is coming."

Michael saw the foal begin to emerge. First, the legs appeared, one slightly ahead of the other. Then the head came, tucked between the forelegs that now extended from the mare's body. The head and neck that followed seemed enclosed in some bluish-white sac. The shoulders passed through next.

Then nothing happened.

"Why has she stopped?" he asked. "The babe isn't fully delivered."

"She and the foal need to rest. Watch a moment. If Morningstar can be patient, so can you," she teased.

They waited a few minutes, then the woman sighed. "I was afraid this might happen. I'll need to help her. Usually the sac breaks on its own, but sometimes a little push is required."

She pulled a dagger from her booted foot and approached the mare and half-delivered babe, cooing softly to them both. Then she made a small slit in the sac. Liquid rushed out. She picked up a piece of straw and tickled around the foal's nose.

"I'm clearing the passage so her foal can breathe," she explained. "We don't want the newborn to suffocate." She stroked the mother reassuringly, telling her what a fine job she was doing.

Michael watched her gentle touch with both mother and foal. Strong emotion flooded him at the tenderness he witnessed before him.

After some minutes, the foal's hips came through. Then the mare took another period of rest before he watched the last of the foal finally appear. Immediately, the mare began to rise. The new foal struggled, and Michael saw the umbilical cord break in the process. He marveled at the wonder of birth.

"We need to watch now for the placenta. 'Tis the last stage and most important to observe carefully. The contractions will continue in an effort to expel it from her body. Poor Morningstar," she said, her voice low and pleasant. "I know, my sweetling. I know. You're hurting now. But it's almost over. Be patient." She stroked the horse gently.

They sat in companionable silence for the hour it took before the placenta came out. The woman retrieved it and examined it closely.

"Good." She nodded, a pleased look on her face. "Nothing broke off, so I won't have to recover any of the missing pieces."

Michael shuddered, not wanting to think what that might entail.

Instead, he focused on the new foal. While they'd waited for the mother to finish the final stage of the birth, the foal had learned to stand on its feet. It pained him when the newborn hadn't been able to do so the first or second time. By the third attempt, Michael grinned as it managed to stand and stay upright, though it swayed slightly.

"Now I need this little one to nurse." The woman maneuvered the newborn toward its mother and the waiting teat. After a little encouragement, the foal latched on to the mother's teat and began sucking enthusiastically. The noise was the only one that filled the stable.

Finally, the woman stood. Her braid had loosened. Honeyed tendrils escaped and surrounded her face. She looked tired but utterly satisfied.

Much like a woman did after he'd thoroughly made love to her.

Michael felt a deep longing for this woman. She had ordered him about, but he rather liked her bossy ways. His physical attraction to her had grown with each hour they'd spent together.

What would Lord Geoffrey and Lady Merryn think if he returned with a bride from this trip?

Michael knew Lady Merryn would be pleased. She'd taken to him and always complimented him when he played with Hal. Mayhap the countess could arrange a cottage for the two of them and his new wife could work with the de Montfort horses.

He couldn't believe such fanciful thoughts danced in his head. He'd risen this morning as a single man. Now the idea of wedding and bedding the woman before him was all he could think of. After the awful example of his parents' marriage, it was a wonder he'd even dwell on such matters.

Yet, he gazed at the woman as she lovingly stroked first the foal, then the mother. She drew close and pressed a kiss upon the flank of Morningstar and then another as she moved to the horse's head and kissed the creature between the ears.

Watching her with these two animals brought a wave of desire that exploded within him. 'Twas unfamiliar . . . yet exhilarating.

Michael realized *this* was what Geoffrey and Merryn had, something so deep that it transcended all else. He wanted it. Wanted it desperately. He would find out who this woman's father was and ask for her hand.

He laughed heartily and the woman glanced at him, rewarding him with a sweet smile for the hours he'd spent helping her.

Michael supposed the first thing he should learn was her name. That might prove helpful when he asked for her hand in marriage.

CHAPTER FOUR

ELYSANDE ROSE TO her feet and used her forearm to brush away the stray hairs tickling her forehead. She looked down at her stained clothing and realized she looked a frightening mess. Though physically worn to the bone, she still could have floated back to the keep. The birth of a foal never ceased to amaze and invigorate her.

She looked to the man who had come to her aid so many hours ago. *Michael.* That was his name.

For the first time that day, Elysande really saw him. Before, he'd simply been an extra pair of hands, making the entire process go more smoothly.

Now?

Everything changed in an instant.

He was well over six feet, with broad shoulders and a massive chest. Thick hair black as night. Cheekbones chiseled as if from stone. Lips full and sensuous. Staring at them made her begin to tingle in a most unusual—but pleasant—way. She had never kissed a man, but the only thought racing through her mind was that she wanted to press her mouth to his.

And keep it there. Forever.

Their eyes met. His piercing blue ones held hers as if she had been taken prisoner by him. Elysande couldn't move. She couldn't breathe.

Wordlessly, she took a step toward him.

"You are in so much trouble!"

The spell broke.

Elysande looked over Michael's shoulder and saw Avelyn there, her hands fisted on her hips, her face grim.

She blew out a long breath. "I might have known I'd find you here. You've been gone for hours. You were absent from the noon meal. You missed meeting—"

"But Morningstar foaled. Look. 'Tis a boy."

Avelyn's face softened into a smile as she spied the mother and foal fast asleep on the hay. Her lips pursed a moment. "I suppose that's an acceptable excuse. But you must come. Now. The evening meal will be served in less than an hour." Then she looked to Michael and dropped a curtsey. "Good day to you, sir. I fear, in my scolding, I misplaced my good manners. I am Lady Avelyn Le Cler. Are you one of my uncle's knights?"

Michael nodded. "I am, my lady. Lord Geoffrey has looked forward to meeting you. And to attending the wedding, of course."

Avelyn smiled. "He's a lovely man and Lady Merryn is so lively. We're delighted they could attend the wedding with such short notice."

"They are kind and generous people, my lady. I'm glad that you have the chance to spend time with them and your young cousins."

"Well, I see you've helped in Morningstar's foaling. Much thanks to you." She looked to her sister. "Please. We must make you presentable. I fear even a foaling will not be an accepted excuse."

Avelyn latched on to her hand and began to pull Elysande away. She called over her shoulder, "My thanks for your help. Mayhap, later tonight, you can come with me to check on the foal's progress."

"'Twould be my fondest wish," Michael shouted to her as Avelyn dragged her through the stable.

"Mother is furious at you for not greeting our kin. And you're filthy. We'll barely have time to bathe you before we dine. Oh, I hope Lord Holger doesn't notice you in such a state. You know how cross he becomes when he sees you dressed in this manner, Elysande."

She didn't care what her stepfather thought. She let herself be tugged through the inner bailey and into the keep. They reached their shared chamber, where a steaming bath awaited her. Avelyn rushed her from her clothes and into the water and began scrubbing her from head to toe.

Elysande sat back and let her sister take charge. Her thoughts turned to her uncle's knight. Michael's laugh had been deep and masculine. Not a thing like Hendry's. Her betrothed's was high and squeaky, as was his voice. Again, she bemoaned the fact that her father had contracted her to a man she already knew she would never respect.

The betrothal had surprised her, for he hadn't asked her opinion regarding it—which was so unlike him. He had treated both his daughters well, allowing them to pursue their passions. Hers had been languages and horses. She could write in Latin and spoke French, though she had a hard time with the difficult spelling of the musical language. Her father had never admonished her for dressing comfortably while she worked with the horses. In fact, he'd encouraged her interest in them. She owed most of her knowledge to his teachings since he loved the beasts as much as she did. They'd spent many pleasurable hours in one another's company in the stables or pastures or out riding the land.

Elysande's thoughts floated back to Michael. His image loomed large as she closed her eyes. That unusual tingling occurred again. She longed to touch her hand to his cheek, where a tiny, white scar had stood out against his olive skin. She wanted to do nothing more than kiss the man—a stranger!

Where did these bizarre feelings come from?

She barely knew him though they'd spent hours together in close proximity. She could recall his scent, a mixture of leather and horse and something achingly male. Elysande shuddered.

"Has the water chilled already?"

Avelyn's words interrupted her pleasant recollection.

"Nay, 'tis nothing."

Her sister held a bath sheet out. "Come. Stand. Let me dry you." She clicked her tongue in displeasure. "We'll never get your hair dry in time. I'll simply rebraid it. And Mother already set out a new *cotehardie* for you. She wants you to look your best when you meet Uncle Geoffrey and his family."

Elysande allowed Avelyn to dress her and redo her hair. She decided not to let her thoughts linger on Michael. It would be foolish to fixate upon another man when she would be married in less than a week's time.

"You look lovely." Avelyn kissed her cheek. Her eyes brimmed with tears. "Oh, Elysande, I'm going to miss you so much."

"Then you must come visit me in the north. Mayhap, my new husband's family will know of an appropriate match with a nearby nobleman. It would be more tolerable living far away in the north—if you could be close to me."

She smoothed the pale cream *cotehardie*, admiring the rich color of the emerald green embroidery. It was one of several that had been sewn for her in the last month in preparation for her wedding and the trip to her new home. Elysande decided to do more than hint to Hendry about finding a husband for Avelyn. If left up to Lord Holger, who knew what bridegroom her stepfather might select for her sister? She'd rather have a hand in helping to choose Avelyn's husband. Mayhap Hendry had some unattached, nearby cousin that would suit if not brothers of his own that might be persuaded to marry her sister.

They left the bedchamber and made their way down to the great hall. Trestle tables had already been set out for the evening meal. Many of the people of Hopeston gathered near them in conversation after a long day's work.

"Elysande!"

She heard her mother's voice call to her. She spied her mother standing with her stepfather and another couple. Elysande assumed the two would be her uncle and aunt-by-marriage. She hurried toward them, Avelyn not far behind her.

Her mother gave her what she and Avelyn called *The Look*. Mary used it only when severely displeased with either of them. Then it vanished as quickly as it came. Elysande knew she had a brief reprieve from the tongue-lashing that would occur behind closed doors, thanks to her absence for most of the day. She put on a smile and greeted their guests.

"Uncle Geoffrey. Aunt Merryn." Elysande gave each of them a kiss. "I'm happy that you could attend my wedding. Mother couldn't wait for your arrival." She paused. "I must apologize for not being present to meet you when you arrived. My horse, Morningstar, began to foal early this morning and I've been with her all day." She grinned. "I'm happy to report that a new male foal now rests with his mother in the stable."

Geoffrey laughed. "You definitely have de Montfort blood in you, Elysande. We do love our horses."

Elysande looked to her mother in surprise. "Truly?"

Mary shrugged. "I spent my fair share of time with Eloisa and the horses growing up. After I married, running a household became more of a priority." She looked to her husband, who gave a curt nod.

Merryn linked an arm through Elysande's. "We're so pleased to be at Hopeston. Come, I want you to meet our children, your cousins. We have twins and then a younger one."

Her aunt led her across the room. Elysande saw a boy and girl chasing after a small child that ran around with a gleeful look on his face as he skillfully avoided them.

"Oh, my!" she exclaimed. "They're miniature versions of you and Uncle Geoffrey."

Merryn laughed. "We hear that all the time. Children! Come meet your cousin."

The twins corralled their brother and came to greet them. The boy was tall and sturdy, while the girl was dainty and graceful. Elysande thought Geoffrey and Merryn must have looked much as these two did when they were the same age.

"Elysande, may I present my son, Ancel, who fosters with the Earl of Winterbourne, and my daughter, Alys, who attends Queen Philippa at the royal court. And for now, they have little Hal in their grasps. Hal might escape at any moment."

The twins greeted her with enthusiasm, asking all sorts of questions. She found them delightful children, while the little one kept Elysande laughing with his antics.

Without warning, she longed for children as bright and lively as these three. Ones that would look like Michael and her as they matured. Her face grew warm at the thought.

Why was she so taken by a man who was practically a stranger?

Elysande noticed people began seating themselves and suggested they head to the dais for the meal. Alys took her hand and had them skipping along as she chattered away.

They reached their seats and the service began. While she ate, Elysande's eyes searched the great hall, hoping to catch a glimpse of Michael. She spotted a table full of knights unfamiliar to her and assumed these were her uncle's men. Then she knew Michael was there because her heart began to beat erratically.

His back was to her, but she would know those broad shoulders and dark hair anywhere. She found it difficult to swallow another bite because of the fluttering in her stomach.

"This venison is so tender," Merryn said, drawing Elysande back to the guests that surrounded her.

She was determined to concentrate on the meal and her new kin. Elysande thought she did a decent job of both.

Even if her eyes wandered upon occasion to the table of knights on the far left of the great hall.

"SLOW DOWN, MICHAEL. You want to leave enough for the rest of us," Hammond teased.

Michael shrugged. "I missed the noon meal, my friend. I must make up for lost time and food. Or so my stomach tells me." He tore off a hunk of bread and popped it into his mouth.

"Where were you? I didn't see you after we left the stables. You missed some delicious rosemary bread and cold ale, as well as a sumptuous meal."

"I was needed in the stables." Michael stabbed another bite of the venison with his dirk and chewed away.

"Was there a problem with one of the horses?" Hammond asked. "I know how carefully you inspect each one after being on the road."

He swallowed. "Nay. Not a problem. I did make sure all the shoes still fit firmly and that each horse had its fill of oats. But a . . . situation came up."

Hammond laughed. "'Tis one involving a pretty maid by the dreamy look on your face."

Michael froze. Did his face truly reveal the longings he had for the unnamed woman?

He'd looked around for her as he'd entered the great hall, assuming she must be one of the serving wenches. Lady Avelyn had strongly rebuked her for missing much of the day inside the keep, especially since guests had arrived at Hopeston. He supposed she'd been derelict in her cleaning or kitchen duties while she'd spent the daylight hours with the foaling dam.

But he hadn't spotted her, and now the meal drew to a close. Poor thing. She was probably being punished by doing the lowest menial task in the kitchen and would have to eat later.

It did cause him to wonder, though. With Morningstar so close to giving birth, why hadn't her father—or one of the other grooms—been available to help her? Or even come with a watchful eye as the horse gave birth?

Michael determined to find her once the meal was cleared away. He had yet to learn her name.

And he wanted to learn even more than that. He longed to wrap the woman in his arms. Drown in her scent. Kiss her senseless. Drive his shaft into her and make her his.

He turned to his companion. While he shared most things with his closest friend, he was not ready to go so far as to tell Hammond he was ready to commit to a woman in holy wedlock. He feared his friend would try to talk him out of such a rash decision.

Michael realized that marrying a lowly servant girl would be frowned upon for the future Earl of Sandbourne. Yet no one, save for

Lord Geoffrey, knew he was to inherit the lofty title one day. He'd gained his knighthood under Sir Lovel, but when he came to Kinwick, Michael decided not to share what his future held with those he encountered. He was a stranger to all but his liege lord. The knights in service to Lord Geoffrey hadn't a clue they toiled beside a future earl. He'd asked Lord Geoffrey to keep his secret and knew no one had learned of it.

Frankly, he didn't care if the woman was highborn or low. Desire for her filled him like never before. When they eventually returned to Sandbourne, no one need even know her father had worked in the stables and she herself served those at Hopeston Castle. As earl, he could marry any woman he pleased. His father hadn't betrothed him to anyone before he left Sandbourne at the tender age of eight. He would marry this woman and bring the bride of his choosing to his home.

Once his father was gone for good.

Michael turned to Hammond. "As a matter of fact, the situation did involve a woman." He smiled. "A very pretty one, at that."

Hammond slammed a fist upon the table. "I knew it. You have all the luck with the fairer sex, my friend."

He sighed. "Actually, she put me to work for the entire day. A dam was ready to deliver, and she required my assistance. We spent the entire day with the horse, watching her foal." He smiled. "'Twas quite interesting since I'd never witnessed it before. Almost like a miracle."

Hammond nodded. "I've watched a horse give birth before. I found it hard to believe that so soon after, the foal could stand on its own."

Michael rubbed his chin thoughtfully. "This one took a few times to gain his balance, but once on his feet? He was sturdy and true." He leaned in. "She invited me to return to the stables tonight after we supped, so we could check on the mother and foal together."

His friend's eyebrows shot up. "Hmm. I wonder what else you might investigate while together."

"I plan to go hunt for her now and find out."

As he came to his feet, he found Lord Geoffrey approaching him.

"Is all well, Michael?" he asked. "I missed seeing you after our arrival."

"No problems, my lord. I gave a hand in the Hopeston stables, is all. I assisted with a dam that foaled a fine little horse."

Geoffrey's eyes gleamed. "Did you?" He chuckled. "You've come a long way from your early days with Sir Lovel, my friend. I remember when you weren't overly fond of horses."

Michael shrugged. "Things change, my lord. I'm glad I grew up and have become the man I am and not that pudgy lad who was slow at everything a page was required to do."

The nobleman laid a hand on his shoulder. "You are the best of men, Michael. I'm pleased that you're in my service." His hand squeezed Michael's shoulder in affection. "But come with me. I would have you meet my sister Mary and my nieces." A shadow crossed his face. "And our host."

They crossed the great hall as groups of people returned the trestle tables to the sides of the large room. As they drew near, Michael saw Lady Avelyn in conversation with Lady Merryn and an older woman he supposed was Geoffrey's sister.

"Ladies, I would like you to meet one of my finest knights. Sir Michael Devereux, my sister, Lady Mary, and one of my two nieces, Lady Avelyn."

Michael bowed. "'Tis a pleasure to accompany Lord Geoffrey and Lady Merryn to Hopeston, Lady Mary." He looked to the younger woman. "And a pleasure to see you again, my lady."

"We met earlier. In the stables," Avelyn explained to the others. "Thank you for your help with Morningstar. Elysande loves that horse as much as she does her own flesh and blood."

Elysande.

At least he had a name for his future wife. And he liked it. Quite a bit. He couldn't wait to address her by name and hear it flow from his tongue.

Just then, Hal came running up to him, being chased by Alys and a woman behind her.

"Michael! Michael!"

He scooped the boy into his arms. "How's my little man?" he asked, tickling Hal under the chin. The boy giggled and squirmed.

Then he sensed eyes upon him. Michael looked up.

Elysande stood a few feet in front of him. His mouth went dry as he gazed upon her.

But his mind tried to understand what he saw.

She wore a *cotehardie* of palest cream, embroidered with a rich emerald green. A delicate gold cross hung about her neck, emphasizing its slenderness. She reminded him of a graceful swan.

This was no servant. This beauty, out of her boyish pants and faded tunic, was all woman—and one highborn.

Michael realized, in that moment, that Elysande was Geoffrey's other niece. The thought pleased him tremendously. He believed Geoffrey would offer whatever support he might need in winning Elysande's hand.

"Ah, Sir Michael, here is my errant daughter, who neglected to greet her family and guests," Lady Mary said.

Elysande's sunny smile lit up the room. At the same time, it pushed everyone but her from his vision. Michael's heart pounded so quickly, he felt as if he'd run a thousand steps in an instant.

"I'm afraid I didn't properly thank you for your help today, *Sir* Michael." Elysande turned to her mother. "This gallant knight helped me with Morningstar and her new foal," she shared, "though he merely introduced himself to me as Michael."

Lady Mary nodded graciously to him. "Thank you, good sir. I'm glad my daughter had your help. She usually is quite headstrong and refuses for anyone to aid her in these matters." She looked back to her daughter. "At least Morningstar gave birth before your wedding, my dear. Now you won't have to worry about her being left behind when you and Hendry travel north next week."

Michael felt as if he'd been stabbed in the gut. His eyes cut to Avelyn and back to Elysande. It wasn't Lady Avelyn who was to wed later this week.

'Twas Lady Elysande.

CHAPTER FIVE

E LYSANDE HEARD HER mother's words. They brought her crashing back to a painful reality.

She had watched her uncle when he went to address his knights as she and Alys playfully chased Hal about. When he led Michael over to meet her family, she gazed at him from afar. He was everything she would want in a man. Intelligent. Kind. Interesting.

And simply looking at him made her go weak in the knees. She stood on shaky legs, just as Morningstar's new foal.

God in Heaven, she wanted this man—and no other. Especially not Hendry.

Her small cousin took off in a blur. Both she and Alys gave chase. Hal ran toward Michael, calling his name, his chubby arms outstretched. She watched as the knight broke into a wide grin and lifted the babe high in his arms. Michael looked so happy, so right, with the child nestled close to him. As if were born to be a father.

Then their eyes had met, and Elysande drew in a quick breath. She could have spent an eternity gazing at his chiseled face. She'd never pictured the Archangel Michael as dark, but this man appeared to have fallen to earth from the heavens high above. She drank him in, a smile immediately forming on her lips.

Her mother ruined any fantasy she had begun to spin in her mind by bringing up her approaching wedding to Hendry.

Elysande watched the stunned look cross Michael's face before it quickly disappeared. If she hadn't been studying him so closely, she would have missed it. In an instant, she realized that he'd believed

Avelyn was the bride-to-be.

And had thought her free.

A thrill rushed through her. Deep within her, Elysande knew this knight was as drawn to her as she was to him.

But nothing could come of their attraction. A betrothal was as good as a marriage. In the sight of God Almighty, she was already a wife to Hendry.

Yet her heart cried out for justice. To meet the man she longed to spend the rest of her life with only days before she wed another? It was a cruel trick on Fate's part.

Elysande threw caution to the wind. "Sir Michael, do you remember that you promised you would return to the stables with me after we dined to check on Morningstar and her foal?"

He nodded stiffly. "I did tell you so, my lady."

"Would you care to accompany me now? I've been thinking of names for the foal. Mayhap you can help me decide upon one."

"Of course." Michael handed Hal to Geoffrey and looked at their circle. "If you would excuse us?"

"I want to go," Alys chimed in. "I love horses."

Elysande bit her lip. Oh, this wouldn't do at all. She wanted a few moments alone with Michael.

Merryn caught her eye. Her brows raised slightly, as if she asked an unspoken question. Elysande gave her a tiny nod, hoping her new aunt might understand.

"I think you've had a very long day, Alys. Find Ancel. I would see all of my children put to bed so that you get a good night's sleep."

"But Mother—"

"No buts, my sweet." Merryn looked toward Elysande. "Mayhap you would take the children to the stables sometime tomorrow and introduce them to your newly-named foal."

Elysande relaxed. "I would enjoy doing so, Lady Aunt."

"You must promise," Alys said solemnly.

Elysande fought back a smile and looked as serious as she could. "I will, indeed. The foal might be a bit shy and Morningstar a tad possessive, but I'll be happy to show both of them off to my new cousins in the morning."

Alys smiled and skipped off in search of her brother. Hal wiggled in Geoffrey's arms.

"Do not even think of letting him loose," Merryn warned her husband. "Let's take the children upstairs. We'll see all of you on the morrow at mass. Good night." She and Geoffrey left those gathered.

Michael held an arm out to her. "My lady?"

Elysande placed her hand atop it. She stiffened her legs with resolve, determined not to collapse and embarrass herself. She wished her mother, Avelyn, and the silent Lord Holger a good evening and allowed Michael to lead her from the noise in the great hall.

At the door, he lit a lantern to light their way. They didn't speak as they exited the keep and went toward the stable. A cool wind stirred the night air about them. Elysande shivered.

"Are you cold, my lady? We can return to the keep for a cloak."

"Nay. We're too close to our destination. Besides, I am eager to see my little loves."

"Then we'll hurry."

They reached the stables. Her fingers tightened slightly on his arm. They had arrived. She should let go. But the warmth emanating below her fingers made her reluctant to do so. Elysande decided to allow her hand to remain on his arm a few moments longer until they reached the stall.

Michael greeted a few of the horses by name as they passed. He stopped a moment and looked down at her.

"My lady, since you are one who enjoys horses, I would like to introduce you to Tempest. We've been close companions since I was a young boy."

The horse, whose mane proved even darker than his master's hair, leaned his head over the stall door. She moved forward and stroked the silky, midnight coat.

"He's a beauty, Michael." She realized for propriety's sake that she should have called him Sir Michael, but it seemed so right addressing him in a more intimate manner.

Michael pulled a carrot from his pocket. Immediately, Tempest perked up and leaned around his new acquaintance, straining to reach his master and the treat.

"Ah, there's my greedy boy." He fed the carrot to the horse, who nibbled it daintily. He gave Tempest an affectionate pat. "Shall we continue?"

He offered his arm again. Elysande didn't hesitate to take it. They walked to the far end of the stable and glanced inside. She saw the foal nursing. She stepped inside the enlarged stall with Michael following closely behind her. He placed the lantern on the ground. Elysande pulled an apple from her pocket and offered it to Morningstar. She gobbled it in an instant.

"Poor thing. She's been through a long day with the labor. I'll fetch her some more oats." Michael left and soon returned with a full bucket.

By then, the foal had come to rest upon the hay. His eyes were closed, a contented look upon his face.

"He looks happy," Michael noted.

"He does," she replied softly. She thought a moment. "I think I'll call him Happy, for I hope all of his future days will be so."

It pained her to think that the foal's future—and hers—rested in the north. Soon she would be wed to a stranger and travel far from her loved ones.

Without warning, a sob escaped her lips. Elysande turned away and stepped into the shadows by the wall. She hadn't meant to show her feelings of despair, much less voice them through tears.

Michael came to her. He grasped her firmly by the elbows and stared into her eyes. His own, the blue so dark they looked almost black in the dim light, searched her face.

His touch had sent a shock through her. A low humming seemed to vibrate between them.

"I know you feel what's between us," he said, his voice low, the yearning unmistakable.

"Aye," she replied, her breath shallow and rapid.

He gave her a crooked smile. "We are but strangers, yet I feel I've known you for a lifetime."

Elysande nodded. "I feel the same way."

"I never thought to utter these words, but I'm already more than a little in love with you," he admitted. A sad look crossed his face. "Yet, I now understand from your lady mother that you are the woman who will wed in but a few days' time. Not Lady Avelyn."

"Aye." Her eyes welled with tears. "We have no future, Michael, and, for that, my heart breaks." A tremble ran through her. "I fear what I'll become, having never known your touch."

His hands tightened on her elbows. "And I don't know how I'll live through each day to come not having you by my side." His hands slid up her arms to her shoulders. His fingers caressed her neck.

Elysande boldly told him, "I've never been kissed, chael. 'Twould be my fondest wish for you to be the first man to do so. I would like to hold that memory in my heart for all time."

He hesitated. She knew if he were a knight of her uncle's that he must be the most honorable of men. He wouldn't act in an unchivalrous manner.

But she wanted him. Here. Now. Elysande knew if she did not have his kiss that she might wither and die.

So she took charge like a knight riding into battle.

Her hands came to rest upon his chest. She felt his heartbeat racing rapidly against her palm. She cupped his cheek, the one with the tiny scar on it. Her other hand crept to his mouth. Her fingertips brushed his lips. Then she took both hands and fisted them in his hair, pulling his face down to hers.

Their lips met. Hot desire, something she'd never known, raced through her limbs, dissolving her bones. Michael's arms enfolded her, drawing her near. His tongue slid along the seam of her lips, teasing her, opening them for an adventure she had yet to experience. Then his tongue thrust into her mouth, dancing with hers, dueling, possessing her with a heat that spread throughout her body. Every sense came alive.

Elysande's fingers pushed deeper into his hair as his hands roamed her back and slipped to her buttocks. He squeezed them, pulling her against him. She felt his manhood, hard against her, frightening her and yet bringing a sense of wonderment. *She* aroused these feelings in him. *He* caused her to burn with want of him.

Again and again his kisses branded her. His lips moved to her throat, burning a hot trail to the swell of her breast. His stubble scraped the tender flesh as his hand cupped her breast. It swelled, filling his palm. Elysande thought she might go up in flames and burn the stables to the ground, so great was the heat generated between them.

Suddenly, it ended. Michael's mouth was gone. His hands fell to his side. A winter's cold seemed to embrace her now that his warmth had fled.

"Michael?" she asked, not knowing how to form any word beyond his name.

He cradled her face, stroking his thumbs against her cheeks.

"You're perfection, my love. My one true love. My sweet Elysande." His last words were but a whisper.

She heard the strong emotion in them, causing his voice to go low and thick.

He kissed her once again, hard and swift, then pulled away.

"God forgive me," he muttered and stormed from the stall.

CHAPTER SIX

MERRYN WATCHED AS Avelyn escorted the children from the great hall. They had just broken their fast, and now Avelyn took them to explore the keep. Mary's younger daughter had taken to her de Montfort cousins as if she'd known them from birth. Merryn knew the girl would make an excellent mother to her own babes one day. Merryn had promised her children that, after their cousin gave them a tour of Hopeston Castle, they could go and meet the new foal in the stables.

For now, she had other concerns. Merryn sensed something was wrong with Elysande as she watched her pick at the bread in front of her. Her new niece-by-marriage had impressed Merryn with her kindness and intelligence. She was glad Geoffrey had accepted the invitation to visit Hopeston. Merryn had looked forward to becoming acquainted with his sister and her two daughters, especially since they were only two days' ride from Kinwick. She hoped to host these relatives and allow Mary to revisit her childhood home. She had no memory of Mary even though she must have been present when Merryn visited Kinwick in her younger days. Being three years younger than Geoffrey, though, she couldn't recall anything from her childhood about his two older sisters. They would have left Kinwick before Merryn turned five. She already felt she had a sister in Mary and had decided to firm up plans for them to visit the de Montfort estate. Mayhap at Christmas. 'Twould be lovely to bring some of the family together.

Merryn glanced over at Mary's second husband. Lord Holger was another matter. She was glad Geoffrey engaged the man now in lengthy conversation as they broke their fast. The nobleman hadn't warmed to his wife's relatives. Merryn had overheard Holger bitterly complaining about the cost of Elysande's wedding and how many guests had been invited. His already reddened face turned a brighter scarlet as he got worked up over the situation.

Geoffrey took her hand, bringing Merryn from her reverie.

"Lord Holger and I are going to ride about his estate. Would you care to join us?"

Her husband gave her a lazy smile and squeezed her hand. Merryn could tell he held back laughter. She had already revealed her feelings about their host last night after they saw the children to bed and lay entangled in each other's arms.

She smiled brightly. "I'll leave riding to you gentlemen. I'd prefer to keep company with Lady Mary and hear more about the wedding."

Holger belched loudly. "Come along then, de Montfort. We can leave the womenfolk to their talk. Though how they can converse endlessly about something as uninteresting as a wedding has me baffled."

The two men left the great hall and Merryn turned to her left. "Elysande, would you like to take a walk about the keep with me?"

The young woman tossed aside the bread she played with. "I'd enjoy that, my lady."

Merryn placed her hand on Elysande's shoulder. "Please. Call me Merryn, for we are family."

She caught sight of the tears that welled in Elysande's eyes. "Family which I'll probably never see again," she muttered, her mouth turning downward.

Rising, Merryn tugged on her niece's elbow. "Show me a quiet place where we can speak privately. I believe you have need of a sympathetic ear."

Elysande stood and slipped her arm through Merryn's. "We could go to my bedchamber."

"I would like that."

They made their way to the room. It had a large bed and two chairs placed under a single window.

"This is a lovely room," Merryn said. "Do you share it with your sister?"

Elysande nodded as she seated herself. Merryn took the remaining chair.

"I can't imagine how you're feeling," she began. "Geoffrey and I grew up on adjoining estates. We knew each other from childhood and were best friends. Our friendship turned into a deep, abiding love." She smiled. "To this day, my husband is still my best friend and greatest confidant."

Merryn studied her niece. "But you are in much different circumstances, I gather."

"Aye," Elysande said, wiping her sleeves against her eyes. Already, they were red and swollen as if she'd cried many tears this morning.

"I know you'll miss your mother and sister. But it could be a great adventure," Merryn said encouragingly.

"That's true. I'll miss Mother and Avelyn beyond words. We're close and always have been. Mother has told me to ask Hendry if Avelyn might come and stay with us." Elysande shrugged. "But I have no idea if that would be allowed. I only met him once, several years ago. To be frank, I didn't think much of him." She gave Merryn a rueful smile. "'Twill most certainly not be a love match as you and Uncle have."

Merryn took the girl's hand. "I am one of the few blessed in that regard. I loved Geoffrey from the time I was only half your age, and our love grows stronger with each passing year. But that doesn't mean that other couples who wed as strangers never find love. My parents did. You and Hendry could be one of those couples."

Elysande burst in tears. She stood and ran to the bed and fell upon it. Her loud sobs and shaking body caused the bed to shake.

Now, Merryn was getting to the root of the problem. Instinctively, she knew what ailed her niece.

She crossed and sat on the bed, gently stroking the girl's hair, murmuring soft words of comfort. For some minutes, Elysande cried as if her heart would break in two. More than most, Merryn knew that kind of pain. The seven lonely years she'd spent without her husband in her bed, not knowing where he'd vanished, gave her a unique perspective.

When Elysande began to quiet, Merryn asked, "So you love another? Is he also from the north, whence you came, or will you leave him behind when you leave the south?"

The girl raised her tearstained face, surprise written across it. "How did you know?"

She took her hand. "Women just do. So who is this man?"

"M-M-Michael."

Merryn had not expected this answer. "Our Michael? Michael Devereux?" She wanted to point out that they'd just met, but she understood the heart wanted what it wanted. Though love usually bloomed slowly, sometimes it sprang instantly between a man and woman.

"Aye." Elysande sat up. "I don't even understand how it happened so fast. He appeared in my life only yesterday. He stayed with me all day as Morningstar foaled."

"You shared a meaningful experience that bonded you in a special way."

"And... and... we kissed," Elysande admitted. "Last night. When we went to the stables to check on the horses. We both feel the same way." Her mouth began to tremble. "Yet we know nothing can come of it."

Again, Merryn found herself surprised, yet it made perfect sense. Both Michael and Elysande were intelligent, attractive, and compassionate souls. They'd been drawn together during an emotional time. It saddened her that they couldn't be together so their new love could blossom.

"*I* kissed him," Elysande shared. "I've never kissed any man, but all I wanted to do was kiss him, Merryn. And he returned the kiss." She expelled a long breath. "It was... magical. I know he loves me and I love him. But then he left, begging God to forgive him."

She jumped to her feet and began roaming the room. "And I'm miserable. I don't want to wed Hendry. I already know how ill-suited we are. I live for horses—and he doesn't even like them! He is weak in spirit and body. We should never have been matched together."

Elysande angrily wiped the tears from her cheeks. "I don't want to go live in the north. And I'm very afraid of Lord Ingram, Hendry's father." She threw her hands in the air. "What am I to do?"

Merryn enfolded Elysande in her arms. "There's nothing you can do. Michael is an honorable knight. A man of his word. He would never come between you and this Hendry." She paused. "You must go through with your marriage. 'Tis what your father wanted. You must honor his wishes and the betrothal contract."

Merryn broke their embrace and looked her niece in the eye. "And you will mourn in your heart for a long time. Mayhap the rest of your life. But your fate is in your own hands, Elysande. Only you can decide to be a good wife to your new husband and a nurturing mother to the babes you'll bear him."

Merryn laid a palm against Elysande's damp cheek. "Sometimes, we must set aside our own longings to serve others. I know that's not what you want to hear, but I advise you to put your feelings for Michael aside. Try and make a new future with your husband. Don't look back. You'll only be miserable if you wallow in something that can never be returned to you. Look ahead."

Elysande buried her face into Merryn's shoulder. "You're right. But it hurts so much."

"I know."

MERRYN SPENT ANOTHER hour with Elysande, sharing a bit of her own story. She explained how she had managed Kinwick in Geoffrey's absence, especially after his father's death.

"I had no one to guide me. I couldn't show weakness. I had to trust my own instincts."

"But you're lucky, Merryn. Uncle Geoffrey came home to you."

"Aye, he did." She gave Elysande a smile. "And who knows? Your own story is yet to be written. It may turn out much differently than what you anticipate."

Merryn rose to her feet. "Come. I need to find the children and see what trouble Hal has caused."

"I'll take them to see Morningstar and Happy as I promised Alys. She is a dear girl."

"That she is. I know she thrives under Queen Philippa's tutelage, but I sorely miss her."

They located Avelyn and all three children near the training yard. They watched the knights at work as Geoffrey's men sparred with Holger's soldiers. Ancel immediately asked if they could go to the stables and meet the new foal. Elysande agreed, never looking at the men close by. Avelyn decided to accompany them. Merryn felt with two adults and two older children in tow, mayhap the four of them could keep Hal in line.

She watched them leave and then located Michael. The tall knight tutored a younger man, holding his sword and demonstrating how to swing the weapon for maximum effect. Merryn's heart went out to the knight. He was a good soldier and an even finer man. She had thought to pair him with a woman only last week. Now, she decided upon their return to Kinwick that she would play matchmaker and find a young woman that would help him forget his brief encounter with love at Hopeston Castle. She believed that if he turned his attention in a different direction and married, he could find some happiness of his own.

Merryn returned to the keep. She found Mary and spent a few hours with her in the solar. The two women sewed as they chatted like old friends. Merryn caught glimpses of her husband in his sister, especially around her mouth.

She finally excused herself, needing to find the children. She'd left them with their cousins long enough. Merryn went back to the inner bailey and found Geoffrey returning from his ride with Lord Holger.

He linked his arm through hers. "Take a stroll with me. We can share about our day." Geoffrey leaned close to her and softly confided, "Mine? 'Twas awful. Holger is boring and as stupid as a tree stump. Frankly, it's an insult to the stump to say that. I'm sure the stump is far more intelligent than Holger could ever be."

Merryn giggled, snuggling closer to her husband as they sauntered along. "I learned something very interesting today. Your niece is in love with Michael and he with her."

Geoffrey abruptly stopped. "*Our* Michael? Michael Devereux? Why, they only just met."

Merryn pulled him along. "Which makes it all the more tragic. She'll marry in a few days' time and he'll return to Kinwick, miserable as she is as she rides away to the cold, barren north. But," she confided, "I've decided to find Michael a wife to help him forget this quick interlude. He's so good with Hal, and he'll make a find husband."

"Nay," Geoffrey warned. "Stay out of it, Merryn."

His words baffled her. "Why?"

"I hate to thwart your plans, but Michael needs to find a special woman to be his bride." Geoffrey sighed. "I hate to break his confidence, but I know 'twill go no further."

His words intrigued her. "What do you know?"

"You remember I told you that Michael fostered at Sir Lovel's with me."

"Of course. He was a page when you became a squire. And then you went to fight as a knight in France and didn't see him upon your return since you came straight to Kinwick."

Geoffrey stopped to nuzzle her neck. "Because I had to come home to you, my love."

His touch thrilled her, but curiosity pulled at her. "So, go on."

"Michael will inherit a title and quite a large bit of property upon his father's death. Our Sir Michael will become the Earl of Sandbourne."

"Michael's to be an earl? Well, I must say that doesn't surprise me. The way he carries himself. His intelligence and kindheartedness. He will make the best of earls. I'm so pleased." She paused. "But why hasn't he shared this? 'Tis nothing to be ashamed of."

"He simply wanted to be one of the men and not be treated differently. So, I'm sorry, but your scheming is no good. Michael will need to marry a woman of his own class, one who'll make a good countess and be his perfect helpmate."

Merryn frowned. "Then it makes me even sorrier that it can't be Elysande. She'd be an ideal match for him. I rather like this feisty niece of ours."

CHAPTER SEVEN

ELYSANDE DRESSED WITH care. Today marked the arrival of her groom and his relatives. She wanted to look her best. She glanced down and admired the dark blue surcoat and the slashes of slate gray that ran through it. She sat on the bed and slipped on the soft leather shoes that came just above her ankles. She supposed she should save them for her wedding tomorrow, but she hadn't wanted to break in a new pair of shoes on such a long day. She'd worn these for a few hours each day for the last week and they finally had begun to feel comfortable. She hoped by tomorrow they wouldn't give her any problems.

Avelyn bounded through the door. "Oh, that color looks lovely on you, Elysande. Hendry is going to fall madly in love with you the moment he sees you."

But she didn't want Hendry to be in love with her.

She only wanted Michael Devereux's love.

Elysande swallowed hard, forcing down what wanted to come back up. She hadn't eaten much the past two days. The little she did manage to eat constantly threatened to spill from her.

"Let me do your hair," Avelyn said, leading her to a chair. "You know how I enjoy dressing it."

Her sister brushed Elysande's long, blond locks and braided her hair before coiling it around her ears and head. Avelyn's gentle touch soothed Elysande. She closed her eyes and tried to focus on the sensation of the brush gliding along.

Yet all she could see in her mind was Michael and his piercing blue eyes. All she remembered was the taste of his kiss.

She forced her eyes open and sat patiently, waiting for Avelyn to finish. Elysande knew that she needed to take Merryn's advice and push aside all thoughts of Michael. Her focus should be on her upcoming wedding and the man who was her betrothed.

"There." Avelyn stepped back and admired her work. "You'll not only steal Hendry's heart but every man's."

They heard the sound of a horn. The pit of her stomach grew cold.

"They're here."

Elysande acknowledged her sister's words with a brief nod. She tried her best to stir some excitement within her as she accompanied Avelyn to the great hall. They entered to a flurry of activity. So many people had crowded into the room, it looked as if they were about to celebrate the Christmas season. Numerous guests had arrived for the wedding during the past two days. She had no idea who many of them were or why they'd been invited. The buzz of so many conversations made her head begin to ache.

Little Hal raced by, a look of mischief on his face. Avelyn excused herself and chased after the boy.

Elysande stepped further into the room and glanced about. She didn't know if she'd even recognize Hendry in this mob. She supposed he would have grown taller during the past four years. She prayed his skinny arms and legs had filled out some. Then she sensed eyes upon her and turned.

Michael stared at her from across the room.

Their eyes locked on one another. Everyone else faded from view. Elysande felt as if only the two of them stood at a great distance in the large space. She drank in his tall frame and remembered those muscled arms about her, holding her in an embrace as he kissed the life out of her. Elysande felt the hot flush creeping up her neck and spilling onto her cheeks. She turned away and headed to her right.

She must avoid Michael Devereux. At all costs.

If she didn't, she might fracture into a thousand tiny pieces that could never be put back together again.

"There you are."

Elysande turned and saw the overweight, red-faced Lord Holger approaching. She supposed he would lead her to her groom and see that they were properly reintroduced after so long a time apart.

Her stepfather took her elbow. "Come with me, child. We must speak of an important matter."

Immediately, she sensed something was wrong. Holger's voice had seemed almost tender. She hadn't thought her stepfather had a compassionate bone in his thick body, but she knew by his tone that something was amiss.

The nobleman led her from the noise of the great hall to a small room down the corridor where his steward kept the estate's ledgers. Holger ushered her inside and indicated that she should take a seat. Elysande did so, still worried about what he would reveal.

"I have some news for you. I'm not quite sure how you'll react. Especially since your father put together the betrothal contract."

He paused. She realized he was uncertain of how to break whatever news he had to tell her.

"I thought it would be better to have some privacy as I shared it with you."

An awkward silence filled the room. Still, he hesitated.

"Please tell me, my lord. Whatever it is, I will handle this news. You may be blunt. I'm not a child that needs to be coddled."

"So be it." He took a deep breath and expelled it. "Your marriage will not take place as was planned."

Elysande's mouth fell open. "What? Why?" A tiny bit of hope filled her heart.

Had Michael spoken to Lord Holger? Had he asked that the betrothal contract be voided so they could wed instead?

Her stepfather placed a hand on her shoulder. "I'm afraid I must inform you that your betrothed . . . Hendry . . . has . . . died."

Died?

She expelled a long breath, one she didn't even know she had held. Hendry. Dead. Relief flooded her. She wouldn't have to marry him tomorrow. She wouldn't have to go north. She wouldn't be forced to leave her mother and Avelyn.

And she was free—free so that Michael Devereux might press his suit.

The excitement she had pretended to feel now became real. Her heart beat quickly. She had to find Michael. She must tell him this news. She was no longer betrothed. She loved Michael. He loved her. She had to let him know. They could marry. They could be together. Forever. They could love long and well, just as Merryn and Geoffrey did.

Elysande came to her feet. She tried to tamp down the joy she felt. She knew it was her duty to first find Lord Ingram and offer him her condolences.

Then she would take Michael aside and share the wonderful news with him.

A strong knock sounded, startling her.

Lord Holger called out, "Come."

Elysande was surprised when Lord Ingram entered the room. He closed the door behind him and came to stand next to her.

"Did you tell her about my son?"

Her heart skipped a beat as she stared up at Hendry's father. The nobleman was still tall, but his hair had gone from the soft gray she remembered to a snowy white in the years since she'd seen him. His skin seemed more weathered, too. He gave her a grim smile, revealing yellowed teeth.

"Aye," her stepfather said. "She took it well."

"And the rest?" the nobleman asked, glancing back at Holger.

"Nay."

Some undercurrent ran through their brief words. Elysande wondered at its meaning.

She decided to address Lord Ingram. "I am sorry for the loss of your son, my lord. I had looked forward to my marriage with Hendry. I hope he did not suffer much." She hoped God would forgive her for such a small lie. She only wished to comfort Hendry's father in his time of grief.

"He was a weakling," bellowed Lord Ingram. "From the time he was expelled from his mother's womb, the boy lacked strength and vigor."

His words took her aback. It didn't sound as if Lord Ingram mourned for his son at all. She felt sorry for Hendry in that moment. The boy had obviously never lived up to his father's impossible expectations.

"I couldn't get a healthy child from my wife. Neither boy nor girl." His eyes gleamed as he studied at her. "But now 'twill be possible."

She was totally confused. "Pardon, my lord? I'm not sure what you mean."

Ingram placed his beefy hands on her shoulders and gazed into her eyes. "I'll be your new groom, Lady Elysande."

Marry Lord Ingram?

Panic swept through Elysande. "But . . . but what of Lady Gloriana, my lord? I cannot be the bride of a man who possesses another wife."

The nobleman snorted in disgust. "Lady Gloriana is as dead as her son. It took long enough to be rid of her. She died the morning we left to come to Hopeston." He chuckled. "'Tis what probably did Hendry in since he was always tied to the woman's apron strings. The boy cried like a babe when I refused to delay our departure in order to attend his mother's funeral mass that afternoon. Frankly, I am glad to be rid of the both of them."

His words stunned her. What man would be so cruel as to speak of his wife and son in such a hateful manner? And to demand that his son accompany him immediately, when postponing their departure to Hopeston by a day could easily have assuaged Hendry's grief and allowed him see his mother properly buried.

It was monstrous. *He* was monstrous.

Ingram's fingers tightened on her shoulders as his eyes gleamed. "As soon as the contract can be satisfactorily arranged, you and I will wed, my lady. And I plan to get you with child as soon as I bed you.

And keep you that way." He grinned, his yellow teeth almost glowing. "We'll have many babes together. And spend many nights making those babes."

His touch sickened her. His words horrified her.

She pushed hard against his chest and stepped away, her entire body quaking in anger. "You, my lord, are the last man on earth that I would wish to wed. I would rather die an untouched virgin decades from now than be shackled to a man like you."

Anger sparked in Lord Ingram's eyes as he took a menacing step toward her. His hands shot out and grabbed her upper arms, the fingers so firmly holding her that she knew she'd have bruises there by morning.

He lowered his face till his nose almost touched hers. "Listen well, my lady. You are a woman, and you'll have absolutely no say in the matter. Lord Holger and I will negotiate the contract in your absence."

His fingers dug into her tender flesh. Elysande bit her lip to stifle from crying out in pain.

"I do not care what the contract calls for," she boldly proclaimed. "I will never, ever marry the likes of you. You cannot force me to say the words."

Lord Ingram looked startled for a moment before he began to chuckle ominously.

"Oh, I shall enjoy breaking your spirit, my dear—but it will be broken. 'Twill be up to you. You can be a docile wife and hold your tongue and do my bidding without question, or I will lock you in the solar and keep you tied naked to my bed while I ravish you over and over till you've lost your defiance and learn how to submit as a woman should."

Lord Ingram glared at her. "The choice will be yours."

Fear unlike any she'd ever known poured through Elysande at the thought of a future with this fiend. She glanced to Lord Holger, who stood with his arms crossed and a sour look upon his face.

With a surge of strength she didn't know she possessed, Elysande broke away from Lord Ingram's grasp and ran from the room. She rounded a corner and hit a wall. No, not a wall—Michael.

His large frame loomed next to her. Those piercing blue eyes dug into the depths of her soul as his hands steadied her.

"Nay!" Elysande slammed her hands into his chest and pushed him away. She gathered her skirts and took off again, running down the corridor and out the doors of the keep.

Following Elysande, Michael's long strides were full of purpose. He'd been standing with Lord Geoffrey and Lady Mary when the wedding party from the north arrived. Lord Ingram barreled through the great hall as if he owned the place. Michael knew of the nobleman by reputation alone and it had done the man justice.

Michael had been in a foul mood for two days since he'd abandoned Elysande in the stables after they'd kissed. He'd used poor judgment succumbing to her kiss, but he wouldn't have changed a moment of their encounter. She was everything he imagined he could ever want in a wife. Her beauty, now fresh and lovely, would only see her age gracefully. She would grow more beautiful in a score than she was now.

But he found her heart and mind to be what attracted him even more than her comely looks. Elysande was intelligent and caring. Nurturing. Playful. Determined and strong.

And he had lost her as quickly as he'd found her.

That was why he'd stormed from the stables after drinking in her sweet kisses. Oh, how he longed to make her his. Hear her cry out his name in ecstasy as he made love to her. Wake beside her every morning, knowing they faced the new day together.

Her betrothal and upcoming marriage stood between them, though. Michael would never dishonor her or his vows as a knight—though he wanted to plunge his shaft into her and plant his seed deep within her belly.

There could never be anything between them, for she would be married to another in the blink of an eye.

Lord Ingram's arrival changed all of that. Without preface, the brash nobleman bluntly informed Lady Mary that his son had died while they'd traveled on the road to Hopeston. Michael thought he saw a bit of relief in her eyes. She had motioned her husband over and shared the news with him.

Learning of Hendry's sudden death gave Michael hope. He'd turned to Lord Geoffrey, who gave him an encouraging smile. He realized that somehow his liege lord had learned of his feelings for his niece. It could only be Lady Merryn's doing. She was astute beyond measure—and he'd seen her huddled with Elysande several times in the last two days. Either Merryn had guessed the truth or Elysande had confided in her aunt of the feelings between them—and Merryn had shared that with her husband.

"You would make a fine husband to my niece," Geoffrey said, his voice low.

But before Michael could reply, he overheard the words that stunned him.

"I plan to wed Lady Elysande in my son's place," Lord Ingram proclaimed to Lady Mary and Lord Holger. "I came this far for a wedding. Might as well be my own so I didn't waste time on this trip."

A gleam came into Holger's eyes. Michael knew the man would not only approve of getting Elysande off his hands, but his greed would cause him to hold out for more now that a new betrothal contract would need to be drawn up.

"Let me find my stepdaughter," Holger said. "I'll share with her that her groom has passed on. I'm sure she'll be delighted to make a new match with you, Lord Ingram. For the right bridal price, of course," he added.

Michael looked wildly about the great hall and spied Elysande entering. He ached at how lovely and vulnerable she looked. He wished to go to her, but she quickly turned and skirted the room, moving away from him. He'd watched Holger approach her and then remove her from the room.

He found a hand on his arm, restraining him.

"Michael. Hold fast," Geoffrey warned. "No contracts have been signed. I'll speak with Lord Holger after he's broken the news of Hendry's death to Elysande and put your name forth as a suitor. I'm sure the man will drive a hard bargain, but I'm certain that the future Earl of Sandbourne would prove a most worthy candidate."

He nodded, taking in Geoffrey's words. Michael never acted rashly. He would remain calm and bide his time.

Until he saw Lord Ingram leave the great hall. Michael's gut told him that the nobleman went to find Holger and Elysande and demand that they draw up the contracts at once. Michael didn't know how long he could wait. He couldn't chance missing out on this opportunity. He turned and saw Geoffrey nodded at him. At once, he exited the great hall, looking for where the trio could be.

As he searched, Elysande appeared, the color drained from her face. She ran smack into him and Michael grabbed her to hold her steady. She pushed him away and fled.

And now he was determined to find her.

Michael kept Elysande in sight as she ran wildly. He knew, even before she probably did, that she headed to the stables. To her beloved horses. She understood them. Had an affinity for them. She would turn to them in her time of need.

He couldn't imagine what her reaction had been when she was told her dead groom was to be replaced by his father. Lord Ingram was a cruel man. Michael couldn't imagine Elysande by his side—much less in his bed. The thought had hot fury coursing through him and he increased his stride. He reached the stables only moments after he saw her duck inside. He nodded to a groom he passed.

She had to be with Morningstar and Happy. He walked the length of the stable, making the appropriate turns till he came to the enlarged stall. Mother and foal still resided there. Happy nursed away as Morningstar stood patiently. Elysande had her arms wrapped about the dam's neck. She'd buried her face in the horse's mane. Muffled sobs came from her.

Without a word, Michael went to her and captured her small waist in his hands, pulling her away from the horse. She twisted around and caught sight of him. Something garbled came from her lips, then she collapsed against him, her hands clenching his tunic.

Michael moved to the corner of the stable. When his back touched the wall, he slid down it into the soft hay, bringing Elysande with him. He cradled her trembling body in his arms, his lips brushing against her hair. He let her cry until she was spent.

When she fell silent, he lifted her chin with a finger. Those large, amethyst eyes hypnotized him, holding him captive for a moment. He'd never seen such an unusual color. He'd never held such a beautiful woman, both inside and out, within in his arms.

Instinctively, his mouth sought hers. Her soft lips, warm and pliable, opened to him. Michael thrust his tongue inside, tasting the sweetness that he associated with this woman. Sparks ignited as their tongues mated, two souls who had connected. He drank her in, again and again, his pulse pounding louder than he thought possible. His arms tightened about her, bringing her close. His hands roamed her back and rose to plunge into her hair, loosening her braids. The long tresses spilled about her shoulders. Their silky feel rivaled the smoothness of her skin.

He wanted her naked—now, beneath him—their flesh hot against one other.

But now was not the time.

Slowly, he pulled his head away. Their mouths parted. Both panted. He leaned back into her, his forehead resting against hers.

"Michael."

Her whispered word brought chills. This was the woman he was meant to be with for all time. He would do whatever it took to claim her.

"Elysande." He loved her name. Loved saying it to her face. Loved everything about her. 'Twas true what the old wives said. Love arrived like a thief in the night and changed everything as a quick strike of lightning might. Michael hadn't known this woman a week ago. He could easily spend a lifetime learning everything about her.

"Hendry's dead."

"I know."

She started. "You do?" Then her eyes turned downward. Long, dark lashes fell against her cheek. He leaned in and kissed each eyelid and thrilled at hearing her sigh of contentment.

"And Lord Ingram offered for you."

Elysande's head shot up. "You know that, too?"

He nodded. "I heard him tell your mother and Lord Holger that he wished to wed you."

The glum look returned to her face. "They are now engaged in hammering out the contracts so that we can be wed as soon as possible."

"Not if I have anything to say in the matter."

She cupped his cheek. "Oh, Michael. Lord Ingram is a powerful man. For me to marry someone so wealthy? It would be a very good match. I can't see Lord Holger putting up much resistance. Lord Ingram is a very persuasive man."

Michael put a hand over hers, hating the defeated look in her eyes. "I can also be quite convincing, Elysande. I may not seem powerful to you, but one day I will be when I come into my title."

Her brows knitted together. "What do you mean, your title?"

"I'm the only son of the Earl of Sandbourne," he revealed, "though we are estranged. I haven't returned home in fifteen years, but I'll become the earl upon my father's death. I plan to approach Lord Holger and your mother and plead my case. Lord Geoffrey has assured me he, too, will put in a good word on my behalf. One day I'll own more land and gain access to wealth that rivals even Lord Ingram's."

"Oh, Michael!" Elysande kissed him with enthusiasm, her breasts pressing against his chest. He longed to worship each of them in good time.

He took her wrists and gently tugged her away. "Come. We need to return to the keep. I don't want Lord Ingram gaining any ground in his pursuit of you." He reached over and pulled straw from her unbound hair.

Elysande gave him a bright smile. "And to think I fell in love with mere Sir Michael Devereux."

CHAPTER EIGHT

ELYSANDE FLOATED BACK to the great hall, her hand in the crook of Michael's arm. Just touching him brought about a strength and resolve she'd never had before. She felt like a princess, chosen by the most handsome prince in all of Christendom. In the blink of an eye, her fate had changed—thanks to the death of her betrothed and Michael wanting to court her and make her his wife.

Finding out he would come into a title and great wealth meant little to her, but it would definitely sway her stepfather's opinion. Elysande whispered a prayer to the Blessed Virgin, hoping that Lord Holger would listen to reason and refuse Lord Ingram's suit since a younger, more powerful earl wished for her hand in marriage. She couldn't imagine a reason for her stepfather to refuse, but she wanted to speak to her mother immediately.

"We need to find my mother," she told Michael. "Mother is the only one that Lord Holger might listen to." She glanced about the room. "Over there."

Michael steered her toward her mother, who stood with Geoffrey, Merryn, and Avelyn. Elysande caught Merryn's eye and saw her aunt glow with approval as they approached. Then Geoffrey winked at Elysande. She believed, in that moment, that everything would work out as planned.

"Mother, I know you have met Sir Michael Devereux."

Lady Mary bowed her head slightly in acknowledgement. "Geoffrey and Merryn have shared with me that the two of you have strong feelings for one another. Selfishly, I would keep you close to me, here in the south, rather than see you return to the cold north with a man like Lord Ingram." She looked Michael over. "And I believe you would treat my Elysande well, young man."

"I would, my lady. She is my life and my light," he said solemnly.

"Oh, my," Avelyn exclaimed. "How romantic."

Merryn gave Michael a subtle smile. "I did not realize you had such a romantic side to you, Michael. You've never revealed it before."

He laughed. "Nay, my lady. I had no idea it existed—till Elysande came into my life." Michael gave Elysande a warm smile that curled her toes.

"Lord Holger has been closeted with Lord Ingram the past hour," Geoffrey shared. "I believe 'tis time to interrupt their negotiations. Michael, would you like for me to accompany you? I'm happy to speak for you in this matter or stand aside and simply lend my support as you state your case."

Michael nodded. "You would be a strong advocate, my lord. I'd appreciate your presence when I speak to Lord Holger."

Michael turned to Elysande and raised her hand to his lips. He pressed a tender kiss upon her fingers. "If you will excuse me?"

"Of course." Elysande watched Michael and Geoffrey leave the great hall. She already missed her dashing knight.

Her mother stepped over and hugged her tightly, then Merryn and Avelyn each embraced her. The three women shared how happy they were for her. Elysande felt as if she drifted through a dream.

Soon, she and Michael Devereux would be wed.

HAVING LORD GEOFFREY accompanying him to the negotiations brought a sense of relief to Michael. Though only Michael's senior by seven years, the nobleman seemed at ease in any situation and would be a strong ally as Michael faced off with Lord Holger and Lord Ingram.

He led Lord Geoffrey from the great hall and around the corner to the room Elysande had fled from earlier. They came to stand in front of the open door and Michael knocked on the frame.

"May we come in, Lord Holger?" he asked. Without waiting for the nobleman's invitation to enter, Michael strolled in, happy to see the frustrated look upon Lord Ingram's face.

Apparently, the discussion had not gone well so far.

Good.

"What do you want?" Lord Holger demanded, glancing at Michael and then to Lord Geoffrey. "Is my wife curious as to what is taking so long? I will share with Lady Mary in good time what has been decided for her daughter."

Michael watched his liege lord close the door and face the two men.

"Lord Holger." Geoffrey acknowledged Elysande's stepfather with a slight nod before looking to Lord Ingram. "My lord, I am Geoffrey de Montfort, brother to Lady Mary." With his hand, he indicated Michael. "And this is my most trusted knight, Sir Michael Devereux, whom I have known since he was a small boy."

"What business have you here?" Lord Ingram demanded, his tone sharp. "I seek privacy while I bargain with Lord Holger for his stepdaughter's hand."

Geoffrey smiled and smoothly said, "'Tis why we have come. Sir Michael also desires to come to the bargaining table and offer for Lady Elysande."

"What?" Alarm filled Lord Ingram's face. He looked Michael up and down, assessing the challenge to his negotiations.

"My sister is saddened by your son's death," Geoffrey continued, "but it gives her the opportunity to plot a different course for her daughter's life. You see, Mary has grown despondent thinking of Elysande living so far away from her. If my niece married Sir Michael, Elysande could remain in the south, closer to her mother."

Lord Holger sniffed. "You may have good intentions regarding my stepdaughter, Sir Michael, but I doubt a mere knight could meet the bridal price that I require from her future husband. Besides, why would I allow my stepdaughter to wed a man in service to her uncle when she could be a countess and mistress of her husband's castle and holdings? That is possible—if Lord Holger meets my terms, of course."

The time had come for Michael to speak. With confidence, he said, "I may be a lowly knight now, my lord, but I am heir to an earldom. In due time, Lady Elysande would be *my* countess. And Sandbourne is close enough to Hopeston, so that it would be a most desirable place in Lady Mary's eyes for her daughter to be settled. That way, Lady Mary could visit often and play with her grandchildren. You, too, my lord, would be most welcome."

The nobleman's eyes widened in surprise. "You are the Earl of Sandbourne's son?"

"Aye, Lord Holger. His only son. So my father's title and vast holdings will come to me upon his death."

"I know it would please my sister greatly to have Elysande nearby," Geoffrey added. "I can also vouch for Sir Michael's good character. He was a fine boy and has grown into a man of honor. My niece could have no better husband than this good knight who stands before you, Lord Holger."

"But he's only a knight," Lord Ingram pointed out, once again joining the conversation. "It could be years before he gains the title and access to his wealth. I, on the other hand, am quite wealthy now. Lady Elysande would have everything she needed by marrying me—without having to wait."

Lord Holger nodded slowly. "'Tis true, Lord Ingram could provide for the girl immediately. He could produce the bridal price immediately. And my stepdaughter would live in the lap of luxury without having to wait months or years."

Tension filled Michael. He saw the opportunity of making Elysande his slipping away. He glanced quickly to Lord Geoffrey.

"The bridal price is no problem," Geoffrey said. "I can give that to you and have Michael reimburse me when the time comes. The two would live in Kinwick Castle, my home, so my niece would lack for nothing."

Gratitude for Lord Geoffrey's friendship and bold proclamation gave Michael confidence that Lord Holger would finally agree.

Instead, he heard, "I think not, Geoffrey. I have found my stepdaughter to be too headstrong for her own good and far too outspoken for a woman, much less a female of her age. I think she needs the firm hand of an older man, such as Lord Ingram, in order to teach her discipline. I fear Sir Michael is much too young and would be smitten by her beauty and give in to her every whim." Holger glanced at Lord Ingram. "Besides, who runs this family? 'Tis not Lady Mary. I do. Not my wife. I refuse to take her wishes into consideration. I need to do what is best for my stepdaughter."

Lord Holger glanced around the room. "And that is a union with Lord Ingram."

An obstinate look set in Lord Holger's eyes. Michael's heart sank. He knew there'd be no reasoning with Elysande's stepfather. The man had made up his mind and would not budge.

"Please leave us, gentlemen. Lord Ingram and I must return to our discussion and arrange the future of my stepdaughter."

With a wave of defeat leaving a bitter taste in his mouth, Michael strode from the room.

As THE WOMEN continued to chat and the men remained closeted, Elysande began to worry.

"Do you think I should go check on the negotiations with Lord Holger?" she asked. "See what progress has been made?"

Before anyone replied, Michael and Geoffrey entered the great hall again. Elysande could tell by the looks on their faces that they had no good news to share.

She rushed to Michael, the others trailing after her. "What happened?"

His face flushed with anger. "Lord Holger is a fool," he said simply.

Panic surged through her. Elysande turned to her uncle.

"I'm in agreement," Geoffrey said. "No matter how hard we beseeched him, he refused to consider Michael as your future husband. He finally demanded that we leave so he could continue to hammer out the details of the betrothal contract with Lord Ingram." Geoffrey gave her a sorrowful look. "I'm truly sorry, Elysande. I fear this time tomorrow you'll find that you're a bride to Lord Ingram."

"No." The word came out barely a whisper. The pendulum swung yet again against her. She'd gone from the low of awaiting Hendry's arrival to the high of hearing of his death. From hearing that Lord Ingram wished to be her bridegroom to learning that Michael wanted to fight for her—and that he had a powerful title to back his quest.

And now, to find out that her stepfather couldn't be bothered with even listening to anyone's suit other than Lord Ingram's? Hatred welled in her heart.

Elysande looked to her mother. "I won't wed that man. I'll refuse to speak the vows. Lord Holger can't force me to do so. He's not my father."

Avelyn burst out in tears. "If you don't marry him, Elysande, what if Lord Holger forces *me* to marry Lord Ingram?" Her sister ran from the room.

"I'll go to her," Merryn said. She paused and took Elysande's hand and gave it an encouraging squeeze before she left.

Elysande stiffened her spine. No one could fight this battle for her. She must intervene. She must be the one to impact the story of her life.

"Please excuse me." She left the great hall and returned to the steward's office for a second time. A closed door meant nothing. Elysande threw it open without bothering to knock. The door slammed against the wall.

She stepped through as both men eyed her warily.

"If you will excuse us, Lord Ingram. My stepfather and I have a grave matter to discuss."

The earl threw his hands in the air. "Try and talk some sense into Lord Holger, my lady. He is one of the most unreasonable men I've had the displeasure of bargaining with." Ingram studied her through hooded eyes. "I hope by this time tomorrow you won't have to listen to him anymore. Once we have wed."

Ingram left the room. Elysande shut the door behind him and gathered her courage.

Lord Holger fell into a chair. "'Tis a stubborn man I am dealing with. First, Lord Ingram owes me payment because his son died." He lifted a sheaf of papers. "That was already present in the first contract, so he must pay up."

"He owes . . . *you*? Because *my* betrothed died before our marriage could take place?"

Holger clucked his tongue. "Technically, the monies would go to your mother. But as my wife, I would hold them for her." He paused. "And Ingram wants more of a bridal payment than your father originally agreed to. I see no reason why I should pay more than your father did to be rid of you."

Elysande's anger grew. "You're treating me as a piece of meat. I am a person, my lord. Your stepdaughter. Even if I've never heard you refer to me by my name. And I tell you now, I will not—under any circumstances—wed Lord Ingram. You may negotiate till you are blue in the face, but I refuse to be a party to this mockery of a wedding."

His eyes narrowed into slits as he studied her. "I always knew you'd be trouble. I told the king that it was too much for me to take on your mother and two headstrong girls. Edward assured me you were already betrothed and would soon be off my hands. I would merely have to find a husband for your sister. The farther away, the better."

Her stepfather rose to his feet, his face bright red. "You have no rights, girl. None."

"My father would never have treated me in such a despicable manner."

"Your father is *dead*. By law, I'm now your father. That man did you no favors. He and your mother. Letting you run wild in boy's clothing. Spending all your time with horses." Holger glared at her. "You better get used to a man telling you what to do. In and out of bed. Women are here to serve men. Nothing more."

He slammed a fist onto the table. "So be off with you. But first, find Lord Ingram. I've decided to agree to his terms without further argument, the better to be rid of you. This time tomorrow, you'll be wedded. Then bedded. And the day after, I'll never have to be bothered by you again."

Holger gave her a sinister smile. "Once Ingram has broken your maidenhead, we'll see how you behave."

Elysande closed the distance between them. They were almost of the same height. She moved within inches of his face and proclaimed, "I will never—never—marry Lord Ingram. Or any man of your choice! I plan to marry Michael Devereux and never set foot in Hopeston again."

His eyes bulged wide as his nostrils flared in anger. "You'll do as I say, you ungrateful cur. I am the man here. I am in charge. And I demand that—"

Holger stopped mid-sentence. His brows knit in confusion. His eyes clouded over. Then an agonizing look crossed his face, which had deepened to almost purple in color. He clawed at his chest. His eyes grew wide. "Can't . . . breathe," he wheezed. He fell to the ground and gasped.

Then fell silent.

Elysande dropped to her knees. Lord Holger lay still. She placed a hand under his nose. No breath left it. She rose unsteadily.

She had killed her stepfather.

Elysande stumbled to her feet and made her way to the great hall. It seemed like a madhouse now. Even more wedding guests had arrived. She couldn't hear herself think through the din. She brushed through the groups of people, trying to locate her mother. She spied Geoffrey and Merryn standing with a handsome man unfamiliar to her. Her leaden feet moved her in their direction.

Merryn reached out to her and captured her hands. "What ails you, Elysande? Your hands are colder than a winter's day. And you have no color in your cheeks." Merryn brushed a hand through her niece's hair. "I know how upset you are about this wedding. Mayhap you should lie down for a bit."

"He's dead. It's all my fault."

"What?" Geoffrey asked. He placed a hand upon her shoulder. "We know Hendry is gone, Elysande. You had nothing to do with it."

She shook her head violently, trying to make them understand. "No. No. *He's* dead. Lord Holger," she said dully.

The stranger took a step toward her and clasped her elbows. He led her to a chair. Elysande sat. She felt physically and emotionally drained.

"Raynor, find Lady Mary at once. Bring her here. Say not a word to anyone," Merryn commanded. "Geoffrey, go see to Lord Holger. I'll stay with Elysande."

The two men hurried away to do her bidding.

Merryn drew another chair over and sat next to Elysande, holding her hands. "Raynor will find your mother. He's a cousin to your mother and uncle. And he's like a brother to Geoffrey. You can count on his discretion."

The two women sat in silence. Elysande was grateful, for no words could have formed on her lips even if she'd tried.

Geoffrey returned first, shaking his head, his mouth grim. Raynor followed behind him, Lady Mary in tow.

At the sight of her mother, Elysande felt the tears begin to stream down her cheeks. She leapt to her feet.

"I killed him, Mother. I didn't mean to. We argued about the new betrothal. I told him I would never marry Lord Ingram. He shouted at me. Told me he was the man and I must do as he said." She tried to swallow, but her mouth had gone dry. "His face turned so dark and mottled. Then . . . he collapsed."

Her mother embraced her. "It's not your fault, Elysande. You can't blame yourself. Holger ate too much and drank even more. His death could have occurred at any time."

"No. I caused it. We argued. If I hadn't provoked him, he wouldn't have become so upset. I'm to blame." She looked wildly about the room filled with people. "Will God forgive me? Can He forgive me for killing a man?" She thought a moment. "Should I enter a convent? Give my life to God to make up for so grievous a sin?"

"A convent?"

Elysande looked over her mother's shoulder. She saw Lord Ingram had joined their circle. He was the last person she wished to see.

"What's this about a convent? No wife of mine will enter a convent."

Lady Mary faced the nobleman and took charge of the situation. "No one is entering a convent. And no one—least of all you, Lord Ingram—is going to marry my daughter. My husband is dead. I have no intention of signing a betrothal contract with you. Today or any other day."

Ingram's jaw fell open. It took him a moment to recover. "How dare you, woman! I shall write the king at once. He will order you to give me your daughter in marriage."

Elysande's anger exploded. She wanted to protect her mother from this man. "And how dare *you*, my lord? My mother has just learned she is widowed for the second time. You've yet to offer her any comfort but only wish to force your own desires upon my family. Do you think I or any other woman would want to marry you? You don't even seem concerned about the death of your only son, which happened but a few days ago."

Lord Ingram looked taken aback at her words. He sputtered, "But . . . but I had my men bury his body before we continued on to Hopeston. What more could I do?"

"You could grieve for the loss of your child instead of cursing his existence as you did earlier. You could return his body to be buried at the only home he knew. You can offer your condolences to my mother and leave Hopeston immediately. Your presence is no longer required here."

The earl glared at Elysande. "I tell you, my lady, you'll be sorry for your bold words. You will bend to *my* will when I take you to wife. I know the king—"

"As do I and my wife," Geoffrey interrupted. "We're close friends with King Edward and Queen Philippa. Our daughter fosters in their royal household. I guarantee that they'll listen to our counsel regarding this situation a thousandfold over your words." His eyes narrowed. "Make sure you never come near Hopeston and my sister and nieces ever again or you'll live to regret it."

Lord Ingram turned beet red, fuming in rage. Without a word, he turned and fled the great hall.

CHAPTER NINE

ELYSANDE'S MIND WANDERED as the priest droned on in Latin. The many guests who had assembled at Hopeston now attended Lord Holger's funeral instead of feasting and dancing at her wedding.

She couldn't shake the feelings of guilt that weighed her down. They pushed at her as if she'd been trapped under a huge boulder that crushed the life from her. No matter how others tried to reassure her, Elysande knew responsibility for her stepfather's death rested at her doorstep. She thought again that she should offer up her life to God in service. By entering a nunnery, she could dedicate her remaining time on earth to all things holy. A quiet life of prayer and meditation. One that would, hopefully, win her forgiveness for her sins.

But that would be a world without Michael.

Elysande couldn't help but think about him. She hadn't spoken to him since her stepfather's death two days ago. Though she begged God for forgiveness while in constant prayer, her thoughts would turn to the dark, handsome knight. She could feel his strong arms about her. His mouth covering hers. Her hands roaming the hard, muscled chest.

God must not think her very contrite for her sins if she couldn't concentrate without her thoughts turning to Michael's image over and over. Giving Michael up might be the exact penance God required from her.

Was she strong enough to follow through?

She looked down at her hands. One rested in her mother's, their fingers locked together. Avelyn held Elysande's other hand in comfort.

What must her mother be feeling now? She had lost not one, but two husbands. Elysande knew both marriages had been arranged, but at least her parents had been fond of one another, if not in love. As far as her mother's relationship with Lord Holger? It seemed a matter of convenience. The marriage had given Lady Mary and her two daughters a roof over their heads after a male relative inherited her father's title and demanded they vacate the estate. Elysande had rarely seen her mother and stepfather engaged in conversation together. She hoped their lack of personal involvement might make this time easier on her mother.

The mass ended. Both she and Avelyn nodded graciously to those who conveyed their sympathy. Her mother made a few comments to the gathered mourners, thanking them for their kind words in such a time of loss. Elysande wondered if a funeral mass would be held for poor Hendry. She found she'd thought of him more in the past few days than she had in the four years since their betrothal. It pained her that his father had been so brusque and unfeeling regarding his only child's death.

Michael stepped forward briefly, along with several knights that had come from Kinwick. He offered few words, but his eyes said all. Elysande knew he now believed her free to pursue. But she thought otherwise. She needed to atone for her sins.

Even though she wished that she could spend the rest of her life with him.

The last of those in attendance filed from the chapel. Only she, Avelyn, and her mother remained. Mary gathered them to her. Elysande relished the comfort of her mother's arms about her.

"I love you, my darling girls. I'm grateful I have you by my side in such a difficult time."

"What will happen to us, Mother," asked Avelyn, "now that Lord Holger is gone? And Lord Ingram." Her sister shuddered. "I'll never like that man. Never."

"Don't trouble yourself over him, lamb," Mary said. "Even if he writes to the king, I believe your uncle, Geoffrey, will take care of things. As it is, both Geoffrey and I have sent missives to King Edward to inform him of the situation. He is on summer progress, so it might be a few weeks before they catch up to him and we receive a reply."

She hugged them tightly. "So for now, we won't worry. I suggest we return to the great hall. A lovely meal awaits us. I saw no need for such a large amount of food to go to waste. Though we aren't celebrating Elysande's wedding, at least we can enjoy each other's company and good food and wines."

They returned to the keep. Elysande ate a few bites each time her mother looked in her direction, but she left the rest of her food untouched on the trenchers. Nothing seemed appetizing. She decided to slip away and contemplate her future.

It seemed natural to turn toward the stables, her haven in times of trouble. She visited with Morningstar and Happy. The foal grew sturdier with each passing day. She returned to the keep and avoided the great hall and its many guests. Instead, she decided to go up to her bedchamber and lie down. Mayhap the solitude would help her confused heart.

She moved down the empty stone corridor. As she passed the room given to her uncle and aunt, she heard their voices. Elysande paused as she overheard her name in conversation. The door was ajar. Her curiosity got the better of her.

"Elysande needs a change of scenery, Geoffrey. She's been traumatized by Holger's death. I want her to come back with us to Kinwick."

"I'm not sure if that's wise, my love. You know of the deep feelings between her and Michael. Elysande seems at a crossroads. I don't know if being in close proximity to Michael is the best thing for her now."

"She is a wounded bird. And you know how I take those in."

Geoffrey chuckled. "Indeed, I do."

"Think of it. All she has been through. She lost her beloved father. She moved away from everything she knew to come to Hopeston. She had the trauma of a forced betrothal, only to learn of her fiancé's death a day before their wedding. Then she almost had to marry that horrid

Lord Ingram—*and* she witnessed the abrupt death of her stepfather." Merryn paused. "Not to mention falling hopelessly in love in the midst of all that turmoil. Elysande needs time to heal, Geoffrey. Kinwick is the place for that to occur. Not some nunnery that would choke all the joy from her."

Her aunt's words made sense. She could escape the shadows of death that seemed to linger at Hopeston. Visit her cousins at their home. Get a new perspective while she figured out the dilemma she faced.

Elysande tapped at the door and nudged it open. The sympathetic look Merryn gave her made Elysande rush to her aunt. She fell into her arms and clung to her. Kissing Merryn's cheek, she turned and hugged her uncle, Geoffrey.

She saw the triumphant look in Merryn's eyes as she turned to her husband. "I'll write the king and let him know that Elysande is under your protection, my lord. I'm sure he'll approve of you stepping in."

"Thank you both," Elysande told them. "I don't know what to say. You're showing me great kindness in my time of trouble."

"This is only temporary," Geoffrey warned. "The king may have someone in mind for you to marry. The same could hold true for your mother and Avelyn, too."

But for now I'll be safe.

And if she saw more of Michael? That might help her, as well.

Elysande looked to her uncle. "May I bring my horses?"

Geoffrey burst out into laughter. "You really do have de Montfort blood in you."

MICHAEL DOWNED THE remainder of his ale. Food held no interest for him. He'd spent two days going crazy with worry over Elysande. Raynor had found him and shared the news of Lord Holger's death and Lady Mary's refusal to complete any wedding contracts, despite Lord Ingram's insistence.

But Elysande had remained closeted in her bedchamber until today's funeral mass.

He wished he could have time alone with her. He'd heard talk of how Holger had dropped dead as they argued and that Elysande blamed herself. Michael had even cornered Lady Avelyn and pulled from her that Elysande's guilt had her talking of retreating to a nunnery to atone for her role in her stepfather's death.

If he didn't feel so desperate, he might have laughed. No one with such zest for life—much less incredible beauty—should be locked away from the world and forced to her knees multiple times a day in hours of prayer and penance.

Yet in a way, Michael understood how Elysande felt. It had been much the same with him. As a boy, guilt blanketed him every time his mother suffered another beating at the hands of his father. Though it usually occurred behind locked doors, Michael believed he should be able to prevent his father from acting in such a manner.

More guilt had rushed through him when he fled Sandbourne and cut his father from his life, knowing that he abandoned his mother. The only comfort he drew came from picturing her in the safe haven of a nunnery, far from her husband's fists and feet.

Michael thought of her often, wondering which convent she'd been taken to. He prayed to Christ Almighty at mass each morning that he would be able to locate her and bring her home to spend her final years at Sandbourne once he became the earl. He would make up for the lost years they'd spent apart.

Time would heal Elysande's emotional wounds. He must give her that gift before he declared his undying love and devotion to her and ask Lady Mary for her hand in marriage. So he'd avoided searching for Elysande—for now.

The time drew near for their departure, though. He thought they might leave for Kinwick as soon as tomorrow. Mayhap he should seek her out and at least have a private goodbye between them.

"You haven't heard a word I've said."

Michael's head popped up as a hard fist punched him playfully on his shoulder.

Raynor Le Roux shook his head. "'Tis a woman who has you in misery, my friend. Believe me, I know of such things." He summoned a serving wench over and had her refill their cups.

Michael greedily downed the cool liquid. "Did Lady Beatrice cause you such misery?" Michael had met Raynor's wife when he accompanied the de Montforts on a visit to Ashcroft shortly after the first Le Roux child's birth. "She seemed like an angel. I can't imagine Lady Beatrice causing you any suffering or unhappiness."

His old friend's face took on a wistful look that surprised Michael. "Everything is different now that I have found my Beatrice. I won't tell you of the many obstacles that kept us apart and put me in such a low state. Thank the Heavens we faced them together." Raynor paused. "Marrying Beatrice was the best thing I have ever done, for our love grows stronger with each passing day. I only wish she could have accompanied me to Hopeston." Raynor finished the ale and set his cup down.

"There you are, Michael." Geoffrey de Montfort came to stand next to their table. "We'll leave tomorrow morning after we break our fast. Be sure the men are ready to travel."

"Aye, my lord. I'll see to it now."

Geoffrey paused. "I should also tell you that my niece, Elysande, will accompany us back to Kinwick. Lady Merryn feels a change of scenery might do the girl some good after all that has passed."

His words shocked Michael to the core.

Elysande. At Kinwick.

Suddenly, Michael wanted to leap on the table and dance with joy. Instead, he kept his face blank as he had so many times when he'd been teased by others.

"Will Lady Elysande ride one of our extra mounts or take a horse from the Hopeston stables?"

Geoffrey frowned. "She asked if she could bring her horses with her. The more I think about it, I believe they should remain behind."

"You're right, my lord," Michael agreed. "Kinwick is too far for the foal to travel so soon after his birth. And the dam must remain behind to nurse. I'm sure Lady Elysande isn't thinking straight. She's had much on her mind."

"Then go find her and convince her we must leave mother and babe behind," Geoffrey suggested. "Better yet, find some groom first and have him promise to coddle the pair. 'Twill reassure her if you arrange that before you speak with her."

Curiosity got the better of him. "How long will the lady reside at Kinwick?"

"That's for my niece to decide. Frankly, her idea of locking herself away in a nunnery is not what my sister wants. We need to persuade Elysande during her time at Kinwick to make the right choice." A ghost of a smile crossed the nobleman's face. "I know you're eager to step up and change her mind. Especially since her circumstances have changed since we first arrived."

"Aye, my lord. I want to give her time, though."

Geoffrey nodded. "Just as her horses need time to come to full strength, so does my niece. Merryn and I are hopeful she'll change her mind about becoming a nun—and we'd be happy for you to help in that process. In fact, Merryn is counting upon it."

He placed a hand on Michael's shoulder. "My wife is a lovely woman, but you do not want to displease her and face her wrath."

Michael broke out in a smile. "I promise I'll do my best and see to it that the situation is resolved to everyone's advantage."

"Good man." Geoffrey walked away.

As Michael rose eagerly to his feet, he caught the wide smile on Raynor's face.

"Now I see what troubled you, my friend. Good luck to you in your quest to capture the lady's heart. I can tell she has already captured yours."

"She has, indeed, my lord. Please give my best to Lady Beatrice."

Michael went to find a groom. He'd grease the man's pockets with a few gold coins to guarantee Morningstar and Happy would be taken care of in good measure.

He exited the great hall with a spring in his step.

Elysande was coming to Kinwick.

CHAPTER TEN

ELYSANDE WATCHED AS the rider her uncle had sent out returned. The knight headed straight to his liege lord. They spoke briefly before he rode off in the direction he originally came from.

"We'll make camp up ahead," Geoffrey told them. He called for two of his men to hunt for some small game to supplement what that had brought from Hopeston.

"May I go with them, Father?" Ancel asked eagerly.

Geoffrey nodded. The trio spurred their horses on as the rest of the party continued south on the road.

Merryn turned to Elysande. "Another reason I'm glad that you're coming for a visit to Kinwick." She tilted her head in Alys' direction. "The twins used to do so much together. I think Alys misses those days."

Elysande looked at her young cousin, who did seem a bit forlorn as she watched her brother ride off without her.

"I'll enjoy spending time with Alys. She's promised to teach me something about herbs and potions."

Merryn laughed. "Alys is eager to show off her knowledge. And I miss having her with me when I prepare my concoctions."

"So you also know about herbs? I thought Alys might've learned about them at court."

"I soaked up every bit of knowledge I could from Sephare. She was the healer at Wellbury, where I grew up. I have a small room where I prepare my herbs and flowers and store them. As mistress of Kinwick, I'm often called upon to help with the sick or birthing of babes. Alys has been my shadow in these endeavors from the time she could walk."

Elysande glanced back at Alys. Her young cousin was conversing with Michael as she had much of the day. Elysande noticed how both Alys and Ancel had ridden close to the knight's side as they journeyed to Kinwick. Michael had listened more than he'd spoken, but she could tell he enjoyed talking with the children.

What had surprised her more was that Baby Hal insisted upon riding with Michael. Geoffrey had helped Merryn mount Destiny and then handed the boy up to her. They'd barely ridden beyond the gates of Hopeston when Hal began squirming in his mother's lap. He held his hands out and kept calling, "Michael! Michael!" Finally, her uncle stopped and asked if Michael would take on the rambunctious tyke. He readily agreed and Hal had been content to sit in the knight's lap and babble away—whether Michael was listening to him or not.

She found her heart touched by his ease with the three de Montfort children. Elysande knew Michael would be a caring father.

And she wished he could be the father of her babes.

There, she'd finally formed the thought that had lingered in her mind all day. Lying to herself did no good. She wanted this man—in every way possible. She wanted to marry him and warm his bed. Give birth to his children. Share a life with him, the good along with the bad.

Was that asking too much?

Elysande didn't know.

The more miles they traveled from Hopeston, the more she felt her burden of guilt being lifted away. True, she'd argued vehemently with her stepfather, but both her mother and Avelyn insisted Lord Holger's death had nothing to do with their harsh words aimed at one another. She realized Lord Holger was not a young man. He was vastly overweight and usually red in the face despite little exertion on his part. She supposed he could have collapsed and died at any moment. It just happened to be one in which they'd been arguing.

Elysande sent up another prayer of thanks that she was free to travel to Kinwick. Her mother could have gone ahead and honored her late husband's wishes and shipped Elysande off with Lord Ingram as her new husband, keeping her in the same family, albeit with the father instead of the son. Instead, Lady Mary had stood firm and sent that loathsome nobleman back to the north.

Her mother didn't pressure her in any manner regarding the future, though Elysande had mentioned her idea of penance as a nun. Lady Mary merely told her daughter to enjoy her visit with her uncle and aunt and to use the opportunity to get to know her young cousins. She would be welcomed back at Hopeston when she was ready to return.

The horses in front of her began to slow and veer off the road. Elysande looked around and saw they headed into a wood. Soon, they reached a clearing which she assumed had been found and inspected by the rider Geoffrey sent out. Knights began to dismount. Her uncle lifted his wife down and then helped Elysande from the saddle.

"We'll make camp here," he told her. "Merryn may need some help with the children. My men will take care of the rest."

Elysande looked around and saw wood already being chopped. Two knights came and gathered the horses, hobbling some and leading a few others away to the stream she heard in the distance.

Hal came barreling her way. Michael was close behind him in mock pursuit as the boy squealed. Elysande scooped Hal up.

"Stay away, Sir Michael," she warned. "I am Hal's protector. I'll keep all monsters from him."

Michael dropped his arms. He looked at Hal. "I'm afraid she's put a spell upon me, Hal. I can't lift my arms." He pretended to try and raise them, groaning as if in pain. "Nay, I can't capture you, thanks to your cousin's special magic."

Elysande set Hal back onto the ground. "You are under my protection, little one. I'll keep this brute away from you."

Hal grinned and took off running again. Alys caught his hand and led him away.

"You're very good with him," Elysande said. "I watched as he rode with you all day. He didn't wiggle or protest. And he loves to talk to you."

Michael pushed a hand through his dark hair. "He's a fine lad. I enjoy his company."

She gave him a shy smile. "I must thank you again for convincing me that Morningstar and Happy should remain behind. I'd forgotten how difficult the roads can be. 'Twas best they stay where they're safe. And Avelyn promised to look in on them each day and take them both a treat."

"The groom I spoke with will also keep an eye on them. He guaranteed me no harm would come to either horse."

She nodded. "I'm sure you did something to convince him. He's never been pleasant to me or gone out of his way to help me when I've been in the stables."

Michael frowned. "I'm sorry I didn't know that. Suffice it to say, he will do his task as promised. If he doesn't, he'll answer to me."

Elysande heard the sound of hooves approaching.

"Ah, it sounds as if our dinner has arrived," he said. "You might wish to help Merryn set out the bread and cheese that your lady mother provided for our return trip."

Elysande watched Michael head toward the other soldiers that had returned. Ancel held a hand up in greeting. He jumped from his horse.

"We caught three rabbits!" the boy exclaimed. "You're the best at skinning, Michael. Mayhap I can watch you prepare them for dinner?"

Elysande went over to Merryn and offered to help. They removed the food her mother had sent along and poured wine from flasks. By the time that task had been accomplished, Michael had the rabbits skinned, skewered, and resting over the fire. Soon, Elysande's mouth watered at the smell of roasting meat.

The entire party gathered in a circle around the fire and ate their fill. Alys entertained them with some stories and songs she had heard at court. Ancel added in a few jokes that he and the other pages fostering at the Earl of Winterbourne's had invented. The meal finally ended and Elysande and Merryn took some of the dishes to the stream to clean them.

By the time they returned, the camp had been readied for sleep. Pallets awaited them and everyone found a place to bed down. Geoffrey appointed two men to stand guard for the first shift. Elysande noted Michael was one of them. She lay down, Alys on one side of her and Ancel on the other. Merryn gathered a weary Hal into her arms and curled her body around him. Geoffrey then wrapped his arm around the two of them.

A quiet descended. It had been a lengthy day of travel. Before long, Elysande heard the snores—some subtle, a few men rattling noisily—but she had trouble falling asleep. Her mind swirled with the events of the past few days. After a good while, she heard murmured voices and saw the guards change shift. She watched as Michael came near her. He added a few pieces of wood to the fire and then bedded down on the other side of Ancel.

Having him near helped Elysande to relax. She closed her eyes and felt the darkness swallow her up.

MICHAEL AWOKE, HIS body taut, as if ready to pounce. He opened his eyes. As his eyes accustomed themselves to the dark, he could see no guards on duty. Then he realized the fire had gone out.

It shouldn't have.

The last thing he'd done before going to sleep was place more wood onto the fire. Not much. Just enough to keep it burning low throughout the night.

Someone had extinguished it.

As his hand went to his sword's hilt, he sensed a nearby presence. He leapt to his feet and drew his weapon as he heard a muffled cry. He could see the outline of a man.

The stranger hauled a struggling Elysande to her feet.

His warning cry pierced the night, alerting the de Montfort knights. Within seconds, men sprang awake. The sound of steel swords unsheathing came in unison.

Michael already strode the few steps to Elysande. He could see a man's hand across her mouth, preventing her from crying out. His other arm had her about the waist as she kicked. Though Michael couldn't be certain, he doubted the man had a weapon out. He trusted his gut and quickly lifted his sword.

The attacker shouted an obscenity and released her. Elysande scrambled away as Michael's sword arced downward in a swift, fatal blow. The man fell to his knees and then face down into what had been the fire.

Michael heard shouts and saw a blur of figures ahead of him. He looked back and found the de Montfort family. Geoffrey had pushed Merryn behind him and held his sword high. Hal wiggled sleepily in his mother's arms. Alys sprang behind her father and crouched next to her mother. Ancel had his small sword in hand, ready to protect his loved ones. Michael thrust a hand out to Elysande. She latched on to it and he pulled her to her feet.

"'Tis over! We've killed the bastards!"

Michael kept her hand firm in his. Elysande took the few steps to him. He wrapped his arms about her trembling body.

Within minutes, torches were lit. Soldiers scoured the area around the camp. Michael tried to join them, but Elysande had a death grip on him. Geoffrey caught his eye and waved him over.

"Stay with them," he ordered, indicating his family.

Michael did, one arm about Elysande, the other holding his sword, as he maneuvered her closer to Merryn and the children.

After some minutes, Geoffrey gathered everyone round. His words were blunt.

"Our two guards are dead. Their throats cut. Both intruders are also dead. Does anyone recognize them?"

Several of his men nodded.

"They were both at Hopeston, but not part of Lord Holger's company of men," one offered. "I saw them in Lord Ingram's colors, but neither bears those now."

Michael sensed Elysande go still and tightened his arm about her.

Geoffrey looked to his niece. "Is that blood? Are you hurt?"

She shook her head. "Nay, my lord."

Michael looked at her and saw that blood trickled down her chin—but no wound was visible. He brushed his hand against it, trying to wipe it away.

Elysande glanced at his hand and shuddered. "When that... man... tried to take me, I... bit him. As hard as I could."

"Then it's his blood," Geoffrey told her. "Did he speak to you?" he asked gently.

"No, Uncle. One minute I slept and the next I found myself jerked to my feet."

"You fought him bravely," Michael said softly. "I saw you kicking at him. You slowed him down enough to alert us, my lady. 'Twas swift thinking on your part."

Elysande's mouth trembled. No words came from her.

Geoffrey came to stand before her. "I suspect Lord Ingram is not pleased at how matters ended at Hopeston. He does not wait to see how the king answers his missive. He would take what he wants. And that is you, Niece." He looked around "Break camp at once. It's almost dawn. We shall hasten to Kinwick."

The men immediately sprang into action. Geoffrey ordered the bodies of the two de Montfort soldiers be secured so they could receive a proper burial at Kinwick.

"And Lord Ingram's men?" Michael asked.

Geoffrey's eyes grew hard as he looked at the bodies on the ground. "Leave them to rot."

Minutes later, the supplies and horses had been readied. Geoffrey insisted each of his family members ride with a trusted knight and not on their own horses. He signaled Michael over.

"Lady Elysande will ride with you. If we come under attack, see that she reaches Kinwick safely. I and the others will tend to my family." Geoffrey gazed steadily at him. "I'm entrusting her well-being to you, Michael."

"I won't let you down, my lord."

"Good." The nobleman strode away, pairing up his children with different knights before he placed his wife upon Mystery, his own horse.

Michael looked to Elysande. He held a hand out to her. "Come, my lady. You're to ride with me."

She gave him a slight nod. He lifted her to Tempest and then seated himself behind her.

Michael hated the circumstances that had led to them sitting so closely together, but he relished her nearness. He wrapped his arms about her, pulling her against his chest as he took up his reins. The subtle smell of violets wafted about him.

"You'll be safe, Elysande," he murmured softly into her ear. "Trust in me."

She looked over her shoulder, her amethyst eyes large. "I do, Michael. Despite what has happened this night, I've never felt more protected."

Michael spurred Tempest on with watchful eyes.

CHAPTER ELEVEN

Elysande awoke to a feeling of peace that washed over her. She'd only been at Kinwick a week, but already she felt part of the de Montfort family. Geoffrey's mother, Elia, had been especially kind to her. Elysande also found the people who worked at the castle and on the surrounding lands both friendly and industrious. They welcomed her without hesitation. It had been far different when she had arrived at Hopeston. From the servants inside the keep and beyond, she and Avelyn believed everyone spied upon them. Her mother laughed at the thought, but Elysande had never been comfortable under her stepfather's roof.

She rose and dressed for the day, deciding on a tawny *cotehardie* and a scarlet sideless surcoat. She wove a scarlet ribbon through her hair, hoping that Michael would notice it.

Her thoughts never strayed far from the handsome knight—in part because he had become her shadow since her arrival at Kinwick. She guessed that her uncle had charged Michael with her care and he took those orders quite seriously.

Elysande dreamily thought back on the ride to Kinwick after Lord Ingram's men had breached their camp. Michael had placed her on his horse and enfolded her in his arms. Though only minutes before she had nearly been kidnapped, she relaxed knowing Michael watched over her. The feel of his armor at her back was like a solid wall of stone that protected her from the world. His arms skimmed her sides. His hands that held Tempest's reins sat firm against her belly, securing her to him. Michael's very nearness caused her head to swim and her breath to rise giddily as she inhaled his masculine scent.

Yet, once they arrived at Kinwick, he hadn't touched her. He kept their conversations to a minimum as he followed her about the castle grounds while she interacted with others.

But his eyes told a different story.

Elysande sensed them on her wherever she went. Often, she would meet them. The blue, heated stare caused her insides to wiggle about in a most delightful way. Sometimes, she would give him a smile and turn back to her task. Other times, their eyes locked for minutes, speaking volumes.

Michael wanted her. Of that she was certain.

And she wanted him.

As each day passed, that became more obvious to her. Elysande observed the happy family that her uncle had and knew she wanted the same for herself. The de Montforts interacted constantly with one another, with everything from encouragement to love. Elysande wanted children just like her cousins, ones that were polite and sweet, who loved to express themselves and were curious about the world. She would miss Ancel, who, after tonight, would return to Winterbourne, the estate next to Kinwick, where he fostered with the earl. She would have more time with Alys, thanks to the royal court's summer progress. Alys and the other younger girls had been excused and would not rejoin the court until it return to London in early September.

Most of all, Elysande had come to adore little Hal. Almost halfway between one and two years of age, the tyke fell into more mischief than most children. But one look at those large, round eyes gave him license to run wild. Even when scolded, his sweet disposition caused him to reward a person with a huge smile and hug and then take off again in search of trouble.

Elysande finished dressing and made her way to the chapel for morning mass. As was his habit, Michael awaited her at the door and escorted her inside. Even within the walls of the castle, he kept a watchful eye upon her.

After mass, they went into the great hall to break their fast. Michael joined a table of soldiers while Elysande went to sit on the dais with the family. She greeted Geoffrey and then became engaged in conversation with Ancel, who was eager to return to his duties as a page. He told her everything he liked to do for the earl and countess, and Elysande became caught up in his enthusiasm.

Once they completed the small meal, Ancel excused himself to go to the training yard.

Alys asked, "Would you like to go to the meadow and into the woods to gather herbs with me?"

"I'd be delighted. You must promise me that you'll tell me all about what we gather and what you will do with it."

"Of course. I learn more every day from Mother." Alys looked around and frowned. "I haven't seen her this morning. I wonder where she could be."

Elysande remembered that Merryn had looked somewhat pale the night before and that Geoffrey had encouraged her to retire early. "Mayhap she slept a bit later since she was feeling poorly last night."

A determined look crossed Alys' face. "I hope she can come with us. If not, I'll fix whatever ails her. For now, I'll go and gather baskets for us to collect our herbs." She thought a moment. "I'll even speak to Cook about taking something to eat and drink with us. Many times we're gone several hours, so we might miss the midday meal."

"Then I'll check on Merryn while you accomplish your tasks," Elysande offered. "We can meet back here."

Alys skipped away happily.

"And what might you do today, my lady?"

She turned and found Michael at her elbow. "Alys and I have plans to go to the meadow and beyond. She wishes to replenish the store of herbs and she's going to teach me a bit about their medicinal nature."

He nodded. "Young Alys is already a healer in her own right. Lady Merryn has taught her well. 'Twill be an interesting day for you."

"So you'll accompany us to the meadow?"

"Aye. When do you leave?"

"Not for a while. Alys has gone to gather her things. I'm to find Lady Merryn and see if she wishes to go with us. Have you seen her this morning?"

"Nay."

"Then I'll check the solar and meet you back here."

"As you wish."

Elysande left, feeling Michael's eyes following her the length of the great hall. She arrived at the solar and paused before the closed door. As she lifted her hand to knock, she heard an awful retching sound. Concerned, she pushed open the door.

Merryn sat in a chair next to the table, a small pail in her lap. She glanced up and gave a weary smile before she bent over the pail again.

Elysande rushed in. "What ails you, Merryn? Should I fetch Uncle Geoffrey or Tilda?"

Merryn lifted her head and swallowed hard. After pausing a moment, she took the pail and rested it on the floor, pushing it under her chair with her foot. She looked very pale as she dabbed a linen cloth to her mouth.

"No, thank you, Elysande. 'Tis Geoffrey's fault to begin with."

"Why would you—" She stopped, realizing what Merryn meant. "You're with child?"

"I am." Merryn leaned back in the chair, a tiny smile crossing her lips. "With the twins, I was sick every morning for the first few months. Then I felt absolutely glorious. I had more energy than ever before. I got more done in a day than most women did in a week. But by the last two months, I barely left my bed."

"Were you sick again?"

Merryn laughed. "Nay. I became as round as a turret. It was too much effort to waddle about. And the twins warred within my womb, kicking away, fighting for space. I worried day and night that they would come out as mortal enemies, but I was proven wrong. They were as thick as thieves from the beginning and always looked after one another."

"They do seem very close."

"They spoke another language known only to them the first few years. And when they finally abandoned it, it seemed as if they could speak to each other without using words. Even now, I catch them glancing at one another and I know I'm missing an entire conversation going on between them." She sighed. "But come. Sit with me."

Elysande took a seat. "Were you that ill with Hal?"

Merryn laughed. "I was a mess with Hal. I was never sick a single morning, but every evening before bed? I couldn't stop retching and was miserable up till the very day I delivered him. Frankly, I couldn't wait for him to leave my womb. I thought once he arrived, the difficult part would be behind me." She gave Elysande a knowing look. "Little did I know Hal would cause as much trouble outside my womb as he did within."

"What about this time?" she asked, her curiosity growing.

"It's proven to be different than the first two times being with child. I seemed my usual self. Only slightly more tired the first two months. 'Twas only since we've returned to Kinwick that I am puny in the mornings. But I think the worst of it has passed for today." She looked to the table. "Would you pour me some of the weak ale? That seems to help. If I keep it down, I can try a little of the bread that Tilda brought me."

Elysande poured the ale into a pewter cup and watched her aunt sip at it. She finally nodded, so Elysande gave her some of the bread, as well.

"How are you settling into Kinwick?"

"Quite well. Everyone has been most welcoming. I've spent several hours in your stables. You may not know, but it's almost time for one of your dams to foal."

"Ah, that would be Hera. She is normally as sweet-tempered as any horse I've known, but I fear you're seeing her at her worst. She's foaled twice before. Both times, her temper has grown until she gives birth, then she returns to the loving, good-natured mare we know."

Elysande nodded. "I'm glad you shared that with me. I may have Hera's groom take her to the pasture instead."

"Why would you do that?"

"I've found with certain horses that being confined in a stall worsens the situation once they're nearing their time to give birth. Hera may prefer being out in the open. It may make the process easier on her."

Merryn patted her hand. "You know so much about horses."

"Father allowed Avelyn and me to pursue our passions." Elysande gave her aunt a sheepish grin. "Mine always happened to be horses."

"I know it was difficult for you to leave Morningstar and Happy behind."

Elysande nodded. "But Michael convinced me it would be too soon for the two of them to embark upon a journey of such length. My head agreed with him, but it saddened my heart. Yet somehow, he convinced a very rude groom to do his best in looking out for them till I returned to Hopeston."

Merryn nodded wisely. "Michael is a most persuasive man. And speaking of him, have you come to any decision regarding your future?" She gave Elysande a wry smile. "Somehow, I don't picture you spending a majority of your hours on your knees doing penance for something that was a natural occurrence."

Elysande sighed. "I've come to see it the same way," she agreed. "My stepfather was in poor physical shape. His health had faded ever since we came to Hopeston. I know now it was not my fault that he passed so suddenly. Besides, Mother would never forgive me if I entered a nunnery for such a weak reason. She's often told me that she wants many grandchildren."

"Have you shared your decision with Michael?"

"No," Elysande admitted. "In fact, we haven't shared much at all. Ever since we returned to Kinwick, we've barely spoken to one another."

"Yet he is almost always hovering nearby."

"Thanks to Uncle's orders."

"Mayhap he is waiting to hear from Geoffrey what the king says." Merryn took her hand. "I know he has strong feelings for you,

Elysande. But he would not press his suit if first, you did not want him to and second, if the king objected." Her aunt squeezed her hand reassuringly. "I think you need to let Michael know you're not opposed to match between you. He's probably still under the impression that you're ready to lock yourself away in a nunnery and suffer most prodigiously."

Elysande laughed. "Somehow, I can't see myself doing that. I believe I was being rash when I made that statement."

"It was natural for you to experience some guilt because of the circumstances," Merryn said. "But I would definitely clue Michael in as to your change of heart. And I hope we'll hear soon from King Edward. I think a match between you and Michael would be ideal. He's a fine man. I know you've seen how good he is with children."

"I've never seen a man more comfortable with them. Especially children that are not his own," Elysande teased.

Merryn laughed. "I must admit that there are some days when I would give Hal away. Can you imagine what that boy will be like as he grows older? The Earl of Winterbourne has it easy now with only Ancel under his care. When we send Hal his way? Hardie might send him back to us the very same day!"

Elysande giggled. "I hope that I can one day have a child as adorable and mischievous as Hal."

"Be careful what you wish for," her aunt warned, though Elysande saw the teasing light in Merryn's eyes.

"If things come to pass—and Michael and I are meant to be together—then I would be happy to have a boy that looked like Michael. Even if he acted as if the Devil himself were his sire!"

They laughed. Elysande decided that she would draw Michael away today and, in private, tell him how she'd decided not to enter a convent.

And when she did? Elysande hoped he would kiss her senseless.

CHAPTER TWELVE

Elysande returned to the great hall. She spotted Michael talking with Tilda. The servant met her eyes as she approached.

"Lady Merryn is staying behind?" Tilda asked.

Elysande nodded. "She's feeling better, but she didn't want to tax herself by being out in the hot sun for so long."

"Lady Merryn is ill?" Michael asked, concern written on his brow.

The two women pursed their lips. Wordless communication passed between them.

"The venison didn't agree with her," Elysande offered. "She had a rough night after consuming it, but she's recovered. She decided she would prefer a day resting in her chambers, but she'll be at the evening meal tonight."

"I'll go tend to her now," Tilda said, excusing herself.

Before Michael could pursue the matter, Alys came rushing up, two baskets hanging on each arm.

"Michael, you need to go to see Cook. She has food for us to take, but you'll need to carry it."

"I'll retrieve it at once, my lady." He bowed formally and stepped away.

Alys giggled. "Michael is so funny." She looked around. "Is Mother coming?"

Elysande decided that Merryn would have to share her news with her family and retainers in her own time. She didn't think a small untruth would matter.

"Actually, your mother said she had many things to do. She hoped you wouldn't mind taking me to the meadow. Merryn said no one knew herbs and flowers as well as her Alys did. She told me I would learn more in your company than hers."

The young girl glowed at the compliment. "I'll try to be as good a teacher to you as Mother has been to me." Alys looked over her shoulder as Michael approached, laden with a large basket.

"Hurry, Michael! We must stop wasting time. I've got so much to show Cousin Elysande."

"I am at your command, ladies."

Alys giggled again and handed over two of the empty baskets to Elysande. They set off. Many greeted them as they passed through the inner and outer baileys and left the castle grounds. Michael followed several steps behind them. Elysande knew he listened to her conversation with Alys, but he didn't join in.

They reached the large meadow, which stretched across a wide spread of land. Many flowers dotted the way. Elysande saw the forest beyond it.

"What are we looking for today?" she asked.

Alys looked around and then pointed. "Over there. See the chartreuse yellow blossoms on tall stems?"

"The ones with a feathery foliage?"

"Yes. That's dill. We need to pick lots of that. And we're down to the last of the rosemary at this time of year."

"I know what that looks like," Elysande said. "What else?"

Alys took Elysande's arm and walked her into the tall grassland. She motioned to their left. "Do you see the cones of lilac-pink bells past the dill? That's spearmint. I definitely want some of that." She thought a moment. "And lots of blackberries for Davy."

Elysande asked, "Who is Davy? I don't believe I've met him yet."

"He's very old now. He lives in a cottage that way." Alys pointed to the south. "Mother told me he's been fighting the flux. His waste is very watery and not solid at all," she said matter-of-factly. "The blackberries will aid his digestion."

Elysande was a little shocked someone as young as Alys could talk of such things which usually were left unspoken, but then she remembered Merryn's practical nature. The lady of Kinwick would never shy away from sharing knowledge with her daughter, especially if it would help one of their tenants.

"The blackberries are at the edge of the woods and just beyond it. Why don't you start with that, Elysande? Pick as many as you like. I'll put the excess in jars since they can't be picked after Old Michaelmas Day."

Alys' words piqued Elysande's curiosity. "And why is that?"

Her young cousin laughed. "If you listen to most people, they'll say 'tis the Devil himself who makes blackberries unfit to eat after October. Tilda swears that the Devil spits on them so that we can't eat them without growing violently ill. But she's wrong."

"How so?" Elysande asked.

"Mother tells me that it's really the wet and cold weather that causes mold to grow on them. That alone makes the blackberries poisonous, not some silly legend."

Elysande thought Alys seemed well beyond her years at that moment. And her next words confirmed that.

The girl moved close to her. "Now go and hunt for those blackberries," she instructed, her voice low. "I'm sure Michael will trail after you. In fact, you might have to step into the seclusion of the woods to find the best ones."

Elysande's jaw dropped. "But—"

"I've seen the looks pass between you two. You remind me of Mother and Father. They still act like a pair of lovebirds. 'Twould be nice for you and Michael to be the same."

Alys touched Elysande's cheek. "I would be so happy if you and Michael were to wed." Alys glanced over at Michael, who still stood on the road. "Michael is my favorite of all Father's knights. He will make an excellent husband." She dropped her hand. "So it's the blackberries that are most important," she said, her voice louder now.

Alys looked over her shoulder and called out, "Michael, go with Elysande. I need plenty of ripe blackberries for Davy. Don't come back empty-handed," she warned.

Michael came to where they stood. "Where will you be, my lady?" he asked Alys.

"Right over there. I have dill to pick. And rosemary if I can find it. Please look for that, too. I'll join you shortly." Alys moved away with a determined step. Once she reached the dill, she knelt and began to place it in her basket.

Michael turned to Elysande. "We have our marching orders. Come, my lady. I know exactly where to find the best blackberries." He grinned. "This is not my first time aiding Lady Alys as she collects flowers and herbs."

He led Elysande to the edge of the woods and beyond. They quickly located a patch of blackberries. She dropped to her knees and began picking the fruit, putting bunches of it in one of the baskets that Alys had thoughtfully provided. Michael sat down on the ground and began adding to her basket.

"You don't have to help with women's work," she teased.

Their hands brushed as he pulled a berry from its resting place. A jolt shot through her. Elysande yanked her hand away as if she'd been scorched. She dropped it into her lap and stared at it. Her mouth went dry. The blood began pounding in her ears.

Then, warm fingers lifted her chin and held it in place. Her eyes became lost in Michael's dark blue ones.

"We haven't really talked since you've come to Kinwick," he said softly.

"I know," she whispered.

"You've seemed happy this past week."

"I have been." His fingers burned into her flesh.

"Lord Geoffrey and Lady Merryn are fine people."

"They are." Elysande continued to gaze into his eyes. She swallowed. "And I told Merryn today how I was mistaken."

"In what?" he asked, his deep voice as smooth as velvet.

"In wanting to retreat to a nunnery."

His eyes sparked with interest. "Indeed?"

"Aye. I don't want to live a quiet life with the pious sisters. I don't think I'm one made for only prayers and solitude."

She watched the slow smile begin to light his face.

"And what might you wish for your life?" he asked lightly, still holding her chin in his hand.

Never taking her eyes from his, she admitted, "I wish for a life with you, Michael. I can't think of anyone else I'd rather spend my life with. I want to laugh with you. Share my day with you. Have babes with you," she boldly declared, surprising herself with her honest admission.

His smile now filled his face, touching his eyes in merriment. "Lord Geoffrey has assured me he's written on my behalf to the king. That he believes it will be a favorable outcome. I was merely waiting for you to come to the same conclusion."

Both Michael's hands cradled her face tenderly. Elysande grew warm at his touch.

"Since I met you, I've thought of no other woman. Before I even knew your name, I'd decided you would be the one for me." His callused thumbs lovingly brushed her cheeks. "I couldn't wait to find out your name so that I could go at once to your father and ask for your hand in marriage. And when I found out you weren't the daughter of a lowly groom but Hopeston's bride-to-be? It nearly undid me."

He slowly brushed his lips against hers. Elysande's heart skipped a beat.

Michael broke the kiss. "Hope grew when I found out your betrothed had died on his journey to Hopeston," he continued. "It died yet again when your stepfather refused to consider my suit. But now?" He gazed at her lovingly.

"I've prayed to the Almighty on High that you would come to your senses. That you wouldn't choose to lock yourself away from the world for something that wasn't your fault. Now I find those prayers have been answered most favorably."

He brought his mouth to hers again. His hands pushed into her hair as his tongue gently coaxed her lips to part. It ran along her lower lip and then slipped inside. It touched the tip of her own, sparking a flame of desire within her. Elysande moaned and brought her hands to his shoulders as he deepened the kiss.

Her heart pounded furiously as their tongues now dueled, mating with one another. Her breathing grew shallow and giddy. Michael's hands ran through her hair and dropped to her back. He pulled her close. Her breasts grazed his chest and began to feel heavy. They ached with need. He placed his palm over one and rubbed the nipple back and forth, causing it to come to life. Her lower region caught on fire. The unfamiliar feeling filled her with a sweet longing.

Elysande locked her hands behind his neck and nestled as close to Michael as she could. Her tongue now warred with his as an equal. She heard his groan of pleasure. It thrilled her that she had the power to make him feel her need for him. Her body began thrumming, pulsating, coming alive as never before. Both his hands now palmed her breasts, squeezing them, lifting them, rubbing them. They felt on fire. *She* felt on fire.

Michael broke their kiss and dropped his hands to her waist. He lifted Elysande to her feet as he stood and backed her against a tree. Once again, his mouth locked on hers, bringing her to a height she'd never found. Then his lips trailed down her throat and lingered at the curve of her breast, nipping and licking at it.

She needed more. Much more.

Elysande pushed the clothing aside, pulling it from her shoulders, pawing at it till it dropped to her waist. Only her smock remained in the way. She saw the heat in Michael's eyes as his head dropped. His mouth fastened on to her breast, warm and wet as his tongue stroked it through the thin material. Then his teeth lightly grazed her nipple, causing a surge to ripple through her.

She cried out from the pleasure. Her fingers buried themselves in his dark, thick hair, bringing him closer to her. He continued to lick and nibble at first one breast, then the other, till the blood sang in her veins. His hand traced a line up her leg, under her skirts, and then came to the apex where the pulsing beat out of control.

Elysande pushed hard against the tree as his mouth continued to tease her breast and his fingers did the same within her womanly parts. His mouth moved up again and closed over hers. Soon his tongue mimicked the actions of his fingers, moving in and out. He continued stroking her in both places till she thought she might go mad.

Then the pulsing turned into a warmth that burst from her as the sun rising on the horizon. She began to shudder violently against his fingers as an intense pleasure enveloped her. Elysande cried out, the sound falling into his mouth as he kissed her. She clung to him, sobbing, riding out the waves as they stormed through her.

The feelings slowly subsided. She panted heavily as his lips parted from hers. Their foreheads fell against one another. Michael leaned into her heavily. She, in turn, used his weight and the tree behind her to support herself. Her legs wobbled beneath her, threatening to fold at any moment.

"Did I bring you pleasure?" he asked, his voice rough and low.

"Aye." The one word took great effort on her part. No more would come.

He cradled her face and kissed her tenderly. "I would do that and much more for you, my lady. If you will but have me as yours."

"I've always been yours," she replied. "From the moment of my birth. I knew not who you were and when we were fated to meet, but now that we have?" Elysande kissed him. "It will always be you. Never another. You are my light and my life, Michael Devereux."

"And I plan for us never to be apart, Elysande Le Cler. I am committed to you, heart and soul. In time, we'll make it official in the eyes of God and man, but I want you to know that I am yours till our dying day—and beyond."

Michael kissed her again, long and slow, till her toes began to curl. Then he released her.

"I think it would be smart on our part to pick a few blackberries, my love, or Alys may wonder what we've been up to."

Michael laughed as he took her hands. She quickly repaired her clothes. They returned to the patch of blackberries and began quickly placing them in the basket.

Elysande's heart beat strong. And with each beat, it said, *Michael. Michael. Michael.*

CHAPTER THIRTEEN

ELYSANDE WATCHED AS Ancel hugged Alys. Though each twin favored a different parent and looked nothing alike, in that moment, she saw a resemblance in their attitude. The two were cut from the same cloth and their time in the womb together had bound them in a way that others would never understand.

"The next time I see you will be Christmas time," Alys told her brother.

"Take care at court," Ancel told her. "Learn from the queen, but remember that you'll always be a de Montfort first."

"And the firstborn of we two," she teased. Alys then embraced her twin once more. She turned away and came to stand next to Elysande.

"I can tell that you'll miss Ancel a great deal."

The girl nodded. "He's the best of brothers. Oh, I love Hal and always will. But there will always be something special between Ancel and me. Sometimes, I wonder if even my future husband will know me as well as my twin does."

Elysande put an arm about Alys' shoulder. "It will be different with a husband, but he'll come to know parts of you that even you don't know exist. You'll discover things about each other together."

Alys looked at Elysande with new eyes. "That's quite sage advice, Cousin Elysande. Mayhap you have discovered things about yourself with your future husband?" She didn't bother trying to hide her smile.

Elysande squeezed the girl affectionately. "Just because you threw Michael and me together yesterday, you already have us paired off."

"What if I do?" Alys challenged. "You've seemed very happy since we returned to the keep yesterday. Although the time we spent grinding herbs has probably fled your mind now. And I'm sure you couldn't possible remember all the tidbits I told you about what Mother and I will do with what we collected yesterday."

Elysande felt her face grow warm. It had been hard to listen and remember everything Alys tried to teach her when all Elysande could think about was Michael's mouth on hers. His hands caressing her body.

And when they could share a repeat performance.

Geoffrey motioned them over to where he stood with Merryn, Ancel, and Elia, who juggled a squirming Hal in her arms.

"Come. Your father wants us," she told Alys.

Elysande watched as Ancel shook his father's hand. Then her young cousin looked to his mother. Merryn had tears in her eyes.

"Mother, I'm only one estate away from you," Ancel chided gently.

"'Tis not that," Merryn said. She looked around at the tight circle that had formed. "Before Ancel leaves, I need to share some news with you all." She took a deep breath. "I'm going to have another child a few months. After the new year begins."

Both Ancel and Alys squealed in delight and hugged their mother tightly. Elysande saw the fond look her uncle gave his wife. Without thinking, she glanced over at Michael, who stood nearby. She could tell by the grin on his face that he had overheard Merryn's words.

"I wanted you to know before you left, Ancel. Alys, too. And I wanted to tell you at the same time."

"It's wonderful news, Mother," Alys said, her eyes narrowing. "I only hope you'll have a girl this time."

"Well, I hope for another boy," Ancel declared. "One even wilder than Hal." He ruffled his brother's hair fondly.

Geoffrey slipped an arm about Merryn's waist. "Our hope is for a healthy child." He glanced at his youngest. "And mayhap for one a bit more sedate than this last one."

"That's why you need another girl, Father," Alys said primly.

Elysande joined in as everyone laughed at Alys' simple logic. Then the final goodbyes were said. Ancel and Geoffrey mounted the horses that had been brought to them.

"I'll be home in time for the noon meal, my love," called Geoffrey.

"Goodbye!" Ancel hollered. "Nice to meet you, Cousin Elysande. I hope you come back with Aunt Mary and Cousin Avelyn to celebrate the Christmas season with us."

"Thank you, Ancel," she replied. "That would be my wish as well."

She watched the riders leave the inner bailey and wondered what the next few months would bring.

ELYSANDE HAD JUST broken her fast when Kinwick's head groom came to her.

"It's time, my lady. Hera exhibits all the signs. Her waxing started last night, with beads on the end of each teat. And now the secretion has gone from clear and watery to sticky and thick."

Elysande stood quickly from her seat on the dais. "Is she still in the pasture?"

"Yes, my lady, just as you instructed. I moved the other horses away from her. They've all been returned to their stalls. Hera will have the privacy she needs to deliver her foal."

"Let me change into something more practical before I go to the pasture."

"Is there anything special you need?" asked Merryn.

"Nay. I've done this many times with dams far less docile than Hera."

Geoffrey laughed. "Hera has been a handful for the past week around everyone but Elysande," he informed his wife.

"We've gotten to know one another. I understand her better than I do most people," Elysande said. "I need to put on my pants and a gypon. It's much more comfortable and easier than having to deal with keeping my skirts out of the way."

Michael joined them. "I hear that Hera is ready to foal. I assume we'll be in the pasture for most of the day?"

She nodded. "You might want to ask Cook for some bread and cheese and a flask of wine. I doubt we'll make either the noon or evening meal."

"I'll see to it," he told her.

Elysande hurried to her bedchamber and slipped from her clothes into the brown gypon, *cotehardie*, and pants that she had brought along in case she needed them. She returned downstairs and found Michael waiting for her by the foot of the stairs, a sack in his hand. She, in turn, had brought a bag with a few things of her own that she might need to use for the foal's delivery.

"Sustenance for our long day," he said, holding up the sack. "Cook was only too happy to provide it for us."

"Then we should make haste to the pasture."

The August day was warm and partly cloudy. Elysande saw Hera standing in a secluded spot under the shade of a large oak tree. As they approached, the horse began swishing her tail angrily.

Elysande climbed over the fence. Michael eased the sack to the ground and followed behind her.

She approached the mare and soothingly said, "I hear you're fussy today, my sweet girl. Are you out of sorts?"

As she spoke, she removed the linen cloth she had brought and moved to capture the horse's tail. Swiftly, she wrapped it before Hera knew what she did.

Michael quietly asked, "What does that do? I can't remember if you told me during our first delivery together." He gave her a smile.

"It will keep the tail from having dirt cling to it when she gets up and down. We need to keep the foal as clean as possible in order for it to remain healthy."

Elysande stepped away and backed toward the fence. She gestured for Michael to join her and they sat on top of it as Hera continued her pacing in the pasture. Elysande's eyes swept over the area. She had instructed that any rocks or brush be moved and saw that had occurred. As they waited, Hera paused to eat a few oats and drink some water.

"All seems to be going well so far," Michael said. "I see droplets of milk falling as she moves about. So we sit and observe quietly for now?"

She nodded. "Some dams like a fuss to be made over them, but I can tell Hera doesn't want us to hover. We're here for when she needs us."

He reached over and took her hand in his. A pleasant tingling began. It caused her breath to quicken, but Elysande remained focused on the restless mare. They sat in the sunshine in silence.

Hera moved closer to them. Elysande saw that the horse had broken out into a sweat which dotted her neck and flanks. She slipped off the top of the fence, pulling Michael along with her.

"It's very warm today. If she'll allow us, we need to bathe her some."

Elysande took out more cloths and went to the water bucket. Plunging them in, she twisted the excess water from each and handed one to Michael. They slowly ran the cloths over Hera's flanks and along her neck. The mare stood patiently and seemed to enjoy their ministrations on her behalf.

Then the uterine contractions became more severe. Hera became jittery. She broke away and nervously paced along the fence line, pawing at the ground at intervals. Then she lay down for a minute and rose, repeating the process several times.

"I can see she's distressed," Michael noted. "Can't we do more for her?"

"Nay. Let her work things out in her own way. Hera is helping position the foal with her movements."

Once again, they returned to sit on the fence and keep their distance. Michael took her hand in his again, entwining his fingers through hers. As they sat in the warm sunshine, Elysande experienced perfect contentment. She didn't know if a day—or any given moment—could be as sweet and wonderful as sitting beside the man she loved. She relished his very nearness as they patiently awaiting the birth of the foal.

Hera drew up suddenly, frozen for a moment, a faraway look in her eyes. Then the sac ruptured. Fluid poured out from the horse. Elysande saw the horse's abdomen began contracting more violently.

When Hera didn't lie down as expected, Elysande leapt off the fence and motioned Michael to follow her.

As they rushed over, she told him, "It's the rare horse that wants to stand to give birth. I think Hera may be one of them."

"What do I need to do?"

"If she remains standing, we need to catch the foal and lower it gently to the ground to avoid injury."

Elysande returned for a large, clean blanket and shook it out, setting it on the ground close by the mare. Michael squatted down, hands ready, waiting to see what would happen. But Hera changed her mind and lay down again.

Some minutes passed. Concerned, Elysande said, "I need to check the position of the foal. I hope it's not breech."

She rolled up the sleeve of her gypon and knelt next to the mare. Stroking her gently, she said in soothing tones, "I must feel for your little one, Hera."

Elysande inserted her hand into the birth canal and moved it upwards. As she suspected, the foal was in the breech position. She turned it as best she could and then slid her arm out. Immediately, Hera stood and walked anxiously for some minutes, pausing once for more food and water.

"Was it breech?" Michael asked.

"Aye. Hopefully, between what I did and her pacing, the foal will be in a better position now to be born."

The horse came again to lie on the ground. She had barely stretched out when the foal's head and neck squirted out, encased in a bluish-white sac. The shoulders soon followed. Then a hoof appeared, followed by another one, as the foal's front legs appeared. Hera rested for a while and then began straining.

After some minutes, Elysande became concerned with the mare's lack of progress.

"I'm afraid we'll need to step in and help her. She's very tired and weak now."

"Tell me what to do."

"We'll each need to take one of the hooves in our hand and hold the foal's leg in the other."

They bent in front of the panting dam. Each took firm hold. Michael looked to Elysande for further instructions.

"On three, we'll both pull gently." She counted and they moved as one, helping to expel the foal to its hips.

"Stop," Elysande said. "Hera will need to rest again before we can continue."

The pair sat on each side of Hera, stroking her gently. When Elysande judged that enough time had passed, she said, "Let's work together again. Pull the foal's hooves toward Hera's hooves. 'Twill help rotate her hips and ease the foal from her."

Again, she and Michael grabbed hold of the foal and pulled. This time, the hind legs appeared and the entire foal came out.

But the small creature wasn't breathing.

"The foal hasn't lifted its head," she warned Michael. "That usually happens when the sac breaks."

He quickly passed her his dagger before she could reach for hers. Elysande tore away the membrane. She reached for a bit of straw in order to use it to clear the nasal passage.

Nothing happened.

Panic swelled within her. She bent over the foal. She hadn't ever attempted this before, but her father had told her he had done the same once when a newborn foal did not begin to breathe on its own.

Elysande firmly cupped her hands over the foal's mouth and nose. She drew in a deep breath and expelled it into the animal's nostrils. She waited and repeated the breath.

"The chest rose and fell," Michael told her. He moved next to her and rested his hands on the newborn's belly. "Try again."

She did. Once. Twice. Tears began to well in her eyes. But before she could blow air a third time, the foal whimpered and sucked in a breath on its own.

Elysande fell back in relief. Michael pulled her to her feet and encompassed her in his arms. Uncontrollable tremors rushed through her. She buried her face in his chest and began to weep.

"What if the foal hadn't taken a breath? What if—"

"It did," he reassured her. "Thanks to your quick thinking. I would never have thought to try and breathe into it like that." He brushed soft lips against hers. "You saved its life, Elysande. You worked a miracle, my love."

She clung to him, trembling as if she had the palsy. He murmured soothing words of solace as he held her tenderly, stroking her back, kissing her hair. Finally, she believed her knees would not cause her to fall. Elysande looked up at him.

"Thank you for being here with me. I couldn't have done it without your assistance."

Michael's fingertips wiped the tears from her cheeks. "I recall we still have more to watch for."

She nodded. "The afterbirth."

They observed the mare for some time, but her contractions didn't expel all of the afterbirth. Elysande knelt and tied it into a knot that hung above Hera's hocks.

"This will prevent her from stepping on it or tearing it away too early," she explained to Michael. "It will also add gentle pressure as it hangs down and help it to come out on its own."

They remained with the mare and foal several more hours. She and Michael cheered as they watched the newborn learn to stand. She allowed Michael to help guide the foal to drink from its mother's teat. As the foal nursed, Hera expelled the afterbirth. Elysande examined it to make sure nothing remained behind inside the mare. She also discovered that the foal was a filly.

As they leaned against the fence for support, watching the foal nurse noisily, Michael turned to her.

"I don't know if Lord Geoffrey had a name in mind for this little one, but I believe she should be named Miracle."

"Miracle," Elysande repeated, liking the sound of it. "It's what we witnessed. Together."

With that, she pulled his head toward hers and rewarded all his hard work with a lingering kiss.

CHAPTER FOURTEEN

MICHAEL LOOKED ACROSS the room and watched Elysande as she danced. Her cheeks were flushed a rosy red. Those bewitching amethyst eyes sparkled as she partnered with Hugh, Lady Merryn's brother. Hugh's wife, Milla, heavy with child, sat visiting with Merryn. The couple had come for the evening meal and to meet Elysande. Hugh had been away on business previously. Milla waited for his return before they traveled to the de Montfort estate to make Elysande's acquaintance.

Geoffrey joined Michael. "She's quite fetching."

He watched Elysande twirl about, laughing. "That she is, my lord."

"I hope to hear from the king any day now," Geoffrey confided. "My rider found the royal progress and delivered my message. He's just returned and said that King Edward promised a long missive to Lady Merryn."

Michael grunted. "Our king is quite taken with Lady Merryn. 'Tis a good thing he has Queen Philippa to keep him in line."

"I agree. The queen puts up with no nonsense. She's very fond of Merryn and Alys, too. I hope the king will share with his wife that Elysande is in my custody and what we would like to see to her future." Geoffrey squeezed his shoulder. "You will make my niece a fine husband, Michael."

"It's my fondest desire, my lord."

The music ended. He watched Elysande make her way over to where Merryn and Milla sat. Hugh came toward Michael and Geoffrey.

"I quite like her, Geoffrey," Hugh enthused. "She's lively and witty. I hope your sister, Mary, will soon visit Kinwick with your other niece. It would be nice to see Lady Mary again. I had a small crush on her when I was a boy. She was older by a handful of years and beyond beautiful."

"Mary has spoken to me about returning to Kinwick for a visit in the near future," Geoffrey replied. "It's been many years since she saw the place of her birth."

Michael's thoughts turned to how long it had been since he had laid eyes upon Sandbourne. Over fifteen years had passed since the day he'd ridden away from his boyhood home, vowing never to return until his father's death. He wondered how much longer he'd wait to come into his earldom.

In truth, he remembered very little about the castle. He'd spent many hours alone in his small bedchamber, playing with toy soldiers on the floor, daydreaming about becoming a great, feared knight who would be respected by his peers. Though his mother had taken him for rides around the estate in his early years, she eventually kept to her rooms more and more. Michael believed she did so to prevent running into her husband. One thing he did recall was going to her airy bedchamber and listening while she read to him and told him tales. He reached into his pocket and stroked the small rock that they'd found on one of their trips walking about the estate. The rock, an unusual pink color, had become the only thing he had left of her. His memories of what she looked like had faded over the years.

Still, determination filled him to find her once he returned to live at Sandbourne. His mother had been such a kind, gentle woman. He knew she would approve of Elysande. He could picture the two women, hovering over a small babe, cooing away. The thought brought a smile to his lips.

"Michael?"

He turned and saw Lord Geoffrey held a bit of parchment in his hand.

"My lord?"

"You've received a missive. From Sandbourne."

Their eyes met. Michael's stomach dropped past his knees. His heart quickened. He reached for the delivered message.

As Geoffrey handed it to him, he said, "Go. Read it in private. And let me know what action you'll take."

Michael nodded, clutching the parchment tightly in his hand. He excused himself and left the great hall, the music that played fading away. He exited the keep and went to sit at the top of the stone steps that led up to its doorway. No activity occurred in the bailey below. Sunset would occur within the hour.

He sat frozen, the missive resting in his lap for several minutes, wondering how his life would change with the words he was about to read.

Breaking open the seal, he unrolled the paper. The summer light was still strong enough to read the message easily.

Sir Michael –

'Tis time for you to make your way home. Your father is near death. He's asked for your return since he has advice to dispense to you regarding Sandbourne and your future.

Please hurry. The healer doesn't know how long he may have.

Houdart

Houdart. So he still served as the earl's steward. Michael wondered how old the man truly was. He'd seemed ancient when Michael was a boy, but one's memory could play tricks. Houdart's hair had been gray at the time, his face lined with wrinkles. But now as an adult, Michael realized certain men aged more quickly than others. Houdart's step had always been quick, as fast as his wit. Michael hoped the steward would agree to stay on because it would make the transition of power go more easily when the time came.

Michael stood. He would make for Sandbourne at first light tomorrow.

"Michael?"

He turned and saw Elysande coming toward him. He rose, his

fingers curling around the missive.

"I saw you leave. Is everything all right?"

Holding up the parchment, he revealed, "I just received word from Sandbourne's steward. He says the present earl is quite ill. I need to return at once."

Disappointment crossed her face, only to be replaced by a hopeful look. "So you'll soon be free to make your own choices when you become the earl," she noted.

"Aye." He dropped the paper and yanked her to him. "I want to marry you, Elysande Le Cler, and make you my countess. I want you by my side always, bearing my children." He paused. "But I know 'tis wise to wait for word from the king before we officially commit to one another."

Her palms rested against his chest. "I believe we've already committed to one another," she said softly. "I love you, Michael."

Happiness burst inside him. "I love you, my dearest Elysande. More than words could ever say."

Michael kissed her with great tenderness. As he pulled away, he saw the spark of mischief in her eye, which made him a bit wary.

"You look as Hal might, just before he's caught in some new devilry."

"So you wish to marry me?" she asked.

A lump formed in his throat. He nodded, not trusting that words would come.

"And we're meant to be together, now and forever?"

Michael nodded again.

"You might be gone for some time with this business."

"I might."

Her lips pursed in amusement. "And I might miss you something awful." Her brows arched. "Especially your kisses," she teased.

He drew her closer to him. "You might."

A smile lit her face. "Then mayhap we should give each other something to remember on our last night together."

Elysande took his hand and began racing down the steps. He followed her lead, her hand warm in his as she hurried across the inner bailey.

After some minutes, she halted in front of the stables.

"You want us to check on Hera and Miracle?"

"Nay, my love." She squeezed his hand. "I want us to find some privacy."

"Ah."

This time he took the lead and led her through the stables, past horses munching on hay and oats. He found an empty stall near the rear and stepped inside. As he turned, Elysande threw herself into his arms. Her hands locked around his neck as her breasts brushed against his chest, causing his manhood to stir.

She kissed him hungrily, greedily, as if they would never see each other again. He responded to her kiss with a like passion, knowing the time spent away from her would seem an eternity. Her hands began to roam his body boldly, causing his pulse to quicken. They moved lower and his member sprang to life at her touch.

She broke away a moment, a surprised look on her face, and glanced down. When their eyes met, she suddenly seemed unsure of herself.

Michael pressed his lips to her forehead. "Your caress has spurred me to want to take action." He cupped her face in his hands and sweetly brushed her lips with his briefly. "But we must stop with our goodbyes."

"Why?" she asked, a longing shadowing her face.

"Because we should be husband and wife before we take our love play further."

"Do you love me, Michael?"

Her question startled him. "Of course, sweetling. You know I do. And when we're wed, I'll tell you that seven times a day. Nay, seven times seventy—or more!"

"Love me," she said simply. "Love me now. I am already wed to you in my heart. 'Tis only a few words we'll repeat after some priest. I want you. Now."

He saw she spoke the truth. Her truth.

Their truth.

Michael thought to their upcoming separation. He didn't know what condition he'd find his father in. Michael might be gone a week or two. Mayhap longer. Looking into Elysande's eyes, he realized he needed to brand her as his.

"Are you certain?" he asked, his voice shaking with emotion.

Her response was to kiss him with a possessiveness that shook him to his very soul. *She* branded *him*. With her touch. With her generosity. With her passion.

Michael swept Elysande up into his arms and carried her to the corner of the stall. He placed her gently on a pile of hay and then covered her body with his, his mouth seeking hers once more. As they kissed, his body seemed engulfed in flames. Desire rippled through him as never before. In his arms, he held the one woman he would pledge himself to from now till eternity.

His hand slid up her slender calf, its sweet curve calling to him. Swiftly, he pushed her skirts away. His mouth fastened on the silky skin of her calf, trailing a line of kisses up to her knee, then her thigh. He continued working his way up to her core and plunged his tongue into it. Her gasp of surprise caused him to smile. He tasted her very essence, moving skillfully, wanting to pleasure her till she went mad. She began to pant, then moan, little cries of happiness that brought him satisfaction. He cupped her rounded buttocks and delved deeper, her fingers now threaded in his hair, holding tightly.

Elysande writhed beneath him as he held her firm. She cried out again loudly and began bucking against him. He felt her tremors and let her ride the wave of passion till she stilled. Quickly, he loosened his pants and plunged into her, his mouth covering hers to capture any noise. She dug her nails into his back.

Michael kissed her deeply, holding himself still, waiting until she became caught up again in their love play. He sensed her body relaxing beneath him. Slowly, he withdrew and slipped into her again. He began leisurely, helping her to figure out how to match his rhythm. She quickly understood what to do. Minutes later, they danced to a melody all their own, increasing their speed. She began whimpering again, moaning, tightening both her arms and legs about him. They rocked together as one.

And then he came as never before. His seed spilled into her and as it did, waves of love poured from him. Their kiss was the greatest one of his life. They'd been created for this moment, together, born as one in love.

Spent, he collapsed against her. Then he feared he might crush her. Michael rolled quickly, bringing Elysande with him till she rested on top of him. He gazed upon her flushed face, those amethyst eyes burning large and bright.

Then, with a satisfied smile, she said, "I think I'll enjoy being married to you, Michael Devereux. As long as we can do this every night, that is."

CHAPTER FIFTEEN

MICHAEL STUFFED THE final piece of clothing into the sack, ready to go inform Lord Geoffrey of his departure. He glanced around the barracks where he had spent the last year of his life in service to Geoffrey de Montfort. He gave a prayer of thanksgiving to the Almighty that he'd heard of Geoffrey's return to Kinwick after a mysterious disappearance of many years, for that had spurred Michael to leave Sir Lovel and commit to the man he'd idolized since childhood.

If Michael hadn't come to Kinwick, then he never would have accompanied the de Montfort family to the planned wedding at Hopeston.

And he'd never have met Elysande.

It seemed impossible that they'd only known each other such a short time. Yet, he couldn't imagine his life without her. The intimate experience of witnessing the miracles of two different foals' birth had bonded them in a unique way.

Or maybe Fate had ordained that they should meet. Whatever the reason they'd come together, Michael only knew being with Elysande completed him. More than anything, he looked forward to their wedded life at Sandbourne and the children they would raise. It struck him how, a month ago, he hadn't envisioned life as a married man, yet now he believed it was his road to happiness. That was the difference now. Because he'd found love, nothing would ever be the same again.

He lifted the sack as Hammond came in. He would miss this loyal friend of his. They'd become as close as brothers since his arrival at

Kinwick. Mayhap Hammond might consider coming to Sandbourne—but only if Michael spoke to Geoffrey about it first. He would never go behind his liege lord's back and rob Geoffrey of one of his best soldiers.

"Lord Geoffrey asked that you come and meet with him before you leave," Hammond informed him. "He's waiting for you in the solar."

Michael offered his hand. "Thank you for your friendship, Hammond."

The knight looked puzzled as they shook. "You act as if this is a final farewell between us, Michael. You only mentioned that your father was ill. Aren't you returning to Kinwick?"

Michael didn't want to go into his family history now. "Things are complicated, my friend. Only know that I've appreciated your every kindness to me since I came to Kinwick, and that one day I hope we'll work together again."

Hammond slapped him on the back. "I can think of no other man I'd rather have by my side in case we had to ride into battle." He reached for Michael's sack. "I'll ready Tempest for your departure and attach this to his saddle while you visit with Lord Geoffrey."

"In return, I'll ask one thing of you before I go."

"What? Anything, Michael. You know that."

"Look after Lady Elysande. Keep her safe."

Hammond nodded. "Of course."

The two men left the barracks, parting as Hammond ventured to the stables and Michael turned toward the keep.

Arriving at the solar, he found Geoffrey scribbling away as he sat at the table.

"My lord?"

"Ah, come in, Michael." Geoffrey indicated for him to take a seat.

"Are you leaving today for Sandbourne?"

"Aye, my lord. The earl is very ill. The healer says he doesn't have much time left."

"I know you've been estranged from him, Michael, but it's fortunate you've received this final gift of time to be with him as he comes to the end of his life."

Michael frowned. "How so, my lord?"

"People can change. Mayhap, your father has. If so, he may ask for your forgiveness—and you should give it to him. Don't let any ill will stand between you as he goes to meet his Maker."

Michael didn't know if he could ever forgive the many transgressions of the Earl of Sandbourne, but he nodded sagely as if he would consider it.

"I don't want you to worry about Elysande while you're gone," Geoffrey continued. "I'll see that she always has a guard with her if she leaves the castle grounds. In these last few weeks, Lord Ingram has made no further attempts to spirit her away. I'm certain he's given up on such a foolish scheme and returned to his lands in the north."

"I won't worry about her safety, my lord. I know you love your niece dearly and would protect her from any harm." He shrugged. "I only fear I may go mad being parted from her for an unknown amount of time."

Geoffrey chuckled. "When I hear from the king, I'll send the news along to you. I am confident it will be as we expect. Though it sounds as if you'll likely bury your father soon, your burden should be eased by your upcoming wedding."

Michael broke out in a huge grin. "I hope so, my lord."

Geoffrey accompanied him to the inner bailey, where Hammond had Tempest saddled and ready for Michael to ride.

Merryn descended the steps and handed Michael a heavy sack. "I have food from Cook. Geoffrey said you'll most likely reach Sandbourne by the noon meal tomorrow, but I wanted you to have something for the road."

Alys skipped up and threw her arms about his waist. Hal trailed behind her, babbling nonsense as he held his arms out. Michael scooped up Hal in one arm and gathered Alys in his other.

"I'll miss both of you more than I should admit," he told them. He kissed the tip of Alys' nose and the soft fuzz of Hal's head before he put them back on the ground. As he did, Michael saw Elysande had come down the stairs with Geoffrey's mother. Both women had joined Merryn.

Michael stepped over to the trio. He took Lady Elia's hand and kissed it. "I thank you for your hospitality, my lady. And for letting me enjoy playing with your grandchildren."

The old woman blushed. "I thank you for your courtly ways, Sir Michael. You'll be missed at Kinwick."

He then turned to Elysande and took her hand in his. He bent and pressed his lips to her knuckles far longer than he should have.

"I will miss your delightful company, my lady," he told her.

"And I will miss yours, Sir Michael," she said sincerely, though her eyes twinkled merrily.

Geoffrey spoke up. "You have much to learn about women, Michael."

"My lord?"

Geoffrey shook his head. "If I were leaving Kinwick, do you think Merryn would be happy with a kiss to her hand or a peck on the cheek? Nay, she's a greedy little thing and would want much, much more."

His hand snaked out and latched on to his wife's arm. Geoffrey pulled her to him in a tight embrace.

Glancing at Michael, he said, "*This* is what a woman wants." He proceeded to give Merryn a lingering kiss.

"Not again," Alys muttered. She looked up at Michael. "You might as well do as Father says or poor Cousin Elysande will feel left out."

Michael looked at the couple and laughed as their kiss continued. He shrugged and moved to Elysande, capturing her waist in his hands.

"I can't ignore my liege lord's advice," he told her before his lips met hers in a searing kiss.

Finally, Michael broke the kiss. "I love you," he whispered before turning and mounting Tempest. He nudged the horse and took off with a wave of his hand.

As he reached the gates, Michael thought about the next time he returned to Kinwick. He would ride through its gates as the Earl of

Sandbourne.

And come to claim his bride.

ELYSANDE CONTINUED TO crush the gray-green leaves before her as Alys had instructed. Her nose wrinkled in disgust, thanks to the strong smell that wafted up from the table.

"And what is mugwort used for again?" she asked her young cousin.

Alys gave her a patient look. "I often use it in foot ointments."

"I can't imagine that," Elysande admitted. "Sweating feet smell bad enough as it is. Adding mugwort to them would only seem to add to the problem to me."

Merryn laughed. "Let me finish with the mugwort. Here, come spend time with the rosemary. Rinse your hands in that bowl and dry them carefully before you touch the new herb."

Elysande did as she was told, happy to trade places with Merryn. She bent and smelled the savory rosemary. "Now this is much more to my liking."

"I like a bit of rosemary floating in a cup of hot water. It soothes my stomach," Merryn shared.

She looked at her aunt, whose small bump seemed more visible today. "Are you feeling better?"

"I am. I haven't been ill in two days now. Hopefully, the worst is behind me."

"I remember how large you got with Hal," Alys said. "Every day for months I would ask you when the new babe would come out."

Merryn laughed. "'Twas nothing compared to my girth when I carried you and Ancel. Two of you inside me seemed to swallow me up."

Alys frowned. "I don't know if I want any babes. Although I love Hal, he's so much trouble."

"When you find a man you love, you'll want to bear his babes," Elysande assured her.

"Are you and Michael going to have many children?"

She felt herself pinken immediately and didn't know how to answer.

"Alys! It's not your place to ask such a personal thing," her mother scolded. "Only God knows what He has planned for a couple."

The girl shrugged. "I was only curious, Mother."

Merryn told Elysande to tie small bunches of the rosemary with pieces of twine that lay on the table.

"What will you do with this rosemary?" she asked.

"You may place a few springs under your pillow at night. It will ward off any nightmares that might occur."

Merryn looked up as Tilda came into the room. "My lady? You asked for me to give you fair warning. The noon meal will begin shortly."

"Thank you, Tilda. All right, let's finish with the herbs we have. We can continue later this afternoon."

Once they arrived at the great hall, Elysande picked at the large meal. All she could think about was that Michael should be reaching Sandbourne soon. She wondered at the greeting he would receive and the condition he would find his father in. Surely, if the steward had sent word for him to make haste, then the end must be at hand. She hoped, despite the bitterness that lay between Michael and his father, that they would have a chance to make peace between them before the earl passed.

And once his father was gone, Michael would become the new Earl of Sandbourne. She assumed her uncle had mentioned that in his letter to King Edward. She hoped the king would be amenable to Geoffrey's request to see a marriage between his niece and the knight who would soon become one of the highest peers in the realm.

Elysande noticed Tilda striding across the great hall with purpose. The servant headed toward the dais, something in her hand. As she reached them, Elysande saw the scroll Tilda carried.

"My lord? A rider from the king has arrived with his." She presented the parchment to Geoffrey. "I've given him provisions and asked him to wait in case you need to issue a reply."

"My thanks, Tilda."

The servant scurried off. Elysande looked eagerly to her uncle.

"Why don't we adjourn to the solar and learn what the king has to say?" he asked.

She leapt to her feet. Merryn rose more slowly, aided by her husband. They made their way upstairs. With every step, Elysande's heart beat more swiftly.

They entered the solar. Geoffrey closed the door and they seated themselves at the table. He broke the seal and smoothed the rolled parchment out upon the table—and started laughing.

Elysande sat forward, wondering why he would do so.

"And how has he addressed this missive?" Geoffrey inquired of his wife, his eyes dancing. *"To my dearest Lady Merryn . . . and that troublesome husband of yours."*

Elysande was taken aback. This didn't sound good at all.

Merryn looked at her. "Oh, don't worry, Elysande. The king likes to tease us."

Geoffrey said, "Our king is very fond of Merryn. He looks upon her as he would a youngest daughter. And I'll tell you now—fathers are never quite satisfied with the men who take their daughters to wife. King Edward likes to poke at me some, but it's all in jest."

"Oh." Elysande tried to relax, hoping the rest of the missive proved to be kinder than its opening.

Geoffrey looked back to the parchment and read aloud.

I am glad to have received your missive, Lord Geoffrey. I know it can be hard to locate me when the royal court is on its summer progress. The queen and I are having a grand time, but I'll warn you both now—I intend to make Kinwick my first stop on next summer's tour. No one's tarts in all of England have ever measured up to those that your cook bakes. You think I come to see the two of you and your offspring upon occasion because I enjoy your company, but I secretly only visit to sample your cook's wares.

"See?" Geoffrey said. "The king is definitely one for a joke."

Elysande nodded, finding it hard to believe their king would speak in such a friendly manner. She'd always thought of him as a lofty figure sitting on his throne, making serious decisions regarding his kingdom and its people. She supposed he was, after all, only a man who liked to eat and drink and enjoy life as much as the next man did, even if royal blood did run through his veins.

> *I'm afraid to tell you I was neither surprised to hear of Lord Holger's death nor sorry it occurred. The man irritated me in an odd way. I'd hoped Lady Mary would be able to straighten him out somewhat. Mayhap 'tis a blessing in disguise that he has moved on. I plan to leave Lady Mary in charge of Hopeston for now. Under her guidance, I pray that the estate flourishes. I will not offer her in marriage at the moment, but leave the land to her auspices.*
>
> *As for her daughters, your nieces? The queen and I discussed this matter and would have them come to court. We so enjoy having Lady Alys in our company, and this would give her a chance to get to know her cousins. I've been told that Lady Avelyn has no betrothal in place, so the queen will look to find her a suitable husband. With Lady Elysande's betrothed dying before their wedding, I know she must be traumatized, so it was good of you to take her under your wing for now. We shall give her some time in which to heal. I will refuse Lord Ingram's request that he take his son's place and make her his wife.*

Elysande nervously twisted her hands in her lap. Why would the king want her at court? Why would he not want her and Michael to marry?

> *You'd advised me that one of your most trusted knights—Sir Michael Devereux, son to the Earl of Sandbourne—wishes to make Lady Elysande his bride. Alas, my court advisers who keep up with such affairs tell me that would be impossible. Sir Michael was betrothed to Lady Albreda, eldest daughter of Lord Lambdin, many years ago when he came of age. I know the two have been estranged for years. 'Tis most likely that he does not even remember the brief cere-*

mony since he would have been but a small boy. But with Sandbourne at death's doorstep now (or so I'm told), Sir Michael must meet his family obligations and wed Lady Albreda—the sooner, the better. If not for that, I would have given my blessing for Devereux to wed your niece.

I look forward to seeing you when we return to London soon. Mayhap when you bring Lady Alys back to court, you can also escort your nieces at the same time. Lady Merryn and Lady Mary are also most welcomed to come and see their daughters off and into the queen's care.

Elysande heard voices, but the swirling in her head left her disoriented.

Michael was . . . betrothed?

He would marry another woman. And she would never see him again.

"I'm going to be sick," she cried out. She reached for the pail under Merryn's chair and quickly lost every bite of her noon meal.

And lost all hope of a happy life together with Michael.

CHAPTER SIXTEEN

MICHAEL SAT IN the woods by the road that would lead him to his final destination. He cut another slice from the small round of cheese and placed it in his mouth. He pulled another piece of the bread off and ate it, as well, before washing it down with a taste of wine. He set the food aside and returned his dagger back into his boot.

He wasn't hungry. Nor thirsty. But he was nervous. He could have arrived at Sandbourne in time to dine at noon. Instead, he'd dawdled and stopped to eat alone, with nothing but the trees swaying in the breeze as his companions. He admitted to himself that he was worried to set foot inside Sandbourne again. Though its earl lay dying, Michael didn't want to see him again. Michael remembered being the helpless young boy whom the nobleman continually berated—when the earl wasn't ignoring his only son.

And Michael had been grateful for that small piece of good fortune. It was easier to suffer neglect than to have his father's sharp tongue make fun of him.

Standing, he brushed aside the feelings from the past. He was a respected knight now. He'd grown up straight and strong and lived by a code of honor. Michael had nothing to fear from a man who never meant anything to him. It was foolish for him to waste time in the forest when he could be home at Sandbourne.

Home.

That's what Sandbourne would become after all these years adrift. It had never been that before. Michael was determined to be a good father to whatever children he and Elysande would have. They would be showered with love. He would take them to the far corners of the estate until they knew every inch of the land. His sons and daughters would grow up confident. Knowing affection. Receiving attention. Praised for their good traits and efforts.

Determination filled him. He was master of the rest of his life and needed to get on with it. That meant returning to Sandbourne with his head held high.

Michael climbed into the saddle and nudged Tempest onward. Some minutes later, he entered Sandbourne lands. No one greeted him as he passed. The workers in the fields gave him a cursory glance, but none stopped to call out to him.

He arrived at the gate and waved to its keeper. "'Tis Sir Michael Devereux. I am here to see the earl."

The gates opened to him without a word spoken from the gatekeeper. Michael rode through the outer bailey and turned Tempest toward the stables. He dismounted when he reached the structure.

A groom stepped out. "I can take your horse, my lord."

"Nay. I'll care for him. You may bring him a good measure of oats once I've rubbed him down."

He led the horse into the stables, looking for an empty stall. As he rounded the corner, he spied a place for Tempest. Then he froze in his tracks.

Michael realized he stood before the very stall that he'd first seen Tempest in. The one where his mother and Sir Thirkell had stood, brushing the horse till his coat gleamed like midnight. Though his memory of his mother had grown fuzzy over the years, in an instant, he saw her, laughing and pretty. He remembered Sir Thirkell with fondness, thinking about the stories of the Knights of the Round Table that he'd shared with Michael.

Bile rose in his throat as his father's accusations toward the couple rang in his ears. Michael could picture his father lashing out at his mother. Her crumpled, trembling body on the ground. How the earl angrily struck Thirkell down. The blood that ran dark against the golden hay of the stall. Michael saw it all as if it had happened only moments ago.

Anger rose within him, a rage that threatened to boil over. He fought to keep his head and worked to control his breathing, forcing himself to inhale and exhale slowly until he felt more in charge of his emotions. No matter how ill the Earl of Sandbourne might be, the nobleman would pick up on any weakness and expose it. Michael needed to bury the past. He would enter the keep with a blank face and a hardened heart. He pushed the vivid memories aside and slammed the door on them.

His priority was to care for Tempest and make sure the groom provided ample oats to the horse. Once his mount began to eat, Michael left and crossed the inner bailey. Again, not a single person spoke to him. He remembered a few of them and almost spoke to the smithy, but the man never even looked his way. The people all worked industriously, but no joy filled their faces, as it did those who toiled at Kinwick. Michael determined things would be different when he became the earl. His goal was to have a thriving estate and happy workers who enjoyed what they did and where they lived.

A long staircase led up to the keep. As he started up it, he finally heard the first voice that spoke his name.

"Master Michael?"

He turned and saw an older knight making his way toward him.

"Sir Charles?" Michael recognized the man who'd been good friends with Sir Thirkell and had shared in storytelling duties when Thirkell spoke to Michael of King Arthur's men.

"Aye, 'tis Charles. I knew you'd come. We all did. We all have hope that you'll stay." The knight looked at him with faded, watery eyes. "And that you will make the changes needed."

"I intend to do that very thing, Sir Charles," Michael promised.

A satisfied look crossed the soldier's face. "Good."

Michael entered the keep and was met by Houdart, who came hurrying down the stairs.

"Greetings, Sir Michael. Did you have a pleasant journey from Kinwick?"

He nodded. "It's not a long ride and the weather was fine. How are you, Houdart? We haven't seen one another in many years."

The steward, his gray hair now totally white, looked pleased that Michael had asked. "I'm well, my lord." A shadow crossed his face. "But I cannot say the same for your father."

"Has he much time left?"

Houdart shook his head. "Nay. But come. I'll take you to him. He's been informed of your arrival."

Michael followed Houdart up the stairs. They passed his former bedchamber and then the rooms his mother had once occupied. A fresh stab of emotional pain ground into him. He stiffened his spine, determined to stay strong. Finally, they reached the solar at the end of the corridor.

Houdart came to a halt at the door. "His joints have hurt him for years and he's had a cough which won't go away. But his greatest ailment is apoplexy. He's now totally bedridden. His right side is frozen. He has no use of either limb on that side of his body. And his speech can be hard to understand at times because the right side of his mouth droops. Sometimes, he tries to say something and is quick to anger if no one understands him."

"Thank you for warning me, Houdart. I'm better prepared to see him now."

"Should I let you visit in private?" the steward asked.

Michael saw the hope in Houdart's eyes and supposed the man had borne the brunt of the earl's wrath.

"I think that would be best."

Houdart sighed in relief. "I'll wait for you outside the bedchamber."

They entered the solar. Though early afternoon, it remained dark except for a lone candle burning on the table. Michael had rarely been granted permission to enter the place. Even now, he felt like a trespasser as he stood inside. He wondered at how different it would be in future days when he walked in. Elysande might be sitting in the chair, sewing or reading. Mayhap she'd nurse a babe at her breast.

Michael would pull a chair close and tell her about his day out on the estate. Recount an amusing story of something that had occurred. She might have wine and cheese resting on the table, waiting to share it with him as they spoke of things to be done the next day.

It was important to him that she redecorate the entire solar with new tapestries and furniture. They would make it their special retreat, away from the worries of the world. It would be here that his family would gather after time spent in the great hall with others. The solar would become a refuge. Michael would make sure that nothing from today lingered to remind him of his miserable childhood.

His eyes fell upon the door to the bedchamber, which he'd never entered. That room was off limits to him as a child. He supposed, at one time, his mother had shared the space with her husband. Now, Michael only remembered servants sneaking from the solar. Young, pretty ones he would encounter in the corridor. It didn't take him long to realize they'd come to pleasure the earl. The thought disgusted him. Michael planned to take his marriage vows seriously. He would never stray from Elysande's bed nor allow her to stray from his heart. They would love one another from the first day they wed until he took his last breath. His decision to be nothing like his father would be the guiding light of his life.

Michael noticed Houdart had taken a seat. The steward gave him an encouraging nod, so Michael crossed to the bedchamber and lifted a hand to knock. Houdart cleared his throat. He looked over to the steward.

"His voice is weak now, my lord. His hearing is also poor. Even if he heard your knock, he wouldn't be able to call out for you to enter."

"I see."

Michael steeled himself for what he would find and turned the knob. He pushed open the door and closed it after entering the room. Pausing a moment, he allowed his eyes to adjust to the dim setting. Dirt clouded the single window pane. Another of many things that he would change.

A candle rested on a table next to the door. He picked it up and used it to guide his way across the large room. As he reached the bed, he immediately masked his features and harnessed his reaction.

The current Earl of Sandbourne lay shriveled among the bedclothes. Even in the faint light, Michael could see how sallow his father's skin was. Always a trim man, he'd grown painfully thin, as if someone slowly starved him to death. His hair had grown sparse, and what little remained shot out wildly from his head in every direction.

The right side of the earl's face didn't match the left. His eye drooped noticeably. That side of his mouth turned down, giving him an odd, perplexed look. Michael noticed how still the entire side seemed, compared to the twitching on his father's left side and the drumming of the fingers of his left hand along the mattress.

"So. You came."

Michael understood the words. "Aye. Houdart told me 'twas time to return."

"Because I'll be dead soon," his father complained, bitterness coating the words.

He remained silent since he couldn't think of a gracious reply.

"I wondered if you'd come home and do your duty."

"I would never neglect my duty to Sandbourne or the king."

An unpleasant look crossed the earl's face. "Wasn't it your duty to return home once you finished fostering with Lovel?"

Michael shrugged. "Being out in the world gave me time to grow to manhood and mature. I'll be a better lord and master to Sandbourne because of the time I've spent away from it. And it probably kept me from killing you outright," he added.

His father wheezed, an eerie sound that lingered. The wheeze turned into a cough that racked his body and shook the bed for some minutes.

When it subsided, Michael asked, "Would you like some wine?"

"Nay. I can't keep anything down these days, be it wine or food."

Silence blanketed the room. The time stretched on. Michael took a seat, but every muscle in his body remained tense.

Finally, his father spoke again. "You want to kill me."

"I wanted to when I was eight," he admitted. "Actually, before that. I wanted to kill you every time you beat Mother."

"That whore."

Michael stood. "I won't have you speak of her in that manner. She was a good woman who always remained faithful to you, no matter what you thought."

Another coughing spell erupted. Michael relaxed his fisted hands and sat again, waiting it out.

"I have much to tell you," the earl said, weariness lacing his voice.

"Save it. If it has to do with how to run Sandbourne, I'll do it my own way in my own time."

His father studied him with interest. "You're more like me than you realize, boy."

Michael kept his voice even. "I haven't been a boy in a very long time—and I am nothing like you."

"You're right. You will run Sandbourne as you wish."

"Aye."

The minutes ticked by. Michael thought his father had fallen asleep since his eyes remained closed for so long a time. Just as he readied himself to stand, he found the earl staring at him again.

"You'll be a better earl than most."

"I intend to be a better one than you."

"Always such a quick reply. But you're not as smart as you'd have me think."

"I haven't cared what you thought for many years now. In fact, I don't think I ever cared what you thought."

A crooked smile crossed the earl's thin lips. "You might believe that, but I still remember the fat, terrified boy you were. The one afraid of me and his own shadow. The one too scared to stand up to me and protect his mother. The one who secretly wished to please me."

Michael winced inwardly but knew his father provoked him. He wouldn't give the man the satisfaction of seeing him squirm.

"As I said, I'm my own man now. Nothing you say can cause me fear. I'm here merely to witness you come to the end of your wretched days. Then I shall marry and fill Sandbourne with many children."

He leaned close to his father. The fetid smell of impending death filled his nostrils, almost causing him to gag. "My children will be loved. Adored. Worshipped by me and my wife. And they'll never hear a word about you."

Michael stared into his father's eyes. *"For you are nothing to me."*

Michael sat back in the chair, wanting to suck in deep breaths of clean air. He couldn't wait to leave this chamber of death.

His father used his left hand to push himself up in the bed. "I've sent for your bride. She arrives tomorrow. You'll wed the day after that. I plan to live at least long enough to witness your marriage. Then you both can dance atop my grave, for all that I care."

Confused, Michael asked, "Elysande arrives here tomorrow? How do you even know of her?"

The earl's lips curled into a sneer. "I know of no Elysande." His eyes lit with malevolent interest. "But I told Lord Lambdin that you'd be here to live up to your responsibilities. He and his eldest daughter, Albreda, should reach Sandbourne by this time tomorrow."

His father's words had begun to slur heavily. Surely, Michael had heard things wrong. "Who is Lord Lambdin? And this Albreda you speak of?" Michael demanded as panic surged through him.

"Why, 'tis your new father-in-law and betrothed, my boy."

CHAPTER SEVENTEEN

THE EARL'S CACKLE ended as another coughing spell began. Michael stumbled from the bedchamber, slamming the door behind him. He wanted to lock away any sight and sound of his father.

Houdart rose to his feet. "Are you all right, my lord?"

"He said... he said... that my *betrothed* and her father arrive tomorrow. That I'm to be married in two days' time."

The steward nodded. "Aye, my lord. You father wished for you to be married as soon as possible."

"But... I didn't know I was betrothed. 'Tis the first I've heard of it."

Houdart went to the sideboard. The steward poured a full of cup of wine and pressed it into Michael's hands. He downed it in a single swallow and thrust the empty cup out for more. A second glass was poured. He drank it greedily and then fell into a chair.

He was betrothed.

Michael's head fell into his hands. He reached into his hazy memory for when the event might have occurred.

THE SERVANT HAD almost finished packing the small trunk that Michael would take with him to Sir Lovel's. He was excited to foster with the knight. He'd met Sir Lovel once before and remembered how tall the nobleman was. He'd had a ready smile for everyone and a pleasant manner. Michael was sure that boys under his care would be the same. He longed to make friends since he had none. He wanted a new life in a different place.

Anything had to be better than continuing his existence at Sandbourne. Every day, it seemed his father found a new way to mock him. He was too fat. Too slow. A stupid, empty-headed boy who'd never amount to anything. Michael avoided the earl whenever possible, lurking in the shadows when his father passed, remaining in his room much of the day, left alone to his own devices.

The door opened and his mother entered the bedchamber. She looked so fragile and lovely. Michael experienced a small wave of regret at having to leave her behind.

She held up a cotehardie and gypon for his approval. "I've made you something new to wear for your final night at Sandbourne. It's also something for your first day once you reach Sir Lovel's." Her eyes glowed with love.

He took the clothing, which was soft to the touch. Both were in shades of brown, the gypon a light tan and the cotehardie as dark as the bark of a tree.

"Thank you, Mother. I'll think of you every time I wear these."

She gave him a long hug. "That pleases me." Looking at the servant, his mother waved her from the room. Once they had privacy, she said, "Don't be reluctant to leave Sandbourne, my son. Sir Lovel is a fine man and you'll learn much from him."

"I'll miss you, Mother."

"And I will most certainly miss you. Seeing you is the brightest part of my day." She embraced him again and Michael felt safe in her arms.

"Tonight we'll have a large feast," she informed him.

Her words caught him off guard. "For my last night?"

She hesitated. "In part. And also because we have guests."

Michael should have known nothing special would be done to commemorate his final night at Sandbourne.

"Come. Change your clothes and let's go downstairs. I want you to meet Lord Lambdin and his daughter."

They went to the great hall. Michael saw his father in deep conversation with another man as they stood near the fire. A girl a few years younger than he was clung to her father's leg. His mother had them go over and his father introduced him. The nobleman shook his hand, but the girl was so shy that she never even looked up.

Michael thought it a shame. He would've liked to practice making a new friend before he left to foster with Sir Lovel.

The lavish meal went on for several hours, as if it were Christmas time. Michael ate till he was stuffed, then regretted that he'd done so. It made him dread getting on a horse tomorrow morning, feeling fat and bloated as they journeyed for several days to Sir Lovel's estate.

His mother touched his shoulder and indicated for him to follow her. Michael did so, leaving the noise of the great hall and going to a small room that served as the space where Houdart kept the estate's records.

As they went inside, Michael saw his father and the visiting lord leaning over a table, concentrating on pages before them. Michael and his mother stood quietly, as did the lord's daughter, who sat at his feet under the table.

Then the Sandbourne priest entered the room. His father nodded, and the priest watched both men sign the paper on the table.

The earl called Michael over and told him to repeat what the priest said. He did so, not understanding why he had to. The girl also had to say a few words but, again, she kept her eyes to the ground, her voice barely above a whisper.

Still, his father seemed satisfied. He'd touched cups with their guest and both men drank. Michael was told he could leave. He did so, skirting by his mother and retreating to his bedchamber. He was eager for tomorrow to come.

He couldn't wait to leave Sandbourne—and his father—behind.

MICHAEL NOW UNDERSTOOD that the two men had pored over betrothal contracts. That they'd decided upon the bridal price and exchange of monies and lands. That whatever words he had repeated after the priest, which he hadn't understood, were the ones that now bound him to a stranger. His duty, by law, would be to marry this woman in a ceremony once she arrived at Sandbourne, her new home.

Fleeing the solar in despair, Michael returned to the bedchamber he'd used as a child. He would give up the title. The lands. Everything associated with being the earl.

If it meant he could be with Elysande.

Yet he knew that to be impossible. The king wouldn't allow him to break the betrothal contract simply because he'd fallen in love with another woman. Michael must be a man of his word and marry the woman who would show up tomorrow.

He paced the room for hours, refusing the food that arrived. When he tired, he fell upon the bed but lay awake all night, too restless to sleep. He'd been so eager to come home and begin a new life.

Now that life would be one of misery—bound to a stranger.

Of course, he knew of some marriages where the couple came to love one another—or at least learned to respect their mates. Mayhap he and Lady Albreda could share a mutual respect after a time. It was the best he could hope for. For in his heart, he knew he'd never love anyone except Elysande.

Michael determined he'd never mistreat his wife as his father had. He would be courteous toward her. Honor her position as the countess of Sandbourne and the mother of his babes.

More importantly, he decided he must hide the hurt in his heart. This wife of his must never know of his deep feelings for another woman. He wouldn't hurt her physically or emotionally by letting her know that, while married to him, his heart would forever lay with another.

It struck him that he should call for parchment and ink to write to Elysande. He needed to let her know of the unforeseen circumstances that had occurred. Michael would rather see her in person to do so, yet how could he ride away without explanation from a new bride and a dying father?

He thought how Elysande would take the awful news if he did stand before her. How he wouldn't be able to wrap her within his arms and comfort her with his kiss. Being married to another woman would prevent that. And if he did succumb to his feelings for her, he'd only fall into a web of deceit and break his code of honor as a knight and the vows he would have barely uttered to his new wife.

No, he couldn't risk seeing Elysande in person. One look and he would be under her spell. And even one kiss between them would be wrong.

Michael hesitated, unsure of what he should do. He finally decided that he would write to Lord Geoffrey and enclose a letter to Elysande that explained the situation. He would beg Geoffrey and Merryn to decide if they should break the news to Elysande or give her his letter and then comfort her afterward.

Michael opened the door and caught the attention of a passing servant. He instructed her to bring parchment and ink at once, knowing he must write quickly before he lost his courage.

As he sat forming the words in his mind and then recording them on the page, he knew this was the hardest task he'd ever undertaken. With each word committed to paper, another piece of him withered and died. He completed his task and pushed the letters aside, his heart broken in two. Tears spilled down his cheeks. He hadn't cried for fifteen years—since the day he'd fled Sandbourne.

Angrily, he stood and wiped them away. He was a grown man, not some weeping woman. He would soldier on as he'd been taught to do. Going to the basin, he splashed water onto his face and dried it with his sleeves.

Then he sat in a chair, his thoughts blank. No spark of life showed.

Finally, he stood. He couldn't put things off. The sooner Elysande knew, the better. He would go downstairs and use the earl's seal to close the missive before he found a messenger to ride to Kinwick and deliver the bad news.

A knock at the door startled him. He quickly pushed the parchment under his pillow and went to open the door.

The same servant he'd seen earlier stood there. "Your betrothed has arrived, my lord."

Michael nodded, his throat thick with emotion. He closed the door behind him and followed the girl down to the great hall. The vast room was empty except for the pair sitting at a trestle table that had been pulled from its place against the wall. As he approached them, he vaguely remembered the nobleman from so many years ago.

But it was the woman that drew his eye.

She sat very straight, as if her back had been attached to a board. She stared out across the room but seemed focused on nothing. Her dark clothing was simple but elegant in its cut. A light-colored caul covered her head and hid her hair, with a transparent veil pulled across her face.

Michael came to stand before them. He bowed and greeted them. "My lord. My lady. Welcome to Sandbourne. I am Sir Michael Devereux."

Lord Lambdin stood. "Many years have passed since we have been here. And the boy has become a man." He inclined his head slightly. "Daughter? Rise. Greet your husband-to-be."

Lady Albreda sat motionless for a moment. Michael wondered if she did so in hesitation or defiance. Then she came to her feet. She was a good foot shorter than he was.

Slowly, her head fell back until their eyes met. In them, he saw pain.

And rage.

She offered her hand and he bent over it. He brushed a quick kiss upon her fingers before he released it.

Albreda blinked and she seemed like a different woman. Her eyes now appeared dull in her face. Her lips neither smiled nor frowned. Her placid expression gave away nothing.

Yet he sensed something churning inside her. His curiosity grew.

"Would you care to visit a few minutes with my father, Lord Lambdin?" Michael asked. "He's very ill, but I'm sure he would like to acknowledge your presence and welcome you to our home." Michael glanced at his betrothed. "Mayhap Lady Albreda and I might remain here and become reacquainted while you do so."

As if Houdart read his thoughts, the steward appeared at his elbow. He greeted Lord Lambdin and said, "Lord Sandbourne would like a word with you, my lord. May I escort you to him?"

The nobleman nodded and excused himself, following Houdart from the great hall.

Michael turned to the woman he would spend the rest of his life with, holding his tongue. He wouldn't blurt out that he didn't want to marry her. That his heart belonged to another. He would make the best of their situation, as so many before him had done. She would be mother to his children. Sandbourne would forever be her home.

Before he could speak, Albreda said, "I will not marry you, my lord. Not tomorrow nor any other day. You must help me put a stop to this ceremony. No matter what the cost."

CHAPTER EIGHTEEN

ELYSANDE AWOKE AND blinked several times, surprised that she had fallen asleep. She sat up, still fully clothed from yesterday, her *cotehardie* damp from her tears.

Yesterday. The worst day of her life. The day she discovered her beloved was betrothed to another. And today—and every day after it—would only bring more misery to her soul.

Could it be true? That Michael had no idea he was betrothed?

She knew of the lengthy estrangement with his father. How the break had occurred many years ago when he was but a small boy. She thought back to herself at that age and found, even with a happy childhood, her memories were hazy at best. Just vague impressions of running about the keep, playing dolls with Avelyn, and spending time with the horses. That made her realize how, without being around any family to remind him, he truly might have forgotten about his betrothal—or not even understood the brief ceremony when it took place. He would have repeated a few words and then gone out to play, no wiser as to the significance the words he'd uttered had upon his future.

She swallowed and found her throat remained swollen from the many tears she'd shed. As much as the situation pained her, at least she'd been able to cry at length and have Merryn comfort her.

Michael would have no such opportunity. By now, his father would have told him of the upcoming marriage. She could see Michael now—stoic, unspeaking, keeping his face a mask as his thoughts churned inside. He had no one at Sandbourne in whom he could confide. No one who could listen to him rage against the unfairness.

So he would suffer in silence. That caused a fresh flood of hot tears to escape. Elysande fell back onto the bed and buried her face into the pillow, allowing herself to wallow in a last bit of misery.

Then she decided she must push it aside. Though she would ache for Michael's touch all the days of her life, no good would come from moping around. She would have to build a life without him. It would be expected for her to marry. She would do as she was told and try her best to honor her husband as best she could.

But her love and her heart would always belong to Michael Devereux.

A sudden thought panicked her. *What if she were with child?*

Part of her was thrilled by the notion, believing that she would always have a piece of Michael with her. That any child born of their single coupling would be lavished with love. She would want it to be a boy who looked just as his father did, dark-haired and handsome, full of kindness and good cheer. He would be the light of her life. The child would give her a small bit of her beloved to cherish over the years to come.

Then reality set in. She was unwed. If she did find herself with child, who would marry her? By the time she arrived at court in service to the queen, the babe might already have grown within her to a point where it would be hard to hide. How long could she keep something like that a secret—especially in close quarters with so many other women?

Elysande was torn. Should she seek her uncle's help and find a husband at once, the better to hide the fact? If she hurried and wed quickly enough, mayhap she could convince this man that he was the father of her child. She'd heard some babes did come early, especially first ones.

Yet the thought of lying beside another man, his hands touching her intimately in ways only Michael had, made her gag.

She fell to her knees in prayer, begging the Christ for mercy. Elysande prayed for a long time. For Michael to put the memories of her behind him. For him to begin a new life as Earl of Sandbourne with a lovely woman by his side. For her not to be found with child.

And for the Living Christ to accept her as His Bride.

Elysande realized that she would never be happy at court. Nor would she ever want another man in her bed. She would give up the idea of having children and escape from this world, one that held too many memories of Michael. She must do as she first had believed was best.

She would enter a convent.

Once she'd changed her clothes and bathed her face, a calm descended over her. Her decision now made, she would need to share it with others. Knowing she'd already missed morning mass and breaking her fast, Elysande headed to the solar. She would tell her uncle and aunt of her plans and ask that she be taken back to Hopeston for a brief visit. It would be important for her to see her mother and Avelyn one last time and try to make them understand her decision.

Elysande knocked on the solar's door and heard Merryn call out. She entered and saw her aunt sewing. Merryn put aside the needle and cloth and came to embrace Elysande. She closed her eyes and relished the moment, wondering if nuns comforted each other in such a way.

Merryn stroked her hair fondly. "Would you like to sit with me? I'm making a few things for the new babe."

She appreciated that Merryn didn't mention Michael's name. If her aunt had, Elysande might have dissolved in tears.

Merryn studied her a moment. "Or better yet, it might do you good to get out. Mayhap we should go and visit Johamma. I might even glimpse Ancel while we're at Winterbourne."

Seeing others and having to make polite conversation was the last thing Elysande wanted to do. Since Uncle Geoffrey wasn't here, she would wait and share her news when he was present.

"I think I would make for dull company, Merryn. Why don't you take Alys with you? I know she'll be leaving soon for London. The two of you should spend time together."

Merryn placed her hands on Elysande's shoulders. "You must put your sadness behind you. Michael must be hurting as much as you, but he doesn't have the luxury of moping about. He will fulfill his obligations and live up to his code of honor."

Merryn then tried to offer some inspiration to the conversation. "You don't think so now, Elysande, but court will be grand. You'll live a different life and experience all kinds of wonderful new things. You'll be together with your sister. The queen will look out for you both. And you should be happy for your mother, too. She's not being asked to marry again and move to another estate. She'll be able to stay at Hopeston for the time being and try to bring stability to the estate."

Elysande nodded in agreement. "You're right. It's not just about me. I realize Michael suffers, too. He is a good man and will hold his hurt inside. I know he'll treat his wife with kindness and never mention me to her." Tears stung her eyes. "Because that is the man he is and why I will always love him. But I need a few days to adjust to everything, Merryn. My world has turned upside down." She paused. "Please, take Alys with you on your visit to Winterbourne. I need the time to reflect and pray about matters."

Merryn kissed her cheek. "I understand your need for solitude. Just don't retreat too far within yourself."

Alys entered the solar. Her mother smiled at her only daughter. "How would you like to go see Johamma today? You'll return to court before we know it, so this will most likely be the last time to see her and Hardie before you travel to London."

"Oh, I'd love to, Mother." She glanced at Elysande. "Are you coming with us?"

"No, I have a few things to do here. Enjoy your visit." Elysande excused herself and returned to her room.

But all she could see was Michael, whether her eyes remained open or were closed. She could feel his lips caressing her neck. Nibbling on her earlobe. His strong hands holding her buttocks as he rocked into her.

"Enough!" she told herself. She needed to get out. Focus on something besides her misery. She decided she would go to see Davy. After picking blackberries for him, she and Alys had visited the elderly man. He had been a bit of a rascal, flirting with both of them outrageously. It might do her good to walk about in the fresh air and sunshine and check on the elderly tenant.

Elysande made her way downstairs and stopped by the storeroom to collect a jar of blackberries in case Davy still suffered from the flux.

As she left the keep, she decided to first seek comfort where she always did—the stables. She knew the smell of hay and sight of the horses would help begin to mend her tattered soul. Elysande walked from stall to stall, greeting each horse that had now become familiar to her.

Then she reached an empty stall. Tempest's stall. Seeing it was like a blade stabbing her heart. She blindly ran from the stables, her throat thick with unshed tears. She slowed and continued on her way, trying to calm herself and act in a mature manner. Elysande forced herself to wave to several people in greeting as she passed, doing her best to smile and put on a brave face.

As she went through the open gates of Kinwick, she decided to stop by the pasture and see Hera and Miracle since it would be on the way to Davy's cottage. The sunshine beat upon her back, causing her to grow warm. She chuckled, thinking she might have to open Davy's blackberries and steal a few.

She reached the pasture and set the jar on top of the fence as she leaned against it to watch Miracle run around under Hera's watchful eye. The foal galloped up and down the fence line and then scampered playfully in circles, constantly turning to see if her mother saw her antics.

Elysande smiled at the bond between mother and child, but it once again caused her thoughts to swirl. Either she would never have the pleasure of bearing Michael's child—or his seed already grew within her. She would never regret her rash action of making love with him before they wed, for she would always have the sweet memories of their love play. But being with child could complicate her plans of entering a nunnery.

She determined to leave the matter in God's hands.

A stick snapped and caught her attention. Elysande turned toward the noise. A sudden, blinding pain caused her to stumble.

Then all went dark.

GEOFFREY ENTERED THE great hall. As always, his eyes swept it for a sign of Merryn. She'd been the shining light in his mind all the years he had been imprisoned in the dungeons at Winterbourne. He could have given up and chosen to die many times but willed himself to go on so he could return to her. Spotting her in conversation with Tilda, he headed toward the pair.

Alys fell in to step with him. "We went to see Johamma today."

He laughed. "Already? And did your mother happen to set eyes upon Ancel?"

His daughter nodded. "She did. Johamma took us on a walk. We happened to come across the pages as they polished armor."

"I hope your mother didn't embarrass Ancel in front of his friends."

Alys giggled. "Nay, Father. We merely nodded a greeting and went on our way. But Ancel was pleased. I could tell by his smile."

"And your mother?"

"She didn't smile until we were gone from their sight."

He ruffled Alys' hair. "We'll leave for London soon. Are you ready to go back to life at the royal court?"

Alys grew thoughtful. "You know I love Kinwick, Father, but I'm enjoying my time with the queen. She is so wise. I have much to learn from her."

"There you are," Merryn said.

Geoffrey swept up her hand and pressed a kiss upon her fingers before he turned her hand over and dropped another one upon her palm. He loved the tingle of pleasure that trickled through him. He gave his wife a smile that promised her more than kisses tonight.

"May I escort you to the dais?" He offered an arm and led her to her seat. He glanced around. "Where is Elysande?"

"I don't know."

"Did she go with you and Alys to visit with Johamma?"

"No. She believed she wouldn't be good company."

Geoffrey frowned. "I know she's terribly unhappy, but brooding will do nothing to solve her situation. I won't have her sulking in her room during the remainder of her visit here. I intend to find her and make it clear that I expect her to come to the great hall at once to dine."

Merryn pulled on his arm, forcing him to sit next to her. "Look at it from her point of view, Geoffrey. Michael is lost to her. For all time." She gave him a pointed glance. "I know how she feels. I lost you for seven years, never knowing if you would return to me. I had no idea where you'd gone. At least Elysande can be comforted because she knows Michael is safe. Even if he will soon be in the arms of another woman."

Geoffrey leaned over and gave his wife a tender kiss. "I'm sorry, my love. You're right." He stood. "But I will go and coax her to come and eat something. She needs to see that she has her family's support." He kissed Merryn once more and rose. "I'll be back soon."

He made his way to Elysande's chamber and rapped on the door. When he didn't receive a response, he pushed it open and found the room empty. Puzzled, he returned to the great hall.

"She wasn't in her room," he told Merryn. "I'm concerned." He motioned Hammond over.

"Have you seen Lady Elysande recently?" he asked.

"Nay, my lord."

"Go look for her. Bring her back at once."

"Check in the stables and out in the pasture," Merryn suggested. "She takes solace in the horses. It wouldn't surprise me if you find her there."

They began the meal, but Geoffrey had a nagging feeling that something was amiss. He kept watching the door, waiting for Hammond to report back.

The soldier returned as Geoffrey finished his wine. "I couldn't locate her anywhere, my lord. I spoke to everyone I passed. No one has seen Lady Elysande for some time." He held up a jar. "But I found this to be odd. A jar of blackberries sitting atop the fence in the pasture near where Hera and her foal frolicked."

Merryn reached for Geoffrey's hand. "Elysande went with Alys to take blackberries to Davy a few days ago. Mayhap she went to see him again and lost track of the time."

"And forgot the very blackberries she took?" Geoffrey demanded. A sinking feeling washed over him. Grimly, he said, "I fear she's been taken from us. And I'm certain Lord Ingram is behind it."

Chapter Nineteen

The horse finally stopped. Elysande felt herself being lifted from it by strong hands. She'd been thrown stomach down across the saddle and bounced about for more hours than she could guess. Nausea rose and she began to gag.

"Quick! Get the sack from her head," a voice warned.

Someone stood her on her feet and ripped away the rough burlap sack that had been placed over her head, falling down to her waist. She tried to draw in deep breaths of the night air. Her stomach roiled again as she swayed unsteadily.

"Cut the gag, you fool. If she drowns in her vomit, where will that leave us?"

A hand tightened about her arm from behind. As she blinked, a man pulled a baselard from his waist and cut away the gag that had kept her from calling out for help. She fell to her knees, her hands still bound in front of her. Elysande rested the heels of her hands on the ground to steady herself as she leaned over and was sick. Spent, she rolled to the ground and lay panting.

She got her first look at her captors. The one who had cut away the cloth bound around her mouth was tall and thin as a maypole. He wore a sour look on his face. The other was short and stout, with narrow lips and dark eyes that studied her. It was the second one that yanked her to her feet and marched her to a tree. He pushed her back against the trunk.

"Sit. Stay there. Do not move. Do not utter a word—else I'll cut out your tongue."

His appearance frightened her more than his words. She had a good idea that these men were from Lord Ingram. The nobleman would want her intact. But she heeded the warning all the same. She would listen and learn as much as she could.

And then do her best to escape.

"Want me to build a fire?" the thin one asked.

"Nay. Even though we're far off the road, de Montfort will have figured out the girl is missing. And more than likely, he'll know who was behind her disappearance and send out men to search. I don't want to risk that tonight. Mayhap tomorrow night we can chance building one."

"But 'tis late, Folc. And we left camp so quickly, we didn't bring anything to eat with us." He gave the other soldier a sullen glance. "Not that we've had much the past few weeks, watching for that one." He tossed his head Elysande's way.

So these two had lurked around Kinwick for weeks. Elysande hoped they were the only two that Lord Ingram had sent.

"Find some berries or edible leaves if you must, Ernis. We can stop and buy food as we travel tomorrow. I promise you'll have a full belly then."

"But what do we do with the girl? If we ride into a village with her slung over a horse, people will remember and tell de Montfort's men. Especially if he waves a coin or two in their faces. I thought that was why we left the road today as we traveled. So that no one would see us with her."

Folc rubbed his chin in thought. "You're right. We can't ride all the miles north with her thrown over a horse like a sack of flour. That won't do."

Elysande took calming breaths as the men fell silent. Being jostled on the horse had left her stomach sore and bruised. Since it was dark now, she'd been on the animal for many hours. Her mouth was tender due to the tight gag she'd worn, while her wrists had been rubbed raw as she'd try to loosen the leather ties. If she couldn't escape before morning, then she hoped these criminals would come up with a better way of travel until she could get away.

"A wagon," Folc finally said. "We need to buy a wagon. Or better yet, steal one."

"But that'll take forever," complained Ernis. "Horseback is much faster."

"I don't care," the one called Folc told his companion. "Lord Ingram said to bring the girl home or don't bother to return. We lost everyone but the two of us in the attack on the way to Kinwick. We've waited a few weeks and finally found the opportunity to snatch our prize. I'd rather be safe and make it home at a slower pace than be caught and hanged by de Montfort and his men."

He stroked his chin again. "We can bind her wrists and ankles and lay her down in the bed of the wagon. Throw in sacks of all kinds. Oats. Flour. Salt. And goods, too, as if we'd been out trading. She'll be covered up. Out of sight. De Montfort will be searching for soldiers on horseback. He wouldn't give us a second thought." He laughed. "I can see him now, riding by us without a glance."

"We look like soldiers," Ernis pointed out. "Two soldiers driving a cart. I say that's a suspicious sight. If he came upon us, he'd stop and question us at the very least."

Folc thought on the words. "Then we'll find new clothes."

"And how are we to do that? Stop at the next village and wait while some woman volunteers to stitch together something for us?" Ernis threw a hand down in disgust.

"No," Folc replied. "We'll simply kill the next men we come across and take what they wear."

A chill brushed Elysande's soul at his quick, heartless words. It let her know exactly the kind of men who had taken her—ones cut from the same cloth as Lord Ingram.

MICHAEL PACED IN front of Tempest's stall. His horse happily munched on an extra measure of oats provided by his master. He wanted the animal ready for the ride ahead.

He reached to pick up the lantern and go look for Lady Albreda but stopped himself. She said she would meet him here. He needed to trust her word.

Michael had never met a more single-mined woman. Once her father left the great hall, she adamantly told him she had no intention of marrying him. And why. After he quizzed her and was satisfied with her answers, they'd come up with a risky plan.

Which would be put into action as soon as she arrived.

He heard a noise and looked up. From a distance, he thought he saw a shape moving through the stables. He lifted the lantern and held it high.

"Sir Michael?" a voice called out.

"Aye." He moved to meet her. The noblewoman was dressed in traveling clothes, the hair he had yet to see still hidden under her caul. She brought nothing with her.

"Come, my lady. I'll saddle Tempest and we will be on our way."

She followed him back to the horse's stall. Michael opened the door and began readying the animal for their midnight ride.

As he did, he asked Lady Albreda once more, "And you are absolutely certain?"

"I have no doubts, my lord. I've wished to be a Bride of Christ my entire life. My mother understood this, as she believed she had the same calling from God. Though she was forced to wed my father, she knew of my deepest longing. I know had she lived, Mother would have convinced my father to void our betrothal contract and see the bridal price returned."

Lady Albreda paused. "Father thinks he's doing what is best for me, but I must follow my heart—and it leads me toward God. He has three other young daughters by his second wife. Once I'm gone, my stepmother will make sure that his focus is on them. He'll be too busy finding them husbands to give me much thought."

"And you think leaving in the middle of the night is the best plan?"

"I do. If I'm led to the chapel at noon tomorrow, I will refuse to go through with the wedding vows." A steely glint formed in her eye. "I have the right to break the contract. Just as I have the right to join a convent and be with my sisters in Christ. No man—not even my father—can keep me from my chosen bridegroom."

He had told her about a convent two hours from Sandbourne when she'd expressed her religious desires to him earlier. Albreda said she had no particular nunnery in mind and would be happy at any of them, as long as she could serve Christ Almighty.

Michael led Tempest from his stall. "Then let us ride, my lady." He lifted her into the saddle and handed up the lantern to her. He didn't know if the moonlight would be sufficient enough to light their way.

The empty bailey seemed foreign to him. He'd never seen it lacking in activity. They cantered through it and arrived at the gate.

"Open. I wish to pass," he called up to the gatekeeper.

After a moment of hesitation, the man did as asked. Michael figured the gatekeeper knew how close the current earl was to death. That being the case, he wouldn't wish to alienate the new earl by asking him pesky questions about where he rode off to in the wee hours.

They rode without conversation. Michael concentrated on the road before them, hoping to keep Tempest from stepping into any holes. The two-hour ride took closer to three to complete, due to the care he took. He would have the advantage of the sun rising and lighting his path on the final hour of his way back. He hoped to return to Sandbourne by the time morning mass began.

They arrived at the walls of the convent. He climbed from Tempest's back and reached for Albreda. She might be small in stature, but she had a heart of steel. Michael admired her commitment to the path she had determined was the right one for her.

But he felt he must ask again before he left her behind, if only to soothe his conscience. "My lady, I need your reassurance a final time. Is this truly what you wish?"

She took his hand and pressed a fervent kiss onto it. "I will not change my mind, my lord. I am where I have always been meant to be."

Michael saw how she glowed in happiness and knew she'd made the right choice. He turned and rang the bell at the gate.

Some minutes later, the thick wooden door that was surrounded by stone opened. He explained to the elderly nun before them why they were there and that he wished to speak to the abbess before he left Lady Albreda in the convent's care. The nun motioned for them to follow her. Once they reached the doors to the nunnery itself, Michael hobbled Tempest and told him to be a good horse. The nun offered to take the horse to the water trough as they conducted their business so the animal would be ready for the ride back, and Michael agreed.

It surprised him to see nuns already dressed and filing through the corridors at this early hour. The bells chimed three, and he supposed they headed to prayers. He wondered when they might sleep.

The old nun returned after a few minutes and escorted them to her abbess. Michael allowed Lady Albreda to state her case, which she did with eloquence.

He spoke up and told the abbess that he would see that the bridal price, which would be returned to his family with the voided contract, be sent to the convent. That would, no doubt, be a welcome addition to the convent's coffers and guarantee Albreda a place for life.

Michael thanked the abbess and turned to wish his former betrothed goodbye.

She surprised him by kissing both his cheeks and then expressed her gratitude, once more, for his help in her great escape.

"God will look upon you with favor, Sir Michael."

At that moment, he believed her words with all his heart. Only yesterday, he had met this woman and was to marry her today. Now, thanks to her calling, she generously stepped aside to unite with Christ Almighty as one of His brides.

Which left Michael free to marry the bride of *his* choice. It was an unspoken prayer that had filled Michael's mind and heart since his father had revealed the news of his betrothal. One that had never left his lips because he knew how hopeless the request was.

Yet now? He had faith that God wanted him to care for Elysande.

To make her his wedded wife. To raise children that would love and be loved.

"I'll never forget you, my lady," Michael swore. "You have a generous heart and will do God's work for many years to come. Of this, I am certain."

A genuine smile lit Lady Albreda's face. "Thank you, my lord."

He left the two women, his footsteps light, and returned to the courtyard where Tempest awaited him. Faint light tickled the dark line of the horizon. His ride home would pass much more quickly.

Two hours later, Michael rode through the gates of Sandbourne, the same gatekeeper granting him access. He returned his horse to the stables and gave Tempest a thorough rubdown before returning to his chamber and doffing his clothes. He washed from the basin and put on a clean gypon and *cotehardie*, as well as pants that did not have the dirt of the road upon them. He left his travel-stained clothes in a heap by his bed—and went downstairs to face Lord Lambdin.

Mass had already started as Michael slipped into the chapel. As he listened to the Latin passages, he glanced about the chapel. This would have been his wedding day. He would have taken his vows and entered this very place a married man.

It occurred to him that he didn't have to send the missive he'd written to Elysande, the one where he revealed they couldn't marry because he'd been promised to another woman. He would leave mass and slice the parchment into pieces before burning it. Then he would stay until his father was no more and he became the Earl of Sandbourne. Michael's first action would be to return to Kinwick and learn if Lord Geoffrey had heard from the king. Michael prayed that the king would've sent word that he looked favorably upon the request. If that was the case, Michael would marry Elysande as soon as possible.

He doubted she would prefer returning to Hopeston for the ceremony since she hadn't grown up there. They could come to Sandbourne, but he thought it best to wed at Kinwick. Lady Merryn would be thrilled with that idea. Michael could escort Lady Mary to her childhood home and also bring Lady Avelyn along for the ceremony and feast.

Then he could return to Sandbourne with his bride by his side and live as blissfully as he saw Geoffrey and Merryn do every day. They looked to be more in love as time passed. He hoped the same would be true for Elysande and him.

Michael left the chapel as mass ended and went to the great hall to break his fast. He was famished after his long ride. He saw Lord Lambdin enter and steeled himself for their conversation.

The nobleman approached the dais where he sat. "I haven't seen my daughter this morning. Have you?" he asked candidly, his eyes searching the room as he spoke.

"I have, my lord. There are certain matters which we must discuss regarding Lady Albreda." Michael paused. "Will you accompany me to the solar? I must speak to you and my father together." He rose and stepped down from the dais.

Lambdin's eyes narrowed. "Say what you have to say, Sir Michael. Here and now."

Michael owed the man that much. "Lady Albreda and I will not wed at noon today."

The nobleman's eyes widened. "What? Where is she? What the Devil have you done with my sweet girl?"

"Your daughter chose to break the betrothal contract, as was her legal right."

"Break it? *Break it?* Surely, you jest, Sir Michael."

"No, my lord, I do not. 'Twas what Lady Albreda wanted and I agreed to abide by her wishes. She didn't want to marry on earth, Lord Lambdin. Instead, she has chosen to become a Bride of Christ and left Sandbourne."

"God's teeth! I knew it! I knew she would find a way." He glared at Michael. "And it seems as if you've helped her in this nonsense. Where is she hiding? I will see her returned at once. This ceremony takes place today, regardless of her wishes," Lambdin said angrily. "Albreda is a foolish woman to attempt to flee this marriage. I would have thought you would have exercised better judgment, my lord, and not indulged her in this fantasy."

Michael stood his ground. "She is far away, my lord. Out of your reach. Lady Albreda has gone to live a quiet life at a nunnery a few hours from here."

"Impossible. She had no way to get there." Then understanding dawned in the nobleman's eyes. "*You.* You delivered her there, didn't you?"

"Aye, my lord. After much serious conversation, she convinced me she would never be happy or fulfilled as my wife. Because of that, I escorted her to her chosen destination."

Lord Lambdin's temper exploded. "How could you have done such a foolhardy thing? To sneak out in the middle of the night with my sweet child and ride in secret to some nunnery? I won't accept it, I tell you. I demand that you take me to her. Now! The two of you *will* be married without delay."

Michael shook his head. "She has been offered sanctuary by its abbess. 'Twould be impossible to force her to leave the convent."

The nobleman's face turned bright red. "I won't pay for her to be there. She needs to wed. She needs to be my good girl. I know what's best for her. I cannot let her go and ruin her life."

"Lady Albreda told me she has a calling to Christ. That her mother understood this."

At the mention of Albreda's mother, all the air seemed to go out of Lord Lambdin. "She's the only thing I have left of my sainted first wife."

"And she's happy now," Michael said gently. "Your daughter has a strength of mind coupled with a strength of character. I have never met a woman who knew such purpose and was willing to sacrifice whatever was necessary in order to live her life the way she believed it should be lived."

Michael placed a hand on the nobleman's shoulder. "You should be happy for Lady Albreda, my lord. It is her desire to give herself over to the Christ. If you could have seen the look of joy on her face and witnessed how content she was in her new surroundings, you would know she had made the only choice possible." He paused. "The lady told me you have three more daughters at home that you should concentrate on now."

Lambdin sighed. "She truly seemed happy?"

"Aye, my lord. She seemed a different person altogether."

The nobleman's natural color slowly returned. "I lost her mother many years ago. I just wanted Albreda cared for, as I cared for her dear mother." His eyes met Michael's. "I suppose you've done me a favor, my lord. I couldn't see what she truly needed. I was blinded by my vision for her. I should be grateful to you."

Lambdin paused and gave him a hopeful look. "I don't suppose you would consider wedding another one of my daughters? That way the bridal price wouldn't have to be returned."

"Nay, my lord. I have other plans for choosing a wife."

The nobleman nodded. "Then I will see that the monies are returned to you."

"To my father, actually. I supposed I must go and break the news to him now. Will you accompany me to the solar?"

Lambdin nodded, though Michael saw the reluctance on the older man's face.

Suddenly, Houdart came rushing up, out of breath. "My lord? 'Tis your father. Hurry."

Michael ran through the great hall and up the stairs. He raced down the long corridor and entered the solar, crossing to his father's bedchamber.

As he entered, he heard the gasps as his father strained to breathe. Michael sat on the bed and took his father's hand in his, the first time either had touched one another.

"Come to see me . . . die?" the earl rasped.

"Aye," Michael said. "And to let you know that I won't be marrying Lady Albreda, nor any of Lord Lambdin's daughters."

"You would defy me?" his father spit out. "Refuse to honor . . . the betrothal contract?"

Michael smiled. "I would. All my life, you have been a man full of malice. You took delight in treating me harshly and heaped your cruelty and abuse on my mother. You never cared for anyone—not even yourself." He released the earl's hand and stood.

"I plan to live my life in exactly the opposite manner of yours. I will wed the woman I love and cherish her each and every day of our lives together. Not only will I honor and respect her, but I will lavish love upon every son and daughter that we make together. My children will never suffer from a lack of attention or love. They will thrive and mature and do great things, all with the support of their parents."

Michael paused. "And their grandmother," he added, watching his father startle at the mention of her. "If it's the last thing I do, I will go to the ends of the earth and find Mother and bring her back to Sandbourne. Once she's danced upon your grave, I will treasure each day that I have with her and watch in happiness as she showers love upon her grandchildren. And no one, at any time, will ever utter your name."

It surprised him when the corners of his father's mouth turned up in a smile.

"I see, despite everything, that you have become a man, Michael. A strong man. One who believes in and lives by a code of honor. Well done, my son. Well done."

Before Michael could reply, his father's head fell to one side.

He would breathe no more.

Michael reached for the pink stone in his pocket. He could now bring his mother home.

CHAPTER TWENTY

MICHAEL'S MIND WANDERED as the priest droned on. He didn't need to hear how righteous a man his father had been or any other lies uttered.

He thought back to Lord Lambdin's departure yesterday. The nobleman had been eager to get home to his wife and other daughters and hadn't wanted to stay for the funeral mass of a man he barely knew. Michael encouraged him to take care on his journey home. The men had parted with no grudge between them. In fact, Michael believed he could count Lord Lambdin as an ally if not a trusted friend if the need ever arose.

The mass finally ended. Workers and tenants alike filed past him, some nodding, others pausing to offer words of comfort. He knew so few of them and determined that would change. Taking Elysande to each cottage that rested on Sandbourne land and introducing his new countess as he grew familiar with his people would be a priority in the weeks ahead. He wanted Sandbourne to be an estate that thrived, but he also wanted to come to understand and know those under his protection.

Michael found himself alone except for the priest as the last of the crowd exited the chapel. He hadn't given the priest any instructions as to where to bury the body and he knew the man of God waited awaited them.

"Bury him where you see fit, Father. I know there's plenty of room set aside for family. I have business to attend to." He wouldn't accompany the body to the gravesite. His father was gone from this earth. Michael would put the bastard out of his mind and never think about him again.

For now, he had two missions to accomplish as the new earl. The first included wedding Elysande. The second would be to locate his mother. He hoped he would find her alive and willing to return to Sandbourne after so many years in a convent.

As he turned to walk toward the chapel doors, he spied Houdart hovering in the doorway and strode over to meet the steward.

"My lord, a messenger has arrived. From Kinwick. He says 'tis most urgent. He wishes to speak to you at once."

"Take me to him."

The two men returned to the keep. Michael saw Hammond standing in the hallway as they entered and went to greet his friend. As he stepped closer, the grim look upon the knight's face gave him cause for alarm.

"What's wrong?" Michael asked.

Hammond took him by the arm and led him to a corner. "I have no missive for you, my lord. The matter was urgent and Lord Geoffrey trusted me to deliver his message since he didn't want to waste time putting pen to paper." He looked about. "Your wife. Is she present? My message is not for her ears."

The words took him aback. "How do you know about her? Not that I'm married. I was betrothed and didn't know it. I should've been wed yesterday, but my bride-to-be broke our contract and left Sandbourne."

His friend's eyes widened. "Lord Geoffrey received a missive from the king denying his request for you to wed his niece. It said you were already betrothed and that your father would soon pass. His advisers told him you would marry your intended and become earl."

"I've just come from my father's funeral mass, but I'm free now to wed the woman I choose. I'd like nothing more than to return to Kinwick with you and claim Elysande as my bride."

Hammond shook his head. "That's the very news I bring, my lord. Lady Elysande has vanished from Kinwick."

"Vanished?" A cold hand tightened about Michael's heart.

"Aye. Lord Geoffrey thought you would be wed by now, but he knew of your tender feelings for the lady. He wanted you to know that something foul took place and that he would see her restored to her family."

Michael gripped Hammond's arm. "When did this happen?" His eyes narrowed. "'Twas it Ingram's men again?"

His friend nodded. "We think so. She disappeared the day before yesterday. I rode as quickly as I could to deliver the news to you."

He pushed Hammond back with both hands as the anger erupted from him. "I told you to watch over her. I trusted you to look after her. You failed me."

Hammond's face flushed dully with guilt. "Aye. You're right, my lord. But no one even knew that she'd left the keep. I would have followed her and guarded her well had I known she stepped outside the castle's walls."

Michael reined in his temper. No good would come by blaming his friend. "How was she discovered missing?"

"She didn't appear for the evening meal and could not be located. I found a jar of blackberries sitting on top of the fence at the pasture where Hera and her foal played. We believe she was taken from that spot."

"Has Lord Geoffrey sent out search parties for her?" he demanded.

"Aye. The master himself led one up the main road north and sent a second northeast along secondary roads. I volunteered to bring you the news."

"Then I ask for you to ride with me and my men, Hammond. We'll head north and join in the search. Lady Elysande must be returned."

He spied Houdart. Michael summoned him over, instructing him to bring the captain of the guard to him at once. He then ordered Cook to prepare bags of food for the men to take on their journey.

"We'll ride out within the hour. I'll gather my weapons and return here."

Michael left Hammond, his heart beating fast. With each step he took, he prayed that they would find Elysande before she reached Lord Ingram's estate.

He arrived downstairs just as Houdart came in with the man he'd requested to see. Michael introduced himself to his captain, a capable looking knight named Imbert. He briefly explained the situation.

"I would like to call the soldiers of Sandbourne together and speak to them."

"I'll assemble them now, my lord," Imbert told him. "Give me ten minutes and they'll be gathered in the training yard." He gave a nod and exited the room.

Michael had a thousand questions, but he knew Hammond had no answers. He made good use of the time by pulling the available maps from the solar. Michael then contemplated different routes that led north to Rudland, Lord Ingram's estate. He rolled the parchments up and turned them over to Hammond's care. Signaling his friend that it was time to go, they made their way outside. As Michael approached, he saw the yard filled with soldiers of varying ages.

He climbed the stairs of a wooden platform that had been erected six feet from the ground. He assumed the elevated space allowed Imbert to observe the men as they trained and offer them advice on improving their skills. It now allowed him to see all those who'd gathered.

"I've come today to call you to action," he said, his voice carrying across the training yard. "Most of you don't know me. If you did, you only knew the boy of long ago—and he no longer exists. I've been gone from Sandbourne for many years. In that time, I trained to be a knight and proved my worth to Sir Lovel and Lord Geoffrey, the noblemen I served under."

Michael studied the gathered men. "I hope to prove to you that I am a good lord and an even better leader now that I've inherited the title of Earl of Sandbourne."

Michael paused to assess the effect his words had upon the men before he continued. "I need to ride out now because love has touched my heart. If you love or have loved, you know how fortunate you are." He saw several of the men shake their heads in agreement, a wistful look on their faces.

"God has favored me. He's given me the opportunity of a second chance. The woman I love—the woman I wish to make your future countess—has been taken against her will. I ride now because her life depends upon it." He swallowed. "Mine, as well. For I am nothing without her."

Michael studied the soldiers before him. "I hope to create something that has been lost at Sandbourne. I wish it to be a happy place. A place of hope. One where everyone feels safe and knows that he or she is valued. I need Lady Elysande by my side if I'm to accomplish this."

Michael paused and looked over his gathered men. "So I ask you, as the men who serve Sandbourne—myself and all those within its walls and living on these lands—will you ride with me and restore to me my one true love so that we may become the place I always envisioned that Sandbourne could be?"

A rousing cheer went up amongst the men. Michael's heartbeat picked up several notches. He never imagined that his words would draw such a reaction. He found resolution and pride in the responses of the men. At that moment, he knew that he had the support that he had desired. Michael hoped they would be in time to save her.

Because in saving Elysande, he would save himself.

He couldn't take every man present with him. Of the two hundred, he instructed Sir Imbert to keep half at Sandbourne. His chief responsibility was to keep his people from harm. He asked his captain to remain behind and take charge of the castle and all its lands while he was away. Michael's father had made Imbert head of his guard for a reason. Michael would have to trust the earl's instincts in this matter.

The remaining men, along with Sir Charles, would come with him as they rode north. He hoped they would find one of the de Montfort parties and unite with them in a show of strength.

Michael prayed they would locate Elysande and rescue her before she found herself inside the walls of Rudland.

MICHAEL WATCHED THE approaching rider wave as he drew near. He hoped the scout had good news. They'd spent two fruitless days on the road north. No one had seen anyone resembling Elysande. There had been no sighting of the soldiers who had abducted her. Since they didn't have a description of the men involved, the Sandbourne soldiers were looking for anyone who appeared out of the norm. None had been identified, thus far.

"My lord!"

Michael held a hand up to cease their forward progress as the scout brought his horse next to Tempest.

"Up ahead. 'Tis Lord Geoffrey and a band of his men. They are but two leagues ahead and will wait for us."

"Then we ride to join them." He signaled the men to continue and set a rapid pace.

A short time later, his troops caught up to the de Montfort contingent. Michael rode straightaway to Geoffrey, who stood near Sir Gilbert, the captain of the guard at Kinwick. He dismounted and joined them.

"Michael." Geoffrey gave him a curt nod. "I was surprised when your rider told me of your presence. I would not have—"

"Circumstances have changed, my lord," he interjected before Geoffrey could continue. "I found myself betrothed when I reached Sandbourne, as Hammond told me you discovered yourself in the king's missive. But the lady didn't wish to marry and instead broke the contract. Lady Albreda wished to join a convent and I helped her in that desire. That freed me to join in the search for Elysande."

Geoffrey gave him a grim smile and placed a hand upon his shoulder. "Then I'm more than satisfied that you're able to aid in our hunt for my niece." He reached into a pouch hanging from Mystery's saddle and pulled out a rolled parchment. "Here is the king's missive. I've brought it to show Lord Ingram that King Edward did not favor his pursuit of Elysande and that the king requested she come to court."

He handed it to Michael. "But I'll give it to you for safekeeping now. In it, the king states he would have given his blessing to your union with Elysande if not for your betrothal."

Hope sprang within Michael's heart. "And so, when we find her, this will be proof that she should come with us."

Geoffrey nodded. "But we must find her first. And better out on the road than within the walls of Rudland. If 'tis a fight on our hands, I'd prefer it to be in the open."

"I agree," Michael said. "Have you learned anything in your travels north? We've quizzed villagers and farmers these past two days and have discovered nothing helpful."

The nobleman shook his head. "Nay. We've stopped along the way and spoken with many people. No one has seen any group of soldiers, much less those traveling in the presence of a noblewoman."

Gilbert added, "All we've heard is the usual village gossip. A cow died giving birth to a calf in one village. A cart and two farmers turned up missing in another. A local priest got a young girl with child. And several bags of feed disappeared from a stack. Nothing that has helped in our search or given us any indication how many men are involved in Lady Elysande's abduction. That is why we've continued to push north toward Lord Ingram's place."

Michael listened to his words and then held a finger up. "Wait," he said, a connection forming in his mind. "We've all been looking for soldiers. On horseback, with a noblewoman."

Both Geoffrey and Gilbert nodded in agreement.

"They must realize we wouldn't let Elysande slip away without a fight. They would know that we'd search for them. Ask others if they'd been seen by anyone along the way. What if they abandoned riding on horseback and hid her in the back of a cart? The stolen cart that you mentioned, Sir Gilbert. They could have ditched their armor or even placed it in the wagon itself, along with Elysande. We would never think to look for them this way."

"But why would they do that?" Gilbert asked, playing Devil's advocate. "'Twould take them far longer to arrive at their destination than by horseback."

"Because we would have ridden right past them," Geoffrey declared. "Not given them a second thought. They would be invisible to us. We've stopped a few travelers on the road, but we only asked cursory questions of them."

"I agree," Michael said. "It would be a clever ruse. But that means we've ridden more quickly. They must still be behind us. That's why no villagers have spotted them. They've disguised their identities." He paused. "I also think that there can't be many of them. If they've hung about Kinwick waiting for an opportunity to spirit Elysande away, I'm guessing there's no more than a handful. If that."

He summoned Hammond over and explained their line of thought. "Because we can't be certain—and since you know what Lady Elysande looks like—you should be sent ahead in case they've slipped past either of our groups." Michael looked to Geoffrey. "Is that agreeable with you, my lord?"

"Hammond can take several of my men with him," Geoffrey said. "You and I can combine our forces and head in the opposite direction. I think the road we took from Kinwick to this point would be their most likely route."

"Then let us ride, gentleman," Michael proclaimed. He prayed that he was right and they would soon find his beloved. He swung into the saddle. With a kick of his heels, Tempest took off at a gallop.

CHAPTER TWENTY-ONE

ELYSANDE ACHED ALL over from being jolted for so long. Each day proved the same. Lord Ingram's men placed her in the cart on her back. They bound her wrists with leather ties and her ankles with rope and tied a gag tightly in place to muffle any sound she might make. Then goods and sacks of grain were packed all around her and blankets thrown on top of her. At first, she thought she might smother under their weight. Instead, the blankets and the summer heat left her sweaty and weak by the end of each day, parched from lack of water.

Every night, Folc and Ernis would stop in the woods, driving the cart off the road. Elysande would be given her only meal of the day. She ate whatever the two men provided in order to keep up her strength. Then Ernis would walk her further into the woods to allow her to take care of her needs. It was the only time he removed the restraints from her ankles. Her hands were always left bound. She found it terribly embarrassing, attending to such personal business in front of him as she squatted near the ground. He turned his head slightly—but never long enough for her to reach for the blade in her boot and have enough time to cut through the ties surrounding her wrists. She would clean herself with a few nearby leaves, and then Ernis would march her back to where they camped. He would refasten her restraints and she would be propped up against a tree or tilted to the ground for sleep.

She realized how careful the two men were. They didn't want to give her any chance to escape from them. Elysande said little and when she did, she tried to sound empty-headed, though she didn't think she fooled them. The soldiers had been tasked with a mission and they desperately wanted to succeed.

She, too, was reaching a point of desperation. The farther north they traveled, the less likely was the chance that her uncle and his men would find her before they arrived at Rudland. Elysande assumed that Uncle Geoffrey would have figured out that she'd been taken by men from Lord Ingram, but with her totally hidden from view and Folc and Ernis now dressed as common workers? The de Montfort search party could have easily ridden past the rickety cart without giving it a second thought.

The vehicle slowed. She could feel it moving off the main path. The jostling increased with the uneven terrain. Within minutes, it stopped. She heard the usual noises that occurred with each night's stop. The fire being built. Someone rummaging in the cart for a pot to retrieve water for boiling whatever small game they would catch. She lay there for a long time as they completed these rituals. Finally, the heavy blankets came off her. Elysande blinked and saw that night had fallen.

Folc grabbed her ankles and pulled her toward him till her legs dangled awkwardly from the back of the cart. He pulled her to a standing position and then lifted her by the waist and carried her near the fire before he set her back against a tree stump. Untying the confining gag, his eyes narrowed in unspoken words. She knew he warned her not to make a sound and to speak only when spoken to.

They ate in silence, which suited her. Each time they stopped, Elysande studied her surroundings. If given the chance, she would make a run for it. She wanted to be as familiar as possible with everything around them.

Tonight, they dined upon a small rabbit which hadn't had much meat on its bones. Eating proved awkward with her wrists tied together, her palms facing one another, but she had managed to learn how to do so. She often dropped her food into her lap. Her *cotehardie* now revealed many greasy stains. After so long on the road, sweating under the blankets, she longed for clean clothes and a hot bath. She'd even asked to rinse her face and hands in a stream the first time they stopped, but Folc had rejected the idea. She chuckled inwardly. Mayhap Lord Ingram would be so appalled by her smell and appearance that he would not want her, after all.

The two men had almost finished eating, so Elysande knew she better hurry. When they were through, that meant she was, too—whether she had food left or not. She quickly downed the last few bites and waited patiently to relieve herself. As usual, Ernis was given this task. Folc was the one in charge and Ernis—though not stupid—simply followed any orders given to him.

He came over now and loosened the ties from her ankles. Elysande was thankful the small dagger wedged inside her boot did not stick out. She prayed this was the night she would be able to use it and escape from Lord Ingram's men.

Ernis gripped her elbow firmly and led her away from the camp. Elysande waited for him to look away before she lifted her skirts as best she could. She had never experienced humiliation before—and she would never forget this feeling. She finished her business and looked about for some fallen leaves. She found a few several feet away. A thought suddenly came to her.

She deliberately tripped as she stepped toward the bunch. As she fell, she curled into a ball and brushed her skirts aside. Elysande slipped her fingers inside her boot and, though it was tight, she was able to pull her dagger out.

In the meantime, Ernis cackled at her clumsiness. He bent to right her. Elysande thrust the dagger into his side and pulled up, feeling the skin tear.

She would never forget the look of astonishment on his face. He dropped his hands from her elbows and clutched the hilt of the knife jammed into his side. She put her bound hands atop his and yanked up again. His eyes bulged as he fell away from her, moaning. As the soldier dropped to the ground, the dagger came out of him and remained in her hands.

Then silence. Ernis did not move. Oh, Blessed Jesu. She'd killed him.

She couldn't waste time crying. Or even thinking. Escape loomed in her mind. She would ask God's forgiveness later. Now, she must flee.

Without a backward glance, Elysande skirted the woods, giving their camp a wide berth. She came to the road they must have been on. In the distance, she heard Folc calling out. Then a shrill bellow pierced the quiet of the night. Elysande knew Folc had discovered his comrade's body.

Elysande darted across the road. She dared not stay on it or she'd be easily seen and recaptured. Instead, she headed deep into the woods on the other side and then began making her way parallel to the road. Though she still carried the dagger, she had no time to stop and free her hands. That would have to wait until later.

She didn't run. She knew not to exhaust herself. Rather, she kept a brisk, steady pace as she weaved through the woods, listening to see if Folc gave chase. Elysande knew he would. She was too valuable a prize for him to lose, especially after all the time he'd invested. She wondered if he'd double back on foot and abandon the cart to search for her on horseback, hoping to chase her down. At this point, darkness was her only friend. She had no way to measure time to know how long she'd been gone. More than anything, she needed to find somewhere to hide. It would be easy to spot her once daylight came.

A loud thrashing behind her caused her heart to race. Folc was catching up to her. Elysande stopped in her tracks, looking around for a place to hide. A thick, fallen log lay several feet in front of her, with another log crossing on top of it. Quickly, she threw her leg high and climbed over them. She crouched low and then slipped under the tree trunks as far as she could.

Just in time.

She heard the horse as it crashed through the dense forest. Folc swore loudly, his hollered threats sending a chill down her spine. Then the hooves approached. Elysande held her breath. She couldn't give her position away. Suddenly in the dirt in front of her, the horse landed, having jumped the logs. Folc rode further and then pulled up on the reins. He twirled in a circle, looking carefully at the surrounding woods. She could see his profile in the moonlight, the hook of his nose, the jutting chin. She squeezed her eyes shut and willed him to ride away.

And he did.

Elysande stayed rooted to her hiding place. She would remain here for a little while. If Folc backtracked this way, she didn't want to risk running into him.

Her fingers ached. She lifted her hands, which still clutched the blade so tightly that it took time for her to loosen her grasp on it. She maneuvered the knife toward her and let it slip down some before she began to saw carefully through the leather ties. Sweat dripped from her brow as she concentrated on her task. Finally, she cut through one of the strands enough to where she could pull and weaken it. The dagger sliced through the last bit. Her numb fingers went cold and then began stinging as if she'd fallen onto a bed of needles. Elysande rotated her wrists and opened and shut her fingers, stretching them until she had full feeling in them again.

Returning the dagger to her boot, she looked out into the dark. At least her hands and feet were now free for the first time in days.

HER BODY JUMPED. Elysande's eyes flashed open. She scanned the area before her. Faint light filtered through the thick trees. In her exhaustion, she must have fallen asleep.

Taking the severed ties, she shoved them under the log that had protected her, wanting no trace of her to be found by Folc. She stood unsteadily, leaning against a tree trunk until she had her wobbly legs under control, then she set out walking. She cut through the woods and found the road again before she fell back. Her plan was to remain in the woods and move through them, parallel to the road.

Even in daylight, Elysande didn't want to be out on the road alone because of roaming bands of highwaymen. She remembered traveling to the south after her father's death so her mother could marry Lord Holger. His soldiers had always remained on guard as they journeyed to Hopeston. She didn't want to fall prey to strangers.

Elysande walked for hours. Her feet ached. Her stomach gurgled in hunger. She remained on a constant lookout, tense, wary, watching for Folc.

As she continued, her heart became heavy. In the long hours, she had time to think on how she had killed a man. Yes, he'd kidnapped her. Held her against her will. He would've taken her to Lord Ingram, where she would have been forced to marry.

Still, that didn't justify her taking a life. Now—more than ever—she would need to give her life in service to God. She might not be absolved of her sins, but dedicating her life to the Christ was the best she could do.

Especially now, with Michael already married at Sandbourne.

The light began to fade. Night would soon fall. Elysande was so tired. So hungry. She hurt everywhere. She dreaded spending another night alone in the woods, which seemed to grow more ominous about her.

Then, in the distance, she saw a structure familiar to her. Her excitement grew. She knew this place. 'Twas the Convent of the Blessed Sisters. Her family had stayed there on their way to Hopeston. It had been one of two nunneries that accepted travelers. She, her mother, and Avelyn had met several of the nuns when they took a brief respite from their travels. One, in particular, had been so kind to them. Sister Shiloh. That was her name.

Surely, they would give her sanctuary this night. And mayhap beyond.

Elysande walked as quickly as she could, though the blisters on her feet made each step more painful than the last. She reached the high, stone wall surrounding the convent and searched for the gate, praying she would be granted access. Finding the gate, she rang the bell a dozen times, eager for someone to answer.

A young nun, no older than she was, answered and invited her inside the walls. As the nun shut the gate behind them and locked it from within, Elysande relaxed for the first time in a week. While they walked to the main building, she explained to the nun how she'd stayed here on a previous journey as her party made their way south.

What Elysande kept hidden from the good sister was the fact that she'd recently been taken against her will. That men might be searching for her and come to the convent. Elysande was afraid if she revealed this information that she might not have been granted admission. So she kept quiet. For now.

"I can show you to a small cell reserved for travelers," the nun told her, never asking why a woman alone showed up in the dark, bedraggled and worn to the bone. Elysande's stomach rumbled loudly. The young nun smiled. "And I can bring bread and something for you to drink."

"Oh, please," Elysande said eagerly. "That would be most appreciated."

The nun walked her to the small cell. As on her previous visit, it held a single bed and a lone chair as its furnishings. "Wait here."

"Is Sister Shiloh nearby?" Elysande asked. "I met her on my first stay here. She was so hospitable to us."

A smile crossed the nun's face. "Sister Shiloh is one truly touched by grace. I'll see that she comes to welcome you." The nun looked her up and down. "I'll also have her bring some water. You look as if you would like to bathe your hands and face."

Elysande touched her face self-consciously. She knew it held small scratches from the branches she'd brushed past as she moved through the woods. "That would be kind of you."

She sat on the small bed and eased her boots off. Her feet, rubbed raw by her long trek, were a mass of painful blisters. Her mind went blank. She was so tired, she couldn't even think.

A knock sounded on the door and Sister Shiloh stepped in. She carried a tall jar filled with water under one arm and a thick towel in the other. The young nun who had admitted Elysande followed the older nun. She balanced a small tray with bread and cheese in one hand and carried a cup in her other. She placed the food down and disappeared, closing the door behind her.

"Greetings, Lady Elysande," Sister Shiloh said. "I remember you and your lovely sister and mother. Are they with you? I would enjoy speaking to them, as well as to you."

Elysande burst into tears at the thought of her loved ones. The nun sat next to her. She wrapped an arm around Elysande and held her tenderly, cooing nonsense while she cried.

After she calmed, Sister Shiloh said, "Why don't we let you wash and eat something? Then I want you to share with me whatever's on your heart."

Elysande nodded and let the older woman minister to her. Elysande ate without speaking, allowing the nun to chat about some of her fellow sisters and the animals she cared for every day. After washing Elysande's face, hands, and feet, Sister Shiloh left briefly. She returned minutes later with a strong-smelling salve which she rubbed into Elysande's blistered feet.

Elysande sighed. Already, she felt welcomed. "I have much to tell you, Sister. And I would ask advice from you, as well. I have grievously sinned, and I seek to repent and change my life. I believe God led me here so that I can join your order."

Sister Shiloh listened attentively as Elysande spoke. She explained of her betrothed dying before their wedding ceremony could take place and how she'd gone to visit her uncle at Kinwick. She told of being taken by two of Lord Ingram's men and how the nobleman wanted to marry her. She explained how she had escaped from captivity, killing a man in the process.

Elysande hung her head in shame. Hearing the words uttered aloud made it seem more real than before. She was guilty of breaking one of the Ten Commandments. She'd taken a life and could never undo what she'd done.

The nun took her hand and gently kissed it. "God will forgive you, my lady. He is ever merciful."

"But I believe I should stay on and dedicate myself to His good works. 'Tis the least I can do to try and atone for my sins."

Sister Shiloh nodded. "I know our abbess would never turn you away, but you asked for my advice."

"I did."

"Then I would discuss this with your family. It's a huge decision to leave earthly matters behind. You should share your thoughts with your loved ones and seek your mother's approval. You must be very certain that you can give up worldly things. And not just those that are material in nature. By becoming a Bride of Christ, you must give up loving a man. Bearing his children. Becoming a mother."

Elysande broke down again, her sobs echoing in the tiny room. Sister Shiloh gathered her in her arms and rocked her.

Finally, Elysande brushed aside her tears and spoke. "I do love a man, Sister, but marriage with him is impossible."

"Tell me, my child. It may soothe you to speak of it."

Elysande sighed. "I fell in love with a knight that serves my uncle. He loved me, too. I knew we were meant to be together. But he received word to return to his family's estate in haste because his father lay dying. They'd been estranged for many years. He told me we would marry when he could claim his title as earl."

Elysande shook her head. "But it's too late for us. We received news that he was betrothed." She swallowed, her misery now complete. "By now, he's already married. And if I can't have Michael Devereux as my husband, then I want no other man."

Sister Shiloh stiffened next to her. Elysande pulled away and saw the shocked look on the nun's face.

"What's wrong, Sister? Have I said something to upset you?"

The nun's lips trembled. "Michael Devereux . . . is . . . my son."

CHAPTER TWENTY-TWO

As they returned south back toward Kinwick, Michael studied everyone they passed. Very few travelers were on the road today and he made sure they spoke to each one. None resembled any of Lord Ingram's men, nor did he see anywhere Elysande could be hidden away. The soldiers also wove in and out of the woods, calling Elysande's name, invoking his and Geoffrey's names to alert her who searched for her and that they were friendly forces.

The sun dipped low on the horizon. He was ready to call a halt when he spotted a lone rider in the distance. The man came from out of the woods, turning his head from side to side as if he hunted for something.

Or someone.

Michael spurred Tempest on, wanting to catch up to the rider and ask what he searched for. As Michael came closer, he spotted the nose that hooked sharply.

He recognized the rider as one of Lord Ingram's men.

Michael had seen the soldier at Hopeston, bragging in the training yard. He had seen the man a second time, flirting with a pretty servant in the keep when they dined one evening.

Then a second rider emerged from the opposite side of the road. He held the reins in one hand while his other hand pressed against his side. The man wore a pained expression. Michael immediately knew this man's long, bony face and thin build. Another of Ingram's men. Michael looked over his shoulder and saw his search party had quickened their pace. Ingram's soldiers also noticed the approaching mass of riders. Both turned their horses and dug in their heels, taking off in the opposite direction.

Michael gave chase. He heard the galloping hooves behind him as Geoffrey and the men caught up with him. The thinner man he followed pulled his horse off the road and halted, knowing he could not outrun the bunch. Michael peeled away from the group and rode up next to him. Michael's own men fell out and surrounded the soldier while Geoffrey led his men to track down the other fleeing soldier.

Michael leapt from his horse as the man climbed gingerly from his, still holding his side. Bunching the man's gypon in his fists, Michael yanked him close. "Where is she?" he growled.

The man quivered in fear. Michael looked down and saw that blood stained his clothing and fingers. Ingram's man had been wounded somehow.

He hoped Elysande was the cause of it.

He dragged the man away from the horses and flung him down in the dirt. "Stay," he commanded. He stepped out to gaze down the road and saw Geoffrey headed back his way, his men galloping behind him.

The nobleman rode up and jumped down. "'Twas one of Ingram's men. I'm sure of it as are the others."

"Where is he?" Michael demanded. "We have the other one."

"Dead. He put up a brief fight. One of my men ran a sword through him."

Michael's hands fisted. "Then we'll question this one." He strode back toward the injured man, Geoffrey following him. His men parted so the noblemen could draw near.

"Where is Lady Elysande?" Michael demanded.

The man looked up at him. "I don't know," he said sullenly. "Where's Folc?" He looked about him. No friendly face returned his gaze.

"Don't worry about him," Michael warned. "Tell me everything you know—now—if you want us to spare your life."

"I'm Ernis, in service to Lord Ingram. We were only following his orders," he sputtered. "We weren't to go back to Rudland unless we had the lady in hand." He looked at the group that surrounded him. "You killed the rest of my lord's men when we attacked you on the way to Kinwick. Folc and I were the only two who escaped."

"And you waited and watched for an opportunity to take my niece?" Geoffrey asked, his voice soft, his tone deadly.

"Aye. The two of us. We waited for weeks, skulking about in the woods. And then she appeared. Alone. We thanked our lucky stars and made off with her in haste." He began to blubber, snot pouring from his nose. "You might as well kill me. Lord Ingram'll do that. And worse. He's a hard man. If I return without the lady, I won't live to see another daybreak."

"So you were looking for Lady Elysande? She escaped from you?"

The soldier nodded. "Aye. She must've had a dagger all along and waited to use it." He rubbed his side and grimaced. "Stabbed me, she did. Knocked me for a loop. I fell back and hit my head on a rock." He reached up to rub the back of his scalp. "Don't know which hurts more. Folc found me. Must've knocked me out cold. I wound some linen around the wound and we've been looking for her ever since."

Geoffrey caught Michael's eye and motioned to him. Michael stepped away from the knights gathered around their hostage.

"So we know she has to be in the area. We'll find her, Michael. I swear it by God's wounds." He glanced over at the man still sitting on the ground, looking miserable. "What would you have us do with him?"

Michael hesitated. "Much as I loathe his actions, he was only following orders. He's certainly scared of Lord Ingram. I say we release him. We have what we need from him."

"I agree," Geoffrey said. "Ingram would only execute him."

Both men returned to their prisoner.

Michael said, "We've decided to show you mercy. Get back on your horse and ride from here. Do not return to Lord Ingram. You can become a mercenary. Be your own man. Find a fair lord to fight for." He spat on the ground. "'Tis better than you deserve."

"Thank you, my lord." Ernis scrambled to his feet, not asking any questions. He mounted his horse and took off without a backward glance.

"I think she would try to make her way back south," Michael said, glancing around to see that night had fallen. The thought of his beloved lost and terrified in the darkness wrenched his gut. It would be fruitless to search for Elysande tonight, especially if she hid deep in the woods, but he had to do something.

"I want twenty men sent to the north and another score sent south," Michael told a grim-faced Geoffrey. "They are to stay to the road since 'tis too dangerous to have them tramp through a dark forest at night. Have them call her name throughout the night. Hopefully, she will be close enough to hear them and respond." He sighed and added, "If she's not found, then when dawn breaks, we should send a small party of men north a few leagues and have them work their way back to this spot. The rest of us can ride south in the morning. For now, the remaining men can make camp here before riding out at first light."

"As you wish. May the Christ be with her and help lead us to her." Geoffrey went over and instructed the men as to which would search for Elysande during the night and how they would divide up if the hunt proved unsuccessful.

They ate and bedded down for the night. Michael lay awake for a long time. He knew a multitude of bad things could happen to unaccompanied women.

He begged God for His mercy in keeping Elysande safe tonight. And promised himself that they would find her before the sun set again.

ELYSANDE WAITED FOR Sister Shiloh's return. The older nun had become overwhelmed last night and excused herself from Elysande's presence, but she'd promised to stop by after early morning prayers. Elysande awaited her after a restless night of sleep, eager to hear more of the woman's story. Michael had never mentioned his mother—much less that she was a nun.

A light rap on the door alerted Elysande to her arrival. She hurried to greet the nun and ushered her into the tiny cell. The two women sat on the bed. Sister Shiloh took Elysande's hands and held them lightly as she spoke.

"I'm sorry I rushed off last night," she apologized. "I was overcome with emotion. I haven't seen my son in so many years." She looked wistfully at Elysande. "I know that it's hard for you to think about him from the little you revealed to me, but I would so like to hear about him."

The thought of speaking of Michael pained Elysande, but she realized that Michael's mother had been separated from him for years. She'd only been apart from him for just over a week. She would tell this woman all that she could and bring her comfort in knowing her son had grown into a good man.

The nun bit her lower lip. "I suppose I should also tell you why I am here."

"Only if you wish to," Elysande said.

Sister Shiloh took a deep breath and exhaled slowly. "I was betrothed to Michael's father at a young age, as many are. My parents had me later in life after many childless years of marriage. They passed within a month of each other and I was immediately sent to Sandbourne to marry. The earl was half a score older than I was and distrustful of me from the start. He constantly had me watched. He beat me for minor infractions and imagined I had dalliances with other men."

The older woman shuddered as she recollected her life. Elysande squeezed her hands in sympathy.

"Michael was our only child. He was a quiet boy. Thoughtful. He liked to play with his toy soldiers and listen to stories. He had no playmates and lived an isolated life. After his seventh birthday, the earl sent him to foster many miles from home." Her eyes brimmed with tears. "I missed him every day he was gone."

Elysande reached up and brushed the tears away. If things had worked out differently, this woman would have been her mother-in-law. Already, knowing what she did, Elysande saw glimpses of Michael in this woman.

"My husband was a cruel man. He did not allow Michael to return for the Christmas season his first year away. He told me it was because Michael needed toughening up, but I fear it was his desire to deprive me of my child's company that was the true reason. And when it came time for Michael to return home for his summer visit, my husband didn't bother to escort him home. Instead, Sir Lovel sent one of his trusted knights to deliver Michael safely to Sandbourne. At least I knew he would be in good hands for the journey home."

Sister Shiloh stood and moved to the wall, leaning on it for support as she crossed her arms in front of her. Elysande saw a faraway look in her eyes and knew the woman looked deeply into the past as she revealed her memories.

"I wanted to do something special for Michael to welcome him upon his arrival. Sir Thirkell, one of the knights at Sandbourne, helped me to acquire a horse as dark as midnight and of a good pedigree. Michael had never been fond of horses, but I knew, since he trained to be a knight, that he would need a good steed."

Her words surprised Elysande. *Michael didn't like horses?* She thought of how he helped her deliver not one, but two foals and how gentle he'd been with them.

"Sir Thirkell and I were in the stables that day, brushing Tempest and feeding him bits of carrot. I didn't know Michael had arrived." Her mouth turned downward. "Suddenly, my husband was there, accusing me, once again, of being unfaithful to him."

Sister Shiloh closed her eyes. Elysande saw she trembled.

"He struck Sir Thirkell down in a jealous rage. He killed him," she whispered. The nun opened her eyes. "He began to beat on me. Kick me. And Michael witnessed all of this."

Elysande's heart broke. She couldn't imagine Michael seeing his mother abused in such a horrible way.

"Michael tried to pull my husband off me to no avail. Then he told Michael that he would never see me again. That I would be sent to a nunnery to spend the rest of my days." Sister Shiloh's eyes met hers. "Frankly, I found his words a blessed relief. With Michael away, I had no reason to be at Sandbourne. No reason to live. My husband thought locking me away in a convent would be a terrible punishment—but to me, it was an escape from his brutality."

She came and sat next to Elysande again and took her hands. "Michael stood up to Sandbourne that day. He told him he'd no longer think of him as his father. My boy promised not to set foot on Sandbourne lands again until the earl's death. He jumped on Tempest and rode off without another word."

The nun smiled at the memory. "Mayhap he had learned to like horses at Sir Lovel's, for he certainly looked sure and brave as he galloped away that day."

Elysande heard the pride in the woman's voice.

Sister Shiloh sighed. "That is my tale, my lady. I have been at the Convent of the Blessed Sisters ever since. But please, I beg you. Tell me of my son."

Elysande smiled. "He's grown to be quite tall, with broad shoulders and a commanding presence. He's very handsome with dark, thick hair and eyes much like yours, a piercing blue that can see into a person's soul."

She saw a happy look cross Sister Shiloh's face and continued. "He attained his knighthood and continued in service to Sir Lovel until recently when he came to Kinwick, my uncle's estate. Michael said he'd been a page when Uncle Geoffrey and his cousin, Raynor, served as squires to Sir Lovel. Michael told me how those two were very kind to him and helped teach him what he needed to know."

"I'm glad he was taken care of by those older boys. But tell me how you met Michael. Was it at your uncle's home?"

"Nay. I was to be married. Uncle Geoffrey brought his wife, Merryn, and their children to Hopeston, my stepfather's estate. Michael was one of the knights that accompanied them to the wedding."

Elysande explained how Michael had helped her deliver Morningstar's foal. Of the hours they'd spent together, neither knowing who the other one was. How they fell in love during that single day. She explained that Lord Ingram had wanted to step in and become her new bridegroom upon his son's death and how her mother had refused. Instead, she'd gone home with Geoffrey and Merryn.

"During my time at my uncle's, I came to know Michael well. You'd be so proud of him. He is brave and considerate to all. A very honorable man. We pledged our love to one another. Uncle Geoffrey wrote the king to let him know he served as my protector from Lord Ingram and how my uncle would be pleased if the king would allow one of his knights to marry me."

She sighed. "Then everything happened so quickly. Michael received word of his father's—your husband's—impending death. He left with a promise that he'd return for me once he became the new earl. We had high hopes that King Edward would grant Uncle Geoffrey's request and allow us to marry since the king is very fond of my uncle."

"But you found out he was betrothed," Sister Shiloh said, her eyes misting over.

Elysande's heart grew heavy as she continued her story. "Aye. He'd been gone only one day when a missive came. The king wrote that he would have acquiesced to my uncle's request, but his royal advisers informed him that Michael was already betrothed. He would marry when he reached Sandbourne. King Edward requested that my sister and I come to court in the autumn when Uncle Geoffrey brought his daughter, Alys, back. Alys is in service to Queen Philippa."

"I'm so sorry, my lady," Sister Shiloh told her. "Michael was betrothed when he was very young. 'Twas the day before he departed for Sir Lovel's. I'm sure he hadn't a clue what went on. He was so eager to escape his father and go out into the world and make friends."

"I understand that now. But I was truly hurt when we received the news. And the next day is when I was taken hostage by men sent from Lord Ingram. You know the rest. How I escaped. How I killed one of the soldiers in the process."

Elysande stood, shaking off her gloom. "That's the reason why I must shelter myself away from the world and atone for my mortal sins." She looked to Michael's mother. "Will you help me in this quest?"

The nun stood and embraced her. "While I wish you could have been my daughter-in-law, I will do everything in my power to help make you a sister to me in Christ. Come. Let us go to morning mass and break our fast. Then I will take you to meet our abbess."

CHAPTER TWENTY-THREE

THEY RODE CAREFULLY, leaving the main road often to hunt for Elysande in the woods. Michael believed her intelligence would keep her off the road to avoid strangers who could turn out to be highwayman—or worse.

After two hours, they came across the Convent of the Blessed Sisters. Geoffrey said they'd stopped at the nunnery previously to ask about any travelers that might have taken shelter within the convent's walls. The nun at the gate said none had visited for over two weeks, but that had been a couple of days ago.

"I suggest we call again on the good sisters. If they have no news for us, then we can pay them for some fresh bread and continue on our way."

Michael nodded in agreement. They turned their horses and made for the convent.

When they arrived, he and Geoffrey left their horses with the men and approached the gate. When they inquired if the convent had harbored visitors in the past few days, the thin nun who'd answered their knock informed them they'd played host to several travelers.

Michael asked, "Might we speak with your abbess then regarding these travelers?"

"Of course, my lord. I can take you to her now if you wish."

She led them across the yard and into the convent. The dark hall they entered was a stark contrast to the strong sunshine they'd left behind. As his eyes began to adjust, Michael soaked up the air of heavy silence that blanketed the place.

The nun set a rapid pace. He and Geoffrey followed her through a maze of halls and up a staircase, passing other nuns along the way who kept their eyes downcast. Michael wondered which convent his mother might have been sent to and what her life had been like since they last saw one another. Once he had Elysande safely in hand, he would turn his attention to locating her. He would start by questioning Houdart. His father's steward knew everything that occurred at Sandbourne. The man would be a valuable asset in running the estate, but Michael hoped the steward would be able to reveal where his mother had been sent those many years ago.

They arrived at a door that was ajar. The nun pushed it fully open and ushered them inside a small antechamber.

"You may wait here for Mother." She indicated an oak door on the other side of the room. "Do not knock on it under any circumstances. Mother may be in prayer or about business. Only when she opens it will she be willing to receive you."

They thanked her for her time. Then Geoffrey asked her if the nuns would be willing to sell any freshly-baked bread to the soldiers that accompanied them.

"Aye, my lord. I'll go to our kitchen and see to it now. May God be with you." She bowed her head and departed the way they had come.

The two men sat in silence. Michael said a swift prayer, asking the Blessed Christ, once more, for help in finding Elysande. Then he pushed aside all other thoughts, for they'd only make him worry about her safety.

He heard muted voices and then watched as the door swung open. An older nun with a wrinkled face but a kind smile stood in the doorway. He supposed this was the convent's abbess. Her dress appeared slightly different from the other nuns they had passed in the hallways and she wore a heavy, ornate cross around her neck.

"May the Lord be with you," she said as a woman walked past her.

Shock resonated within him as he recognized her. "Elysande?"

She turned. Her smile lit up the bare room. Her clothing was heavily soiled and she had scratches across her face and hands. He supposed they came from running through the woods as she escaped from her captors.

"Michael!" she cried joyfully.

He leapt to his feet and took a step toward her—then froze.

Another nun followed closely behind her. She looked at him with eyes of crystal blue. Eyes that he could never forget, no matter how much time had passed.

The color drained from the nun's face. "Michael?" she asked softly.

He couldn't speak. A thousand emotions rippled through him. He closed the small space between them and wordlessly wrapped his arms around her. Tears swam in his eyes. Pulling away slightly to look into her eyes, a fresh wave of raw emotion surged through him. More than anything, Michael relished the love running through him and hoped she knew how much he did love her.

Elysande!

Michael finally relaxed his hold and parted from his mother. Elysande stood nearby, watching him with a pleased look on her face.

"Elysande," he murmured as he held out his arms to her. She stepped into them, wrapping hers tightly around his waist. Michael embraced her, his hands running up and down her back, touching her, making sure it was truly her.

Then he kissed her. Once. Twice. Three times. Each one hard and fast, as if he must get in all the kisses they'd missed.

"Oh, my love, I was so worried about you," she said.

"You worried about me? I was frantic when I received the news that you'd been taken. I rode out the minute I heard." He cupped her face tenderly. "And you escaped. My brave, strong, beautiful Elysande." He brought his mouth to hers again in a searing kiss.

Michael felt a hand on his back and broke the kiss. Turning, his face grew warm as he saw the convent's abbess staring at him, her eyes narrowed in displeasure. He looked to his mother and then Geoffrey and saw their approval, which eased his embarrassment somewhat.

"It seems we have a rather complicated situation," the abbess declared. "I will give you some privacy in order to sort things out."

"I'll join you," Geoffrey said. The nobleman looked at Michael. "I'll be waiting outside the gates." He and the abbess exited the room.

Michael kissed Elysande again for good measure and then released her to hug his mother once more. He brushed a kiss on her cheek and then stepped back.

"God is good. He has led me to the two women I sought." He saw a shadow cross Elysande's face. He reached for her hands. "What's wrong, sweetheart?"

She tried to pull from his grasp, but he held firm.

"Michael, it's wrong for me to have kissed you," she said. A look of pure longing crossed her face as she stared at him. Then she dropped her eyes. "A missive arrived from the king after you left."

He knew it had, for Geoffrey had given it to him. He also knew the king would have agreed to his marriage to Elysande.

"It matters not," she said. "You of all people should know why. We learned of your betrothal. I assume . . . I assume you are married by now."

He laughed deep from within and caught her up in his arms. "Nay, my love. It's true that I was betrothed, but when my intended arrived, she told me her fondest wish was to become a Bride of Christ. She had never wanted to marry, even from a young age. She broke our betrothal contract and I took her to a convent a few hours' ride from Sandbourne. I left her there, happy, with a glow about her that told me I'd done the right thing."

Her jaw dropped. She searched his face. "So . . . so . . . you are not married?"

Michael pressed his lips to hers in a lingering kiss. "Nay, sweetheart. 'Tis why I'm here. Searching for you." He cupped her cheek. "I am not whole without you in my life, dearest. You are the part that completes me. Since the king is amenable, I wish to marry you and make you my countess."

Elysande broke out in a radiant smile. "The king will agree. I'm sure. If not for the impediment of your betrothal, he said he would have given us his permission."

Warmth spread throughout him. Then he felt her stiffen in his arms. She pulled away, wrapping her arms around her as if she were suddenly cold.

"Elysande? What—"

"I still can't marry you," she said softly. "I must remain here. I've asked the abbess if I may join the convent and become a Sister in Christ."

"What? But nothing—"

"Hush." She placed a slender finger against his lips. He burned with desire at her touch.

"I've done something awful, Michael. So terrible that I must give my life to Christ to atone for this grievous sin." She bit her lip. "I . . . I killed a man. That's the only reason I'm here and not still on the road traveling to Lord Ingram's estate with the wicked men that abducted me."

Michael realized what she was talking about. "Nay, my love. You killed no man."

"But I did!" she insisted, her eyes sad beyond measure.

"Was this Ernis you believe you killed?"

Shock crossed her face. "How do you know? Did you find his body? Did you find Folc?" She shuddered as she mentioned the soldier's name.

"Folc is dead," he said bluntly. "And we came across Ernis, who is very much alive. You did wound him in the side, but he didn't die from it."

"But he fell back and did not move. I ran. He did not holler out and warn Folc that I was escaping."

"Ernis told us that he hit his head on a rock, my love. He had quite a large knot. The blow knocked him out cold. It was speaking to him that let us know you'd escaped and were somewhere in the area."

"Where is he now?" she asked.

"We let him go." Michael caught her frown of disapproval and rushed to explain. "He was frightened to return to Lord Ingram without you. He even begged us to kill him instead. Geoffrey and I decided to show him mercy. We told him never to return to Rudland again. To go and offer his services elsewhere as a mercenary." He laughed. "Ernis took off quickly. I have no doubt you will never lay eyes upon him again."

His mother placed her hands on Michael's and Elysande's shoulders. "See? You are meant to be together. While this convent has proved a refuge to me, 'twas because I had nothing and no one." She smiled at Elysande. "You have my son. I see how happy he is with you. I will do whatever it takes to convince you to leave here and marry him. Don't waste your life behind these walls when you have the love of a good man."

"And you, too, must come with us, Mother." Michael took his mother's hand. "I swore an oath as a boy to find you and return you to a place of honor at Sandbourne. 'Twas my next quest once I found Elysande and knew she was safe."

His mother shook her head. "I would only be in your way, my son. You and Elysande will create a family of your own." She smiled. "Besides, I've come to relish this quiet life, away from the world."

Her words cut him to the quick.

Before he could protest, Elysande said, "I insist you return with us, my lady. I will need your guidance in my new role as countess." She glanced at Michael. "And I don't think Michael would ever be truly happy if you remained behind."

He saw that his mother wavered and gave one last, impassioned plea. "I need you, Mother. Even as a grown man, I admit that I need you. You have so much love to give. I hope you'll help us raise our children—your grandchildren."

Michael reached into his pocket and pulled out the pink stone he always carried. He took her hand and placed the small rock in her palm.

"We found this one day when we walked around Sandbourne."

"I remember," she said softly.

"I kept it always as a way to remember you. Please, Mother. Come home. Come to Sandbourne with us. I beg you."

Tears spilled down her cheeks. She nodded in agreement, too emotional to speak for some minutes. Finally, she uttered, "Aye, I'll accompany you home."

"We'll need to stop first at Hopeston to call on Elysande's mother," he said. "Though I have the king's permission, I would ask Lady Mary for her daughter's hand in marriage." Michael gazed into Elysande's eyes. "And I have a suggestion for our wedding."

"You do?" The sparkle in her eyes held just a hint of mischief, causing his heart to skip a beat.

"You have no strong ties to Hopeston since you grew up elsewhere. I would like for us to marry at Kinwick. I believe your mother would appreciate returning to her childhood home and seeing the ceremony take place from there. Besides, Lady Merryn enjoys nothing more than to hold a feast with the great hall bursting from the seams with people and plenty of good food."

"That's a lovely idea," Elysande told him. "And we can go from Kinwick to Sandbourne." She threw her arms around him and kissed him soundly.

His mother laughed. "I suppose I'll need to break the news to Mother that she is losing the both of us."

CHAPTER TWENTY-FOUR

THEY WAITED IN the antechamber while Sister Shiloh spoke with the abbess. Michael held Elysande's hand in both of his.

"I'll never let you go," he promised her.

She giggled. "So I'll accompany you to the training yard? You'll hold your sword in one hand and my hand in your other as you instruct your men," she teased. "Or mayhap you'll hold my thread while I weave a tapestry. You can make sure nothing tangles."

He nuzzled a soft spot just below her ear, sending wondrous chills through her. "I'll do all of that. And more." He gave her a wicked grin. "I'll accompany you into your bath, my lady. And sit ever so close to you in the water. My hand will never leave yours. Unless you can think of better places for it to rest."

She remembered his fingers pleasuring her and felt the heat rise up her neck. The thought of him in her bath with her, touching her, brought delicious tingles.

"I see the idea grows on you," he murmured, his teeth tugging on her earlobe.

"Michael!" she protested, pushing him back. "We're sitting in a convent. The abbess is in the next room. She could step out at any moment."

He raised her hand to his lips and brushed them along her knuckles slowly, causing her insides to warm, reflecting the happiness and love she felt for this man.

"She's already seen us kiss, sweetheart. I think she knows what passes between a man and a woman. Especially when they love one another as much as we do."

Her resolve began to weaken.

"I see a smile tugging at the corners of your mouth."

She let the smile grow.

"And I see—"

The door opened. Michael sat back in his chair, but he kept her hand in his. That small gesture pleased Elysande to no end. This man—this honorable knight—would soon be her chosen husband. They would be a love match from the start.

She remembered how he'd made love to her. How he'd done things that she had never dreamed existed.

And how she couldn't wait to be with him again, their bare skin touching, their bodies joined together as one.

The abbess approached them. Michael's mother followed behind her, a peaceful look on her face.

"Sister Shiloh has fully explained the situation to me. I agree with her that this is not the place for you, Lady Elysande." Her eyes flicked to Michael. "I would wish for you to treat your wife-to-be with honor and respect, my lord."

"I'll do my best, Abbess."

"And your mother has also decided to leave our sisterhood and accompany you to Sandbourne." The nun looked over her shoulder. "We will miss your loving presence, Sister." Her eyes twinkled. "But I believe you'll be an asset to your family and help raise your grandchildren to be loving servants to Christ Almighty."

The abbess kissed Sister Shiloh on each cheek. "Go say your goodbyes to the others. Godspeed to you all."

The trio left the abbess. Sister Shiloh stopped along the way at a small cell. "I have a few things to gather. It won't take me long."

She rejoined them minutes later with a small bundle in her arms. Elysande realized that Michael's mother had very little in the way of material possessions and determined to see her clothed and jeweled as the lady she was. She knew Michael would agree.

They gave her some time with her fellow sisters to say their farewells. When she returned, her eyes were bright with unshed tears. Elysande supposed it was hard for her to leave the women who'd given her shelter and companionship all these years, but Elysande knew the future would prove bright for them all as they stepped into the warm sunshine in the courtyard.

"I suppose I'll no longer be known as Sister Shiloh," she told them. She looked at Elysande. "You should call me Orella. My, I haven't said my name in so many years. I'd almost forgotten it."

Elysande put an arm around the former nun's shoulders. "You'll get used to hearing it, my lady."

They reached the oak gate and stepped through it. Elysande froze in her tracks as her eyes swept across a huge group of soldiers amassed outside the walls of the nunnery.

"There are so many!" she proclaimed in wonder.

Michael took her hand. "They're all here for you, my love. Your uncle and I both brought many men to search high and low for you. Come. Let's rejoin them."

As they moved toward the gathered soldiers, a cheer went up. It rang loud and long. Though Elysande knew she pinkened in embarrassment, it thrilled her that so many men had devoted their time to rescue her before she reached Lord Ingram's estate.

Geoffrey stepped out to meet them, along with a man she didn't recognize. She saw he smiled at Michael's mother.

The knight bowed low and took the noblewoman's hand, pressing a kiss to it. "Lady Orella. 'Tis been many years since your beauty graced Sandbourne. You were sorely missed."

"I thank you, Sir Charles." Orella turned to Elysande. "This is Sir Charles, one of Sandbourne's most trustworthy knights. He is the one I told you of."

Elysande smiled at the older man. "So you're the famous storyteller, Sir Charles."

The knight beamed with pride. "I do know a few stories, my lady. Mayhap, once you're ensconced as mistress of Sandbourne, I'll tell you one as we sit by the fire some evening." He grinned. "Or mayhap, I'll wait and tell my tales to your many children."

She found herself blushing again as Michael laughed aloud.

Geoffrey said, "The men we sent north have now reunited with us." He looked to Michael. "Would you like us to accompany you to Sandbourne?"

"Nay, my lord. We have two stops to make before returning there. First, we travel to Hopeston to see Lady Mary. I would hope that you'd join us."

Geoffrey nodded. "I assume you wish to speak to my sister about your upcoming marriage."

"We will." Michael looked to Elysande.

She said, "We would like to bring Mother and Avelyn back to Kinwick. It is our desire to wed there, with your permission, Uncle."

Joy filed Geoffrey's face. "Ah, Mary will like that, indeed. Merryn, too." He thought a moment. "And from there, I can take Alys and Avelyn to London. The king and queen will have returned by then."

"My thoughts exactly," Michael added. He looked at Elysande and then his mother. "Then I will take the two most beautiful ladies in the land home with me to Sandbourne."

"I like this plan," Geoffrey told them. "Come. We ride to Hopeston."

Sir Charles held out a hand to Lady Orella. "My lady? Would you care to ride with me?"

She placed her hand in his. "I'd like that very much, Sir Charles."

Michael led Elysande to a waiting Tempest. "And you'll ride with me," he said, a smile lighting his handsome features.

He lifted her into the saddle and mounted behind her. Strong arms came around her and drew her closer to him. She leaned back, inhaling the wonderful mix of leather, horse, and man.

Her man. Her honorable knight.

"Oh, my," came Lady Orella's voice across the space separating them. "Is . . . Is that Tempest? I see the resemblance from when he was a colt. I gave him to you on the last day we were together. The memory of watching you ride away on that horse has helped sustain me all these years. I always remembered your bravery that day, my son."

"Aye, Mother," replied Michael. "He's more than just my trusty steed. He's another treasured memory, along with the stone, that has helped keep you in my thoughts all these years."

Lady Orella smiled warmly at her son. With that, they were off.

They rode the rest of that day and through half of the next. Elysande remembered journeying along the same route when her family had come to Hopeston. This time, circumstances were vastly different. Before, she had been a girl who'd seen little of the world. Now, she arrived at Hopeston as a woman. One in love with the most wonderful knight in all of England.

They rode through the gates and across the baileys. She caught sight of Avelyn and her mother. Both lifted their skirts and came running to greet them.

Michael jumped down and then lifted her from Tempest. Elysande fell into her mother's arms, then Avelyn's, kissing them both.

"Such a large army of men," Lady Mary remarked. "Whatever is up, Brother?"

Geoffrey kissed his sister's cheek. "We have much to tell you, Mary. Can you feed our men? We've been on the road for many days. I know the men are famished."

"I'll see to it at once. Please, invite everyone into the great hall for ale. I'll have the servants bring bread and cheese, and then we can dine once Cook has calmed down and organized the kitchen to feed such a large group of soldiers." Lady Mary parted from the group.

Elysande linked arms with Avelyn as they started walking up the stairs to the keep. "I have so much to tell you."

Her sister smiled. "And does it involve a certain knight you rode in with?"

She nodded. "But it also involves you." Elysande couldn't contain the news any longer. "You're going to court. At the king's request."

Avelyn's eyes grew large. "Me? At court? You do not jest?"

"King Edward specifically asked Uncle Geoffrey to bring you when he returns Cousin Alys to London. You'll be in service to Queen Philippa." Elysande paused. "Even better, the queen is going to find you a husband."

Avelyn crushed her in an embrace, squealing for joy.

"I see you've shared the news with your sister," Geoffrey said.

"I couldn't help myself, Uncle. Avelyn has long dreamed about going to court."

"You'll have to promise me to keep an eye on Alys," he said to his niece. "As bossy as she's become, she'll probably try to give the king advice on how to run his court."

Avelyn beamed. "I will, Uncle. May I tell Mother?"

"Of course," he said.

She ran off in search of her mother. Elysande watched as the Kinwick and Sandbourne men pulled the trestle tables from the walls of the great hall. Servants quickly brought pitchers of ale and food for them to eat. Lady Mary returned and invited them to the solar.

Once there, her mother said, "You must tell me everything. I feel quite a lot has happened since I last saw my girl." She gave her daughter's hand a squeeze.

Elysande looked to her uncle and nodded. Geoffrey recounted their original trip to Kinwick and the attack on the road, which they knew came from Lord Ingram's men.

Her mother gasped when she heard this. "But I'd rejected Lord Ingram's suit. I can't believe an honorable man would go against my express wishes and try to kidnap my daughter and force her into marriage."

Elysande met Michael's eyes. He took up the tale.

"Speaking of marriage, my lady." Michael took Elysande's hand. "I have fallen madly in love with your daughter. We've come today, in part, for me to ask your blessing upon our union. I would seek to make Elysande my countess."

"Countess?" Her mother's eyes widened. "You are . . . an earl?"

"I am, my lady. My father, the Earl of Sandbourne, recently passed. I have taken the title." He looked to where his mother quietly sat, still in her nun's garb. "And this is my mother, Lady Orella. She will return to Sandbourne after many years away."

Lady Mary grew flustered when she caught sight of the woman in the corner. "I am sorry, my lady. I did not even see you sitting over there. I was so caught up in being with my child again. Forgive me for not acknowledging your presence."

"'Tis quite all right. And please. Call me Orella." She waved a hand down her body at her dress. "I'm sure you're wondering about this nun in your midst."

"I'm wondering about a great many things now." Her mother chuckled. She looked over at Michael. "But as to my daughter?"

"Aye, my lady. Lord Geoffrey wrote the king, and he is agreeable to the match—if you are."

Her mother's eyes met Elysande's. "I have only to look at my daughter and see the happiness that radiates from her. I think a marriage between the two of you would be a very good match, indeed."

"We thought, mayhap, we could marry at Kinwick," Michael added. "'Tis your girlhood home. Lady Avelyn has yet to see it. Lady Merryn always welcomes a wedding when it comes her way. Would this please you?"

Lady Mary nodded in approval. "It would. Let us drink to the marriage of these two." She stood and raised her cup. "To my darling Elysande and her charming husband-to-be. May you and the earl live a long and blessed life, and may your union be one filled with love and many children."

A cheer went up and they all toasted the happy couple.

Geoffrey took up the story and told his sister of Elysande's abduction from Kinwick, at the hands of Lord Ingram's men. He explained that she escaped her captors, glossing over the details, and how they found that she'd taken sanctuary at the Convent of the Blessed Sisters. He went on to describe how the king wished for Avelyn to accompany Alys to court in order to serve the queen.

"I'm quite overwhelmed by all this incredible news," Lady Mary proclaimed. She glanced at her daughter. "Still, I feel everything is as it should be." She took Elysande's hand and then Avelyn's. "I will miss each of you beyond words, but you'll start a new life away from Hopeston. I know God richly blesses you both."

"I can't wait to meet the king," Avelyn said, excitement in her voice.

Lady Mary asked, "Have you met him, Geoffrey? They say he is a good man and that the queen is the kindest of women."

"I have, Mary. The royal couple has come to Kinwick on summer progress in previous years. The king wrote that they will return again next summer. Mayhap you would like to visit then and meet them?"

"As long as they don't come to Hopeston afterward," she said. "I've heard it's quite costly to entertain the royal court."

Geoffrey groaned. "My coin purse is still empty from their last visit." He looked at Elysande. "You and Michael would also be invited to visit at the same time, Niece. I think the king would enjoy meeting you since he will already know your sister."

"To think by then I'll be a married woman—and one meeting the king." She smiled. "I think I'll enjoy that, Uncle."

THEY SET OUT the next morning for Kinwick with two wagons in tow. Trunks held all of Elysande's clothing and personal items that she wished to take to Sandbourne, while others held clothes for Avelyn to take to London. Lady Mary promised to send coin with her daughter so she could have some new clothes made at court. Michael laughed at Avelyn's concerns about being in fashion.

He rode with Elysande in front of him, once again. His arm rested against her waist, holding her close. She had wanted to ride Morningstar, but he'd selfishly rejected that idea. He convinced her it would be unnecessary to bring the horse and her foal all the way to Kinwick, only to double back and go to Sandbourne. Michael promised her that once they settled in at Sandbourne, he would send for her horses. She had readily agreed, which let him know she secretly enjoyed the time spent in his arms on the road.

They'd traveled no more than a few hours when he heard the restlessness that came in waves from the back of their small army. His senses went on high alert as he looked to his left, where Sir Charles rode with his mother. The knight's face showed his concern as they heard the first clash of distant swords at the rear.

"Something's afoot," he told Geoffrey. "We must secure the women."

Michael motioned to Hammond, who rode behind him, Avelyn in the saddle with him.

"Gather the women now," he ordered. "I want a guard of no less than ten surrounding them."

His friend gave a curt nod and called out to several behind him as he slipped from his horse and pulled Avelyn from the saddle. Michael did the same with Elysande as Geoffrey leapt from his horse and removed his sister. Charles already had Michael's mother on firm ground and hustled her over to the other women.

Michael placed his hands on Elysande's shoulders. "Stay together. Don't stray from the men who protect you." He ushered her to a thick oak standing near the side of the road and waved for the other three women to join her. Immediately, a ring of knights formed around them, their swords drawn.

His gut told him who approached and engaged them.

Lord Ingram.

CHAPTER TWENTY-FIVE

ELYSANDE PUT HER arm around Avelyn and drew her close. She felt the tremors of fright running through her sister's body. They echoed those she experienced. Her hands trembled uncontrollably. Even her teeth began chattering as fear paralyzed her. Both her mother and Lady Orella joined them, their faces white as ghosts. The women huddled together, their backs against the large oak. She recognized a few of the knights that closed ranks and encircled them from her stay at Kinwick, including Hammond, a friend of Michael's. The others wore the colors of the Earl of Sandbourne. Though she was not yet their countess, she knew these men would protect her with their lives.

She leaned forward, trying to see through the thick wall of men that surrounded them. They stood shoulder to shoulder, their long swords drawn as they awaited action. Elysande saw how still their bodies were, yet she knew they were coiled and could spring into action in the blink of an eye.

The clanging of swords rattled the peace of the early September day. Guilt poured through her. The fighting that went on around them was because of her. Lord Ingram had some twisted wish to make her his bride, despite denials from her mother and the king. The nobleman had unleashed his men against those from Sandbourne and Kinwick.

And that meant men would die this day.

Her legs shook so that she didn't trust herself to remain standing. She slid down the tree, bringing Avelyn with her. Her sister buried her face in Elysande's shoulder, not wanting to see what went on.

Elysande stared ahead and found she could observe what happened from ground level. The height of the knights in front of them and their wide shoulders that had kept her from viewing the action as she stood no longer blocked her sight. Each soldier's stance left his feet slightly apart, ready to move quickly. It was that gap that allowed her to watch the fighting.

Elysande found she couldn't tear her eyes away from the brutal action. Men swung swords and maces, landing horrific blows against one another. The ground ran red from so much blood. Loud, hoarse cries became swallowed by the screams of those injured. She reached down to her boot and withdrew the dagger that she'd used against Ernis. She doubted the guard surrounding them would allow anyone near enough for her to put it to use, but it calmed her to clasp the weapon in her hand.

It was hard to tell which side might be winning. She had no idea how many men Lord Ingram brought with him. Elysande knew from what Michael said when they'd left the Convent of the Blessed Sisters that they numbered about two hundred strong. She squeezed her eyes closed and begged God for nothing to happen to Michael or Geoffrey. She couldn't believe so much loss was laid at her doorstep and prayed for forgiveness.

When she opened her eyes, she searched for Michael in the melee. She finally spotted him, thanks to his great height. He held his bastard sword in both hands, cutting through men faster than she could count. His determined face showed no mercy to his opponents.

Then she spied Lord Ingram in the fray. The nobleman headed toward Michael, grim resolve hovering about him. She wanted to scream out and warn Michael, but she knew her voice wouldn't be heard above the battle noise. Elysande held her breath and gripped her blade.

MICHAEL CUT A swath through his opponents, moving swiftly with a fluid motion. His years of training took over instinctively. It was as if he and his sword were one as he brandished it against his enemies. Anger raged through him at the thought of Lord Ingram trying to steal Elysande from him. Harnessing the anger, he focused it against every man that stepped into his path.

He plunged his sword into the heart of one man and sliced it across the neck of another soldier. He lifted it high above his head and struck a death blow to another man's head. Whirling, he ripped his sword across the throat of the next man that crossed his path. Michael continued cutting his way through the hostile crowd, focusing on the battle at hand. He longed to glance over to see if Elysande remained safe, but he had to trust that the men who protected her did their job and kept her and the other women secure.

A sixth sense had him turn and duck at the same time. A blade whizzed above him where his neck had been only moments ago. He drove his sword up into the gut of the soldier who stood next to him and then finished off the man's companion before the soldier could raise a weapon against him. Michael kept on fighting, plowing through as many as he could.

And then he saw the man responsible for the day's bloodshed.

Lord Ingram spied him at the same time. Without thought or word, Michael rushed in the nobleman's direction.

He raised his sword as he approached his sworn enemy. Ingram did the same. Both men swung at the same time. The ringing of their steel meeting seemed like music to his ears. Michael brought his sword forth, again and again, sometimes parrying and evading Ingram's blows, other times pushing the older man back with the force of his weapon as much as his rage.

Michael knew his opponent had begun to weaken as time passed and their duel intensified. Ingram lacked strategy. He'd begun to breathe heavily and sweat profusely. The nobleman from the north no longer initiated strikes. Instead, he had to defend himself from them. Michael took command of the fight. He sliced the nobleman's upper arm and heard a howl then twisted low and jabbed his sword into Ingram's hip, pulling it halfway across the man's belly. With that second strike, Ingram stumbled backward and fell to the ground.

Michael planted a firm foot against the nobleman's wrist. Ingram was forced to release his sword. The nobleman's free hand clutched his bleeding belly. Their eyes met and Michael had the satisfaction of seeing defeat on Ingram's face.

As he placed his sword's tip against his fallen enemy's throat, a trumpet sounded in the distance. Michael kept his weapon in place and looked around the impromptu battlefield for the first time since his fight with the lord of Rudland began. He saw that most of the soldiers wearing Ingram's colors had fallen. The trumpet blared again. Fighting ceased.

He glanced over his shoulder to where the women had been led and almost laughed aloud. Elysande scrambled through the parted legs of a very surprised Hammond. She sprang to her feet and gripped her skirts in her hand.

And ran to him.

Love burst within him, its warmth like a hundred suns coursing through his veins. She slowed as she reached him, not wanting to interfere with his pinned his opponent. Michael reached his free hand out to her. She took it. He squeezed her hand, hoping it communicated all the love he felt for her at this moment.

Elysande looked down at the fallen nobleman, a look of disdain on her face. "You're the cause of this bloodshed today, my lord. It need never have occurred. 'Tis your ego that brought about the death of many men this day." She spat on the ground next to him. "I hope you rot in the bowels of Hell."

Geoffrey appeared to their left. "The king approaches. I've spoken with his scout. The royal court is returning to London from their summer progress." He glanced at Michael's prisoner. "He'll want to speak with this one."

"If I live long enough." Hatred blazed from Ingram's eyes. Despite the man's defiant words, Michael saw the pain he suffered.

"Lay down your swords," he bellowed. "All of you, whether from Sandbourne, Kinwick, or Rudland. Put them to the ground now. The king comes."

Michael looked around and saw those still alive obeying his command. He did likewise but made sure his weapon was out of Ingram's reach. He also kicked his prisoner's sword away, finally releasing his boot from the man's wrist. Ingram remained flat on the ground, both hands now cradling his wounded gut. Blood leaked between his fingers. Michael knew it was only a matter of time before Ingram succumbed to the fatal wound.

Minutes later, the royal entourage came into view. Michael had never laid eyes on the king, but he would have known the man to be royal merely from his noble bearing.

Edward marched through the waves of bowing men and came to stand in front of him, Elysande, and Geoffrey. The men bowed as Elysande made her deep curtsey.

"What have I come across, Lord Geoffrey?" The king casually glanced around, but Michael saw that no detail would be missed by this man.

His eyes came to rest on the prone nobleman. "Lord Ingram? I gather 'tis you."

"Sorry I cannot greet you properly, sire."

The king's eyes flicked back to Geoffrey. "Explain what goes on, my lord. The queen and I were enjoying a lovely day with our retinue when we stumbled across this killing field. I didn't think any English lords made war upon one another at this time."

"Sire, it's because of me."

Michael turned and saw that Elysande had taken a step forward. Her mouth trembled, but she held her head high.

Edward studied her with twitching lips. Michael thought the king hid his amusement.

"Identify yourself, my lady. And then please clarify your statement."

"I am Lady Elysande Le Cler, daughter of—"

The king interrupted, looking at Geoffrey. "This is the niece you spoke of? The one you wanted to marry your knight, Sir Michael

Devereux." His eyes turned to Michael.

"I am Michael Devereux, your majesty. Now Earl of Sandbourne." He moved to Elysande's side and took her hand in his. "My father recently passed away, and my betrothal fell through."

"Is that so?" Edward looked at their entwined fingers and sighed. "And you wish to marry, I assume." He glanced over Michael's shoulder. "Greetings, my ladies. Come join us."

Michael watched as his mother, Lady Mary, and Avelyn came forward and curtseyed to the king.

"Ah, another young lady. I'm thinking this is your other niece, Lord Geoffrey. The one scheduled to come to my court. Lady Avelyn, I believe?"

Avelyn nodded. "Yes, sire," she managed to say before falling silent.

Geoffrey took over. "And this is the girls' mother. My sister, Lady Mary, whom you've left in charge of Hopeston Castle for now."

The king appraised her. "I've heard excellent things about you, my lady."

"Thank you, sire." Lady Mary demurely lowered her eyes, which Michael thought was a smart move on her part.

"And this last woman. A nun, I see. Why are you traveling with this group?"

Michael released Elysande's hand and went to take his mother's arm. "This is my mother, sire. Lady Orella Devereux. My father sent her away to a convent many years ago. I swore a vow to find her once I became the new earl."

Michael saw understanding dawn upon Edward's face. "And so you have." The king studied the gathered group a moment before he brought his attention back to Lord Ingram.

"I see the Sandbourne and Kinwick forces united against you, my lord." Edward gave the nobleman a harsh look. "I thought I expressed my wishes clearly and concisely when I denied your suit toward Lady Elysande."

"You did, sire," Ingram said with great effort. His face contorted as his body spasmed. Then he grew still.

The king looked upon the dead body with disdain. He glanced back at Michael.

"I suppose you're happy with Sandbourne, my lord. Would you also like Rudland? I believe Lord Ingram will no longer be needing it."

Michael hid his shock. "No, sire, but I thank you all the same. Sandbourne—and Elysande—will be more than enough for me."

Elysande moved to stand by him again. Michael caught her hand in his.

The king nodded sagely. "I will have to find someone else worthy enough to claim Rudland then. So I assume your wedding will be soon?"

Geoffrey said, "We travel to Kinwick now, your majesty. Elysande and Michael wish to be married there."

Edward clapped his hands in delight. "Lady Merryn will be thrilled, no doubt, when she discovers she has a wedding feast to plan." He paused, lost in thought. Michael thought he might actually be considering whether or to attend their wedding, but then the king said, "I wish the best to you in your upcoming marriage and life together."

"Thank you, sire," both Michael and Elysande replied at the same time.

The king looked to Geoffrey. "And once this wedding is over, you're bringing Lady Alys and Lady Avelyn to court?"

"I am, sire."

"It seems you have things well in hand, Lord Geoffrey. The queen and I will be on our way. Give my best to Lady Merryn. Remember, she's welcome to come with you to London." He looked around. "See that Ingram's men return to Rudland. I'll have to think about who'll receive the estate next."

With that, the king swept away, a true force of nature.

After his departure, Geoffrey had the surviving Rudland men gather around. He explained to them they would soon have a new liege lord, but for now the king had instructed them to return to their home. They went without protest, first placing the bodies of their fallen comrades upon horses to be returned for burial.

Geoffrey and Michael had Charles and Hammond do the same for their own soldiers who had died in combat. Michael assigned Charles to lead a small contingency back to Sandbourne with the bodies as the remaining Sandbourne knights traveled on with them to Kinwick.

As Michael went to place Elysande upon Tempest's back, he brought his arms around her in a tender embrace.

"We now have the king's blessing, my love. I plan on a long life so that I can love you thoroughly each and every day."

"And I will return every bit of that love to you, Michael Devereux," she said, her eyes shining with that promised love. "You may count on it."

Elysande pulled his face to hers in a lengthy, heated kiss.

As Michael returned it, he heard the approving cheers ring out.

EPILOGUE

MICHAEL AWOKE, AS he did every morning, with a smile on his face and Elysande in his arms. Her cheek nestled against his bare chest. Their limbs entangled so closely that it was hard to tell where one ended and the next one began. He held the woman who had become more precious to him than any amount of gold and thought of all the ways she had changed his life in the past few months.

He glanced around the bedchamber of the solar, thinking how he'd been forbidden to enter it as a child. He'd left Sandbourne so many years ago, an angry, friendless boy. But in truth, his father had done him a favor by helping drive Michael from his home.

He had learned—and then thrived—under Sir Lovel's tutelage. Michael had gained the friendship of the older squires, Geoffrey and Raynor, who impressed him with not only physical lessons regarding swordplay and weaponry but the moral life lessons they taught that helped him become the man he was today.

Elysande stirred slightly in his arms. His hand stroked the soft waves that tumbled about her shoulders and spilled across his chest. He thanked Christ Almighty that he'd heard of Lord Geoffrey de Montfort's return to Kinwick—for if he'd never heard the news, Michael wouldn't have sought out Geoffrey and offered himself in service to the nobleman. Without that, Michael never would have traveled to Hopeston and met his future wife.

Elysande moved again, this time stretching as lazily as one of the barn cats in their stables. Her head tilted back as her amethyst eyes opened and fastened on his. Her love for him shined through as a beacon guiding a traveler on a dark night.

Michael gently kissed her. "Are you ready for our travels today, Wife?" he asked as he ran his fingers lightly down her face, caressing her long, swanlike neck and milky white shoulders.

"I am more than ready, Husband," she said, a teasing light in her eyes. "I look forward to seeing my mother and Avelyn and all of my kinfolk at Kinwick. I'm grateful that we've been asked to spend the Christmas season with the de Montforts."

"I agree," he said, "Thought I would love to play host to them at this time next year. By then, I hope to have all the changes completed at Sandbourne. I'll be pleased to show off the estate to them."

She smoothed her thumb across his cheek, a smile tugging at the corners of her mouth. "I think that would be best. I know this year it would've been hard for Merryn to travel to Sandbourne since she's is heavy with child."

"When does the babe come?" Michael asked.

"Probably two months into the new year," she replied.

Again, he caught the smile that threatened to dance across her mouth. "Do you have something to tell me, Elysande?" he asked.

She pressed her lips to his in a sweet, lingering kiss and then pulled back. "I do have news, my lord husband."

"What news do you wish to share with me, my lady?" he asked formally.

She took his hand and brought it to rest against her bare belly. "I'm certain that our child grows within me even as we speak."

His eyes widened in amazement and fell to where their hands lay resting together.

His child. Their child. Nestled deep within her belly.

She said, "This time next year, we'll have our own babe in our arms, my love. I would wish for the others to come and celebrate Christmas with us at Sandbourne as we start new traditions with our own family."

"You couldn't have given me better news, my sweetest Elysande,"

Michael said, excitement brimming within him. He thought to the many happy hours he'd spent playing with the three de Montfort children. Now he would have a child of his own.

He cupped her face tenderly. "We'll raise our child with an abundance of love, be it boy or girl. And I hope many more babes will follow. I want to fill the halls of Sandbourne with happy children who run through them, laughing and playing."

"We will, Michael," Elysande promised, "for out of our love will grow many more lives."

He kissed her again, with love and desire, with longing and reverence. This would be a good life they would share. Together. Forever and always.

The End

About the Author

As a child, Alexa Aston gathered her neighborhood friends together and made up stories for them to act out, her first venture into creating memorable characters. Following her passion for history and love of learning, she became a teacher who began writing on the side to maintain her sanity in a sea of teenage hormones.

Alexa's historical romances use history as a backdrop to place her characters in extraordinary circumstances, where their intense desire for one another grows into the treasured gift of love.

She is the author of *The Knights of Honor*, a medieval romance series that takes place in 14th century England during the reign of Edward III and centers on the de Montfort family. Each romance focuses on the code of chivalry that bound knights of this era.

A native Texan, Alexa lives with her husband in a Dallas suburb, where she eats her fair share of dark chocolate and plots out stories while she walks every morning. She enjoys reading, watching movies and sports, and can't get enough of *Fixer Upper* or *Game of Thrones*. Alexa also writes romantic suspense, western historicals, and standalone medieval novels as Lauren Linwood.

Alexa loves to hear from her readers. You can connect with her through FB, Twitter, and her website, alexaaston.wordpress.com.

Facebook:
www.facebook.com/authoralexaaston

Twitter:
twitter.com/AlexaAston

Newsletter sign-up:
madmimi.com/signups/422152/join

Amazon Page:
amazon.com/author/alexaaston

Made in the USA
Middletown, DE
21 April 2017